AS SEEN ON TV

Chris Kerr

AS SEEN ON TV

Weidenfeld & Nicolson
LONDON

First published in Great Britain in 2005
by Weidenfeld & Nicolson

A CIP catalogue record for this book is available
from the British Library

If the author has inadvertently quoted from any text
in copyright, the publisher will be pleased to credit
the copyright holder in all future editions.

ISBN 0 297 60749 9

Typeset at The Spartan Press Ltd,
Lymington, Hants

Printed in Great Britain by Clays Ltd,
St Ives plc

Weidenfeld & Nicolson
An imprint of the Orion Publishing Group
Orion House, 5 Upper St Martin's Lane,
London WC2H 9EA

www.orionbooks.co.uk

The Undying Myth of the Nuclear Family

Jimmy Thurber © MMI *Sidney Herald*, and syndicated to the *Sunday Times*, London.

If we know something well, we use an expression derived from the word 'family' – we say we're 'familiar' with it. This usage presumes we *know* our own family, and *the family* that everyone talks about as being the basic unit of human society and the moral rock upon which any civilisation's foundations are laid. We know *the family* because it is an idea that permeates pop culture – in plays, poems, songs, novels, TV programmes and movies. Family implies love, compassion, security, cordiality – that's what you're traditionally supposed to get at home from two God-fearing parents, one male Dad, one female Mom, and any siblings you might be lumbered with.

Enter *Roseanne*, enter *Married With Children*, enter *The Simpsons*. Here are TV programmes that seem to break the mould, aim to become the opposite of the normal family sitcom, the anti-family sitcom. We laugh at these shows because the humour comes from the viewer knowing what the family *should* be like and how, say, having Bart as a brother or Al Bundy as a dad is way different. Humour after all, is a socially acceptable method of saying what can't be said seriously because of taboo.

So does this give these shows licence to do anything, to put to death the myth of the functional nuclear family? The answer is no. The reason why is this – these shows actually reinforce the idea of a normal family unit by portraying its opposite. *Roseanne* doesn't deal with domestic violence, or the fact that you're more likely to be killed by a member of your own family (the dad Dan) than by a stranger. *The Simpsons* doesn't tackle issues like child abuse by portraying Homer as the family's live-in patriarchal rapist. *Married with Children* doesn't have an episode satirising sibling incest with Bud and Kelly getting it on.

Why? Because what happens in the family on TV or in the real world is not allowed to interfere with the basic idea of normality, this behaviour model that is the myth of the nuclear family. We admit it – the dysfunctional family exists, in fact we likely came from one, but at the same time, we deny that very fact every time we think 'I wish I'd had a better family.'

If we know something well we say we're familiar with it. We use an expression which seems at first and second glance to link the words 'family' and 'liar' closely together.

Episode 1

I have a problem. No one else can help. Except maybe
the likes of Hannibal, Face, B.A., Murdock, and hooray
for Hollywood feminism, Triple A. Yep, I want to hire
The A-Team. Call me Howling Mad – that's one better
than barking – if this here problem of mine doesn't
raise its bull-ugly head in the middle of Tuesday
night, 24 April. There I am, in my Hollywood bed,
experiencing a wakeful dream about selling a script
to Spielberg himself. I'm pitching the learned-by-
rote résumé I say to everyone out here, even the
people in my dreams. 'My go-project is *The A-Team*, Mr
Spielberg. The door to this was *The Six Million Dollar
Man* movie – even though they got some A-hole to
rewrite me and retitled it *The Bionic Dude*. The key to
that door was my spec script *Zombie Moon* – it's all
about how Zylon, an experimental space-age gas, makes
the international crew of astronauts on Moon Base
Alpha die and come back as undead brain-eaters.'
    Yep, I'm doing the business all right, telling
Spielberg that script-wise I want to adapt something
original, from definitive DreamWorks like Kafka's *The
Castle* or *The Trial* or even *Amerika*, if he wants to,
you know, and he is nodding, he's definitely nodding,
when the damn phone, the landline, BLEEP-BLEEP, BLEEP-
BLEEPS.
    Eyes shut and groaning at the loss of the
opportunity to sell myself properly, I roll off my
back, onto my right side, and lunge at the handset by

5

my pit. I grapple with it, BLEEP-BLEEP, BLEEP . . . and
fumble it up to my ear. 'Yep?'

   'Kirk?'

   'What?'

   'It's me, your mom.'

   'Oh,' I groan.

   'Sorry to call you so late.'

   I open my eyes. The dim red digits of my alarm
clock are right in front of me. They're the only
things I can see in the darkness; I'd long since
declared war on all outside light sources that could
spoil my precious productive dream-sleep. 'It's three
a.m. here,' I say.

   'Well it's only twelve here and I have some bad
news.'

   I should emphasise that three a.m. bad news from
Mom is not the same as three a.m. bad news from anyone
else. Cruel fact: Mom and Dad have been waging a war
of affairs on each other for twenty-five years. Mom
fancies anyone who looks like my first stage namesake,
Kirk Douglas. Dad isn't that fussy – even BV (Before
Viagra) anything in or out of a bikini would do. This
should explain why I tell her to 'Hold on' as I put the
handset down on my pillow, sit up straight and
slapstick myself across the right cheek, then the
left. 'OK, I'm ready for it. Dad's frigging around on
you again?'

   'It's Denise.'

   A problem with my younger sister would, of course,
have been my next guess. 'What's she done now?' I
ask.

   'She's disappeared, Kirk.'

   'Yep, you don't say?'

   'She left a note this time.'

   That's a new one. 'A note?'

   Mom starts to weep. Being an amateur drama queen,

an ex-Pinewood Studios extra, she's had a lot of practice at weeping to create guilt. Dad, in Dick Van Dyke mode, the eternal happy chappy, always says that given an onion Mom could cry for his old family home, Ireland, and everybody with half a brain knows that's a river of tears even if they don't know where the place might be on our *As The World Turns* globe spinning through space.

'What did it say, Mom?'

But Mom is sobbing her heart out.

'Tell me.'

More sobs from Mom. 'It said she is going off dialysis to try something new called Death Therapy.'

'Death Therapy?'

'It said she mightn't be back. And she loved us.'

'When exactly did she leave?' I ask her, and I ask because Denise has bunked off the dialysis programme loads before to try alternative healings like natural herbalistic remedies, shaman drumming therapy, New Age psychic surgeons. All these times she'd come back reeling in less than a week.

'It's dated today, I mean yesterday – Monday the twenty-third.'

'Have you called her girlfriends, and ordinary friends?'

'I don't know any of them apart from Len. I thought you might be able to talk to him.'

Len was my buddy at film school. 'I haven't been in touch recently.'

'Kirk son . . .'

I read her next line so I rattle off, 'She'll turn up. This Death Therapy's just another one of her . . . *things*, you know?'

Mom says it anyway: 'Kirk son, this time would you come back and help us find her?' She said *this time*

7

because last time, when jet-setter Denise had collapsed on her Next Look *Models Inc.* talent scouting in London, I didn't go home to see her being brought back in bits.

'Sure, Mom,' I answer her straight, 'when I'm negotiating the biggest deal of my life tomorrow. No problem.'

'This is a family emergency.'

'Since when did Denise ever—'

'Do it for me, will you?'

I pause (beat) for special effect, not thought – Hollywood *hamartia.* 'I tell you what,' I say, 'if she hasn't turned up by the weekend—'

'The head nurse at the dialysis centre says she's got a maximum of two weeks.'

'Two weeks to what?'

'To live. If she doesn't dialyse.'

Mom has to go making it life or death, a time-locked tragedy in the making. She sounds like a producer, and all I can do is sigh at that. 'Look Mom, this isn't on. I mean what can I do about this, realistically?'

'Help.'

'Just like that?'

'Just like that!' Mom says, and puts the phone down.

I SLAM my handset down too. 'Who needs this?' I yell, and fling myself back down into my pit. What is Mom playing at – laying soap operatic guilt trips on me age thirty-one? And what the hell is Denise playing at putting me in this double bind? I can't even begin to understand. The only thing I know for certain is that my *Big Deal* is just too important to mess up. I mean I'd worked all my life – the bit called a 'career' in the Industry – to get to this point. So, I lie there with my eyes open. The darkness around me seems complete, barring the alarm clock. I BLANK out everything else. I've a special talent for BLANKING things – a Rush family trait.

Episode 2

I get up next morning, alarmed at 5.45, as usual. I
haven't slept much so I have a throbbing in my temples
and the usual rib-constricting, breath-restricting
backache. I lie there for a moment, letting the pains
give me the necessary motivation to get up and onto my
physiotherapist-approved green gym mat to do my
every-day-in-life routine of Pilates exercises. It
takes twenty bloody minutes to fulfil the mission
parameters and do all the stretches and crunches. I
really resent every minute and yet I know that,
without doing it, I'd fall apart. My spine is weak,
you see. Somewhere along the time line of my life the
dorsal arch on Lumbar 4 snapped off, and this led to
spinal instability. I could have helped myself if I'd
known about and obeyed the screenwriter's golden rule
'Always protect your spine,' but I didn't like doing
physical stuff as a kid, because:

1. It hurt.
2. I was weedy compared to other kids.
3. It took me away from watching TV.

So that's why I didn't develop the extra
musculature required to stop the spiral of decline.
Scoliosis. Kyphosis. Scheuerman's disease. Thorassic
outlet syndrome. It wasn't till I was twenty-three,
when I had a year-long attack of chronic back and
acute shoulder pain, that I was diagnosed with all
these conditions. I suppose that was the turning

point for me. I was forced to truly inhabit my body in a way I'd always avoided. Instead of wallowing in self-pity, I decided to get physical like the people around me in Miami; I wanted my body to be more than the way I felt then, thin and bitter and twisted.

After my exercises I put on my black Speedo shorts and go down to the pool. I usually meet the only other dawn-riser in Sherman Oaks' Sherman Sunrise Craftsman-rip-off-style apartment complex. Sure enough, today is no exception. There's Sindy, the spit of Cindy Crawford in her green wow-G-string bikini, practising her diving. She's been on CBS's *The Bold and the Beautiful* for a year. Give her half a chance and, wide-eyed, in that 1000-yard stare people get here, she'd educate you on how her supporting caricature, Helen Troy, is gradually being fed more storyline. So unless they kill her off in a ratings war, or this year's threatened Screen Actors' Guild strike bites, she'll be able to afford the extortionate $1600 per month rent here a while longer.

As I walked down the polished-maple steps to the poolside, I watch her bouncing on that diving board, leaping gracefully, streamlining her implant-curvy *Baywatch* body as much as she can, entering the water and going down deep, coming back up towards me, breaking the surface.

'Hi,' I boldly say to her as I set my towel down on the wooden sunlounger.

'Hi,' she beautifully says to me from the blue of the pool.

'Nice day,' I say. It was eternally a nice day in LA, bar the odd Chandleresque fog-out or Ellroyesque smog-out, but still, originally hailing from four-seasons-in-one-day England I can't help-making small

11

talk about the weather. It's in the genes, those
selfish genes.

'Yeah, sun's up,' she replies, and pulls her *Wonder Woman*, doll-like body up the pool ladder out of the
water.

One kiss, what I would have done for one screen
kiss, one *Hollywood Connection*. 'How's things?' I FLIP
off my flip-flops.

'Fine. You?'

There's a *Split Second* when I think about Denise,
and the meeting at 2.00 p.m., then BLANK. 'Can't
complain.'

'Still writing away?' She sashays back towards the
diving board.

'Yep. Still acting away?'

'Uh-huh,' I hear her say, *He Said, She Said*.

'Good,' I say, and get into the pool nice and easy.
The swimming is not something I ever enjoy – am I
The Man From Atlantis, nope! But I religiously stick
to my strict regime of forty lengths every morning
except Sunday, staying in the water like I've gills
long after way-out-of-my league Sindy has gone and
the extras – uglier, pudgier swimmers – arrive. I'm
still trying to rebuild myself like your man Colonel
Steve Austin had to, only with no help from the OSO
(Office of Strategic Operations).

Work starts with a Big Orange big orange, some
bagels, a cup of Irish tea and a Celebrex pill. I sit
down on my chiropractic chair, eat my healthy and
painkilling feast in my ergonomically perfect, teak-
lined study while reading over what I'd written on the
computer the previous day, or the day before that if I
was dry of words, or the week before if I had a meeting
coming up. And I have a big meeting coming up, so I'm
technically dry, Mojave Desert dry. Death Valley dry,
even. Yep, that there screen is a total goddam white-

out BLANK. There's literally nothing for me to edit,
so I do the only thing I can do: make sure I have my
nostalgic yet novel pitch down to a T by speaking it
into my trusty silver Dictaphone again and again.
(Pitches have to be done verbally because in
principle anything a screenwriter puts in writing has
to be paid for by the producer: Writers' Guild of
America rules OK).

I hate selling, but I'm hoping this script won't be
such a hard sell as the last; the meeting has, after
all, been called by none other than Biff McMurray, the
'hot-shottest' studio exec (with his own production
company) in the Industry right now. I've heard from my
agent, Death-cigarette-smoking Harvey Guck, that
Biff has personally made it his mission in life to
make this movie. That's why Biff has teamed up with
Universal – because they made *The A-Team* for NBC and
still hold the rights to the concept and most of the
characters – and that's also why he's tied in with the
comic book and computer game concern Mad Bull Inc.
which has snagged some of the rights.

Harvey has assured me that if I come up with a
'pure A-Team' storyline Biff will 'drop his pants and
take it like a man'. I'm not sure at all about that
analogy, but the three-against-six-million-dollar
fee I have in mind for the job is a lot of money. If
I've to give Biff a good boffing, I may just do it.
Maybe, if it comes down to prostitution with a capital
P. This is Hollywood after all.

But then again, maybe not.

Episode 3

I leave *The Bachelor* pad early, at 1.00 p.m., not
because I'm scared of being late, but because like
every Angeleno I consider walking evil and am
addicted to driving.

On the way down to my own personal space in the
Sherman Sunrise underground car park, I put my bags
down on a step and slide on my yellow-tinted Armani
driving shades.

I CLICK my wristwatch com-link on too: you see I
have special reason to be an automobile addict – down
there in the darkness a likeness of the Knight
Industries Two Thousand is waiting for me. A classic
black '82 Pontiac Trans-Am, worth $35K. KITTSCH was
what I'd bought with the main part of the $125-
against-$250K earnings from *The Bionic Dude* script.
It's really great to burn about Hollywood pretending
to be Michael Knight championing the innocent and
powerless against criminals who operate above the
law.

'KITTSCH ol' buddy,' I say as I get into my car,
'Take me to Universal City.'

The indestructible car answers back in that queer
sneer, 'Yes, Kirk. And good afternoon to you too.'

KITTSCH takes off with a SCREECH of tyres, for
show, as usual.

I swipe my security card on the gate control and
exit.

I choose to get off the boulevards, drive up Laurel

14

Canyon onto Mulholland Drive – taking a gas-guzzling way to the lot, the kind of exit-the-Valley scenic route I use a fair bit. What does gas matter when a gallon of 98 octane is $1.89?

After a fair few miles of calming palms, eucalyptus trees, pines and glimpses of up-and-coming porn stars' mansions (*The Big Valley*, more specifically Van Nuys, is the porn capital of the world, see *Porn, A Family Business*), I finally head for the Ventura Freeway. Linking up to the seemingly obligatory lunchtime-anytime traffic jam, I keep my eyes peeled for criminals operating above the law, secure in the pretence that KITTSCH is being backed up by old Devon Miles, Dr Bonnie Barstow and politically correct series four addition black mechanic TC3, all travelling in the FLAG MU (The Foundation for Law and Government Mobile Unit).

'Let's get there in one piece,' I say to KITTSCH, who is speed-weaving through the cars and killer la-la-land smog and doesn't answer.

Yellow haze. The Hollywood Freeway is nothing but cars and yellow haze, although that may just be the ultra-trendy tint of my Armanis?

To cross over into Universal Studios Lot I've to get past the security guards and the gate arms. All this takes me back to the not-dissimilar journey I had to make every night for the year I worked in À Votre Santé bistro on the garish City Walk, a veggie place that had 'Carate', a 3-D carrot pumping iron, as its chain logo. I was on $7.00 an hour plus occasional tips; boy did I goddam hate it. But Harvey was right, being there, right place right time – a wired studio exec blabbing away about the concept under my nose got *The Apprentice* a crack at the $6 million script. Field intelligence. That was my Turbo-Boost.

Speaking of which, it would have been so good, so

dramatic, so hubristic, for me to press that button and for KITTSCH to Turbo-Boost over the gate arm. But real life isn't like that; I have to stop as a guard flags me down, and wait like everyone else.

KITTSCH slides my window down.

'Good afternoon, sir,' says the mean-looking guard politely, more politely than they did up the hill when I was a waiter-wannabe-writer. 'May I have your name?'

'Kirk Rush. I have a two o'clock with Biff McMurray.'

The guard looks meanly at his clipboard. 'OK, sir,' he says. 'Here's a guest pass. Drive on.'

I take the paper pass.

KITTSCH drives through, up into the multi-storey, up to LEVEL 3, and SKID-parks, precisely.

I get out of the car.

'Good luck, Kirk,' KITTSCH says. 'You'll need it.'

'Thanks for the confidence Turbo-Boost KITTSCH,' I say and, taking the stairs, leave the multi-storey.

Once out in the eternally nice daylight, I navigate my way through the labyrinth of crap-brown, massive, warehouse-like sound stages, avoiding the VIP and not-VIP tourist trams, walking through the higgledy-piggledy suburbs of the city nobody really lives in to where, thanks to Harvey's precise instructions and my own crypto-amnesiac memory, I find the Happy Crappy Revival-style bungalow, tucked away in a small tropical garden, where I'm supposed to be.

I'm fifteen minutes early. Instead of going right in I stand out on the porch watching and waiting for a tram to go by.

Sure enough, one does. I lean against the wall, casually looking lean and mean. I do *not* wave. Only the *Average Joe* waves, waiter-wannabes. I stay still. Star-striking still. *Joe Millionaire* still.

16

The tourists must think I'm somebody important in
the Industry an *American Idol* because they snap their
digital photos, take their home movies. That's good.
I feel like somebody important in the Industry,
somebody real.

That is before I meet the Angelina not-Jolie
secretary indoors, who abruptly reminds me I'm just
another nobody-writer in a town full of nobody-
writers.

Episode 4

Biff McMurray looks like a gay, *Thirty-something* Robert Redford in an immaculate blue Versace suit. We meet at the door to his way-plush, light and airy office, and we shake hands firmly, like real men are supposed to. 'Good to meet you, Kirk. Loved your Bionic script. Shame they can't get it green-lit, that bionic dick scene is a gut-buster.'

'Thanks, Biff.'

'Harvey tells me you're nearly as big an A-Team nut as me.'

'Yep. I am that disturbed.'

Biff laughs. 'Take a seat.'

So I do. I sit down on the 'write' side of his enormous ash and glass desk. The leather visitors' chair is nicely padded around the lumbar region.

Biff goes round to his side, the 'wrong' side, but instead of sitting down he rolls his beige leather exec's chair out from behind the desk and right up to just in front of me. Then he sits down. 'What do you have for me?'

'A pretty jazzy idea, Biff,' I say, feeling a little more pressured by his proximity than relaxed. '*The A-Team* meets *The A-Team*.'

'We're not talking clones here are we?'

'No. We're just not going to bastardise it with anything else.'

'Keeping it real!' Biff CLAPS his hands. 'I like it already. So, hit me with the jazz, my man.'

18

So I hit him: 'In 1991 a Delta Force unit is sentenced by a military court for a Gulf War crime they did not commit . . . but witnessed. Colonel Decker and his unit were the guilty parties in the massacre of a small party of Marsh Arabs. *The A-Team* tried to stop the killings but tragically couldn't, and Decker framed them before they could testify against him.'

'Uh-huh?'

'Hannibal, Face, B.A. and Murdock – who is convinced he has Gulf War Syndrome – promptly escape from a maximum-security stockade to the Los Angeles underground. And today, mid-1995, still hunted by the incompetent Lieutenant Colonel Lynch, they survive as soldiers of fortune and wait to meet Decker again. Their chance arrives when Ayesha, an Albanian refugee to the US, has a problem which no one else can help her with.'

'Which is?' Biff asks.

'Her family is just one of many in Kosovo who have been taken prisoner by a terrorist army of bad-guy Serbians who are into trafficking human organs for profit.'

Biff is squinting. 'Organs?'

'Kidneys. Livers. Hearts. Limbs. These people kill the donors – those with universal type O blood and tissue – if the price is right in the West.'

'Ouch. And Decker?'

'Decker is one of the terrorist mercenaries who guards the camp, so the Team get to go on a mission to redeem themselves.'

'Where would we set this?'

'LA, and wherever in the US looks like Serbia, and Iraq.'

Biff nods. 'Keeping it cheap and nasty like the series?'

'Why not? The important thing is the audience get to enjoy *The A-Team* kick ass as the world policeman Uncle Sam should, fighting for truth, justice and the American way – without killing anyone.'

Biff is nodding. He's definitely nodding, when the damn phone BLEEP-BLEEPETY-BLEEPS the start of 'Lies (Through the 80s)' by Manfred Mann.

'Sorry, I've been waiting all morning for this call,' he says and takes the call. 'Hi, Sam. I won't dress this up – the answer is no.'

No? I don't want to hear that word. Any more than the protesting director Sam does.

'I'm not going to argue. I'm in a meeting. Come in on budget. Next Thursday I want *The Fantastic Four* ready for cutting.'

More protesting from Sam means more Nos when yes is what I want to hear. Yes. Yep. Yeehaw. Biff will love it, really! He'll drop his pants and buy it for how much? How much? How goddam much – think six million, positive!

'Bye,' Biff says, and puts the phone down.

Maybe right off the back of that no to Sam – when it can only be the legendary zombie master Sam Raimi – isn't the best moment, but I have to ask. 'What do you think of the show so far, Biff?'

Biff comes round the desk to me. 'Heard enough. *The A-Team* meets *The A-Team*.' He holds out his hand. '*I love it when a plan . . .* you know the rest.'

In shock, I shake his hand and stand up; shaking away in other places too, like I'm suffering from my own personal San Andreas quake.

'One condition, Kirk,' Biff says. 'Just make Face bisexual and the bad guys die, all right?'

Face bisexual? Bad guys die? That's two conditions and goes against the spirit of the show. It's a kids'

show, a big kids' show, my kind of show, but I say,
'Uh, OK.'

'I'll phone Harvey and we'll talk.'

Episode 5

What a meeting! It almost never happens this way;
studio execs never ever give the affirmative unless
there is no alternative. I'm so over the moon that
KITTSCH has to Auto-Cruise me back from Universal
City, through Hollywood and past the old real estate
sign on the hill, across West Hollywood, skirting
Beverly Hills to Westwood, to *B. L. Stryker*'s, the
dingy Irish sports pub I go to when I want to connect
in some weird way with the fleapit flat I started out
from five years ago in 1996, with the West Wood, Key
Biscayne – the name that drew me to live here – and
with England, my previous life.

The whole way to *B. L. Stryker*'s I'm thinking, Come
on, Harvey. Get me those six-by-six zeros!
$6,000,000. Wow! Eat your heart out everybody, and it
was virtually everybody I ever met, who ever doubted
me.

Eat your liver out the US Immigration Service, who
dicked me around over my US citizenship, and while I
was a bum-cum-waiter/writer threatened to make me
fly back 'home' to England every ninety days despite
my pathological *Fear Factor* of flying. I was treated
like an illegal alien – and this in my own adopted
country that I'd been resident in for fifteen years.
So what if I didn't bother to become a bona fide
citizen all those years! Who needs a passport in
the good ol' USA?

Eat your kidneys out those absentee landlords and

bosses who made me work like a dog in dodgy bars and as a waiter in À Votre Santé bistro all that time!

Yep, I'm a money-mad moon-zombie high on Zylon gas, coming back from *The Dead Zone* of no writing, craving my pounds of flesh.

When I get to the bar proper, I order six Black Bushes from José the dumb barman who reportedly had his tongue cut out by one of *The World's Most Dangerous Gangs*, the Bloods.

I stand there looking in the mirror. The Luke Duke of Hazzard lookalike there – slightly hunchbacked though and with mullet-less short hair – starts to knock each shooter back in one, folks.

Cheers.

'Eat your brain out, Angela, you bitch!' Lukealike me toasts. 'Bet you're sorry you left me now.'

I'm on my fourth when I hear my wristwatch com-link: 'I hate to drag you away from your sordid little soul sale, Kirk, but we do have a mission.'

I BLANK KITTSCH.

'Remember, your sister is in *Jeopardy*?'

I turn the com-link off and finish my last two drinks.

Strictly against the Californian social code – unofficial Prohibition – I order another six shooters. And *Cheers*, I get through them too.

Not surprisingly, due to alcohol abuse and BLANKing, I can't remember much of that afternoon, evening, or night – everything turns into the shadowy world of the *Knight Rider*.

Good buddy KITTSCH gets me home somehow.

Episode 6

I wake up early, as I always do, restless drunken sleep or not, 5.00 flashing red on the alarm clock. I try to move. That hurts, ow. My poor temples. My aching sinuses. It feels like I've been shot. Shot in the forehead. And if you've been shot in the head you're usually dead. But somehow I'm not? Maybe I've survived because I already have a metal plate in my skull where I was shot, like Michael Long, the cop who was gunned down by the baddies only to return to life dead: remade by flagging Vigilante billionaire Wilton Knight into the crime-fighting son he hoped to have – Michael Knight.

It hurts so bad to think. Why-ow-why did I do this to myself? Why could I not learn from my bloopers? Or, the prohibitions of others? You'd think having been shot twice in the head, once in Vietnam, once in California, would be enough to make anyone keep their head down? But nope, not brain-damaged Michael Long, and not me.

I get up out of the Hollywood bed and stagger into the kitchen. I can't take my Celebrex without eating so I take two plain codeines with yuck, multi-recycled LA tap water. My oesophagus and stomach heave as the hard pills and chill liquid go down; it's disturbing how you can feel bits of your body you don't normally feel when you're ill, how it grounds you.

I pass my green gym mat on the way back to bed.

24

Colonel Steve Austin tells me, You can't break the
training habit of every morning for three years.
Always protect your spine, buddy.

That kind of reinforcement works for me. I lie down
on the mat. I feel deadly weak and hung-over but I can
and do try. I'm a trier – if I'm anything. I do one
crunch. My abs wring my stomach tight and I feel a
surge of barf coming up. I hurriedly sit up.
Swallowing in exaggerated gulps, I hold it down.
Sometimes there's too much pain in life, or maybe the
wrong kind of pain, for it to be of any bloody use to a
body or mind whatsoever.

But I'm not going to just lie down and die, am I? A
swim! I'll do my forty lengths and then come back,
refreshed, to do my exercises afterwards. I can break
the routine and still complete the mission. I hunt
down my black Speedo shorts and struggle into them. I
walk down to the pool, slowly and unsurely.

To my relief, there is no one at or in the pool. I
put my towel down on my usual wooden lounger. I stare
into the blue water. It makes me feel all chilled
inside. I know the only way I'm going to get my body in
there is head first. I FLIP off my flip-flops and walk up
to the diving board.

That's when Sindy in her green wow-G-string bikini
sashays down the steps, bouncing all the way. 'Hi,'
she says beautifully.

'Hi. You're up early today,' I say as boldly as I
can, bouncing myself a little on the board like merman
Patrick Duffy would, then regretting it hugely
because my guts are on the move.

'Yeah,' I hear her say over the stuff SLOSHING,
THRASHING, MASHING in my stomach. 'How's things?' I
barely manage.

'Fine. You?'

There's a split second when I think about the

25

six-million-dollar deal, my hangover, Mom, Denise,
then I heave and BARF . . .

The brown puke-fall froths and seethes as it hits
the calm blue surface of the pool. I gag, then my
stomach racks itself again. My jaws stretch to-the-
max as the Yellowstone geyser exits my mouth.

I'm acutely aware that oh-so-kissable Sindy is
watching, but I can't stop the heaves. The retching.
The spin-spinny-dizziness. The fuzziness. It feels
like I'm going to pass out. BLANKing out when you're
being sick is another lousy family trait, inherited
from my dad, or at least the Rush side of our family
tree.

Pausing for special effect (beat) I should state
that I see all of the following from a POV (Point of
View) on the diving board, OK?

OK.

Believe it or not this is pure mind/body
dissociation, a chemical if not *Millennium*-type
spiritual split, OK?

OK.

Now, Sindy doesn't want to, but in good conscience
has to admit that the only way to rescue me from
drowning is to dive into the spreading ripples of my
puke. I watch her bouncing off the poolside, leaping
gracefully, streamlining her implant-curvy body as
much as she can, SPLASH, entering the water, and going
down deep like the dolphin Darwin in *Seaquest DSV*,
grabbing the sunken me, getting a hold of my head,
pulling me back up to the surface and, with some
effort, dragging me to the side of the contaminated
pool.

Once over there, she SLAPS my face a lot and yells
into my ears for people to come help us.

No one comes. So Sindy grabs hold of the step rail
and tries to pull me up out of the water herself. I'm

too heavy. Too dead-heavy. I want to help her, I'm over here on the board, not over there in the body.

After what seems like an eternity, Sindy's practised actress screams bring four other Sherman Sunrise residents out of their plush apartments. Two familiar female faces, *The Gilmore Girls*, mother and daughter body doubles. Along with some *Melrose Place*-trendy *Studs* with gleaming handguns who I've never seen, let alone met.

When they see what is going on the *Studs* put down their guns and haul me out of the pool.

Sindy orders the erstwhile rescuers to roll me onto my side, which they do. She pushes down on my diaphragm to flush out the water in my lungs.

Sindy turns me back over. She beats into my heart, compressing it with her palms: beat, beat, beat . . . CPR counting: 'One, two, three, four, five.'

She sets my head back, looks for obstructions in my mouth, and sticks her lips on mine. She does not seem to notice that her bikini top has worked loose . . .

I see Sindy's bared breasts swell, and her breath enter and expand my chest. Yep, the kiss of life fills me. It is our long-awaited first kiss. And what do I do in response? Face-Man-slick, I puke again, right into her mouth, that's what, and then BLANK.

My POV reverts to normal and I, one of the living dead, am looking up into her revolted, brown-barf-covered, bold and beautiful-beyond-belief face. When she sees I'm conscious again, Sindy covers up her tits with her perfectly toned and tanned arms, and gets off me.

I stand up under my own steam, a bit shaky. My head hurts like hell, even more hung-over than before.

Both the rescuer *Studs* CLAP my back like we're old buddies already. 'Far out, dude!' they say.

27

'Thanks Sindy,' I say, trying but failing miserably to avoid the guys' winding back-blows.

I don't know if she hears. The familiarish females are tending to her, trying to get her clean of my puke, and then hugging hero-her.

'Everybody, thanks,' I say, but I don't know if they hear.

The rescuer guys are picking up their guns and group-hugging her too.

'He should be checked up by the paramedics,' Sindy is saying to them, but the *Studs* are too busy pressing against her saviour tits, barf or no barf, to listen. *The Dating Game*.

'No paramedics, no doctors,' I say and sidle away from the feel-good huddle. I'm fine. I'm tired and in pain, and nearly dead, and at the end of the day I'm *The Man From Atlantis* unable to save myself, but I'm OK and I'm up the steps and on my way to my apartment before I hear them calling for me. No one follows me though. I guess that's because no one knows my name or where I'm *Living Single*. Not even Sindy.

I get into my apartment and I pour a glass of yuck tap water – to wash the puke-taste out of my mouth and to take two Advils. I figure I've left the last two codeines in the pool. Then I crash into my pit. I'm determined to sleep and let my poor body recover in its own time. But as I lie there in the near-darkness, looking at the grey-dappled ceiling around the curtains, I surprise myself by starting to cry. Funny thing is it's only my eyes, my eyes, which seem to let go, to stream. In a kind of shocked silence I let the tears roll down my temples and pool in my ears. It sounds like I'm under the water again.

Episode 7

I awake to the BLEEPETY-BLEEP-BLEEP-BLEEP of the
cellphone, the beginning of Ultravox's homage to
David Bowie's 'The Man Who Sold the World'. I roll off
my back, onto my right side, and lunge at the handset
by my pit. I grapple with it and fumble it up to my
ear. 'Yep?'

'Kirk, *amigo*, are you in bed?' asks the high-tar
voice of Harvey Guck.

'Yep, Harv.'

'It's three p.m.'

'Jesus.' I open my eyes. The dim red digits of my
alarm clock are right in front of me. They're the only
things I can see in the absolute darkness apart from
the image of Harvey as the fat Gene Hackman playing
Popeye Doyle in *The French Connection 2*.

'Why aren't you working on the treatment?' Harvey
asks.

'I nearly, eh, died this morning.'

'Yeah? You had an NDE? What was it like? Why didn't
you tell me?'

'I nearly bloody died this morning!'

But Harvey doesn't hear my pain. 'Did you see the
white light?'

'No.'

'Did you see your dead relative spirit guides?'

'No.' I suddenly feel like my near-death
experience hadn't been radical enough by Hollywood
standards, that other people had had more down to *The

29

Wire experiences, life-changing experiences.

'OK,' Harvey says, disappointed, 'Well, eh, right, now that you didn't die, be thankful – because I have some good news for you.'

'Good news?' I say. And it registers. Three p.m. good news from Harvey is not the same as three p.m. good news from anyone else. Agents don't phone unless they have really good news. That's why I sit bolt upright, alert and alive as I can be, without even the need for a slap across the right and the left cheeks. 'OK, I'm ready for it, you and Biff talked this morning and—'

'Long or short?'

'Short.'

'I got you three hundred K on acceptance of first draft against six hundred K on green light. More if you do the rewriting.'

Half a million dollars plus, man. It's a *Big Deal*, a *Jackpot*! salary for any screenwriter, but it isn't my dream figure of six million. I have to ask: 'Any profit share?'

'You're kidding.'

'Any merchandising share?'

'What the Guck!' Harvey nearly chokes on tar-glued phlegm. 'Merchandising. Listen, this is a great deal I got you. How's about some serious gratitude?'

'Thanks, Harv.'

'Jesus kid, but you're hard to please.'

'I said thanks.'

'I heard you. Listen, come down to my new club tonight and we'll talk about what this really means to you. Yeah?'

If we have to talk face-to-face that means there's a catch. 'What's the catch?'

'Don't worry. I'll get a limo to pick you up at eight and take you to the club.'

30

'A limo?' I ask. Harvey isn't dirt cheap like most agents because he has Dick Leck (who'd just sold the script of *Buck Rogers in the 25th Century* for $500K) and Francesco Alvarez (who'd been contracted to write the movie of *CHiPs* for $250K) and Chucky Nightingall ($1 million dollar writer of *The Fantastic Four*) on his books but this, this is way OTT. 'A club?' I ask.

'Later.' Harvey rings off.

So $600,000 is there for the taking if I do whatever it is Biff wants: boffing, buffing, buggering. But 600K isn't going to make me *The Six Million Dollar Man*. I decide I can live with that. Till next time. I think about phoning home to tell Mom about *The Sale of the Century*, but then I remember Denise. I think about getting in touch with my best mate from UM – the University of Miami – again (after UM, who knows how many years?) but Len is a mutual, neutral friend of both Denise and me. So, there's no one to call nationally and there's no one to call locally. Everybody I know in LA is in the Industry – waiters, agents, writers, directors, producers. And I can't talk about the deal because it doesn't do to have wagging tongues at such an early stage. Too many things can go wrong. *Who Do You Trust*? You can't trust anybody.

I have to take my mind off the deal, BLANK it and my NDE. Writing is the answer. My work is my whole life in LA, or should I say play is my whole life? Because screenwriting is *Child's Play*, structured play for big kids.

I hit the universal *Remote Control*. Up comes my character research: run VT (a laser disc, actually) of *The A-Team* strutting their knuckle-headed stuff. No bull, ever since I was a kid growing up in the '80s – a natural process that seems to have failed in my case – these five iconic characters have fascinated me. And I know this sounds dumb but, when I started to analyse it, I understood why: for me these avengers had come to represent different archetypal patterns of what it is to be human: these fugitives from earthly justice, these pursuers of a higher moral calling, these soldiers of fortune:

Colonel John 'Hannibal' Smith represents the Thinking Leader: inspirational, zany-but-brainy, above all honourable in his soldiering.

Bosco 'Bad Attitude' Baracus represents the Fixing Fighter: raw aggression coupled with hands-on mechanical genius.

Lieutenant Templeton 'Face Man' Peck is the Lying Lover.

Captain 'Howling Mad' Murdock is the Flying Trickster in the pack.

Amy Amanda Allen 'Triple A' is the Triple Goddess, the soul or whatever, of the team.

I still want to be a member of *The A-Team*, A-hero, aged thirty-one. I'm still watching them. Trying to be one of this *Band of Brothers*, the key, I think, to all of them – Howling Mad Murdock. Dwight Schultz's characterisation is the main focus of my attention. I listen to his maniacal dialogue, his delusional rants, his multiplying split personalities. Say, are we a groovy, happening bunch of guys or . . . what? You know I think that big angry guy is getting worse. Be careful with that mud pie – it took me hours to make and bake it! I'm convinced through his TV schizophrenia I will get into the hearts and minds of the others.

Episode 8

The white stretch limo comes at 8.00 on the dot. I'm
all researched out and more than ready for it at the
entrance to the apartments. I don't know where I'm
supposed to be going so I'm dressed in smart but
casual Versace black slacks and a red shirt *à la
Magnum P. I.*: both of which I'd purchased in Style
Clones, the new 'Cool Britannia, Britannia waves the
rules' outfitter based on *Rodeo Drive*.

'Where are we going?' I ask the suited driver as
soon as I get in the back.

'Venice,' he answers in a heavy-duty Mexican
accent like Benicio del Toro.

That strikes me as odd because there's no clubs in
Venice; there's nothing in Venice at night but
bottle-breaking bearded bums. 'What's the name of
this club, *comprendez*?'

The driver says, 'Disease.'

'Do what?'

'Disease. Off Main Street.'

I've been to the Beach area – the rollerblading,
jogging, biking, posing capital of the daytime world
– many times with Angela-X, but I've never heard of
Disease. Certainly Harvey hasn't mentioned it. But
then, like all early-born Generation X-ers, he's too
into chasing the latest fad in town, too intent on
being one of the first to experience something new to
have time to let anyone else in on stuff.

Disease is the 'Pure Cheese Club' or so the

33

strap-line on the neon sign set over the entrance of
the three-storey mock Art Deco building proclaims.
Lit up there, in glowing red and yellow, is a cheese-
ball that looks like a piss artist's impression of the
HIV retrovirus.

When the limo draws up a big black bouncer comes to
the kerb and opens the door for me. 'You're here to
see Mr Guck?'

'Yep.'

'Follow me, sir,' says the bouncer, who looks like
high school basketball coach, Mr Cooper.

Hangin' With Mr Cooper, I notice he has bullet
holes in his suit and blood oozing from them. 'Are you
all right?' I ask him.

'Oh yeah.' The bouncer shrugs. 'It's Street Art.'

I get out of the limo. '*Gracias*,' I tell the
driver.

There's a small queue to get in but the shot-but-
not bouncer ushers me straight past the roped-in
mainly male crowd and through the front door, celeb-
stylie. 'Mr Guck is in The Ladies' Room, sir,' he
says.

I'm reluctant to enter. The Ladies' Room has a
taboo Lady's WC sign on the door.

'Go on in, sir.'

'OK. Fine.' I go in.

The Ladies' Room is Ghetto Revival, much like you'd
imagine a washroom to be like in Downtown or South
Central - real beat up. Every surface painted or tiled
in a faded shade of blue. Large graffitied cubicles up
one wall. Chipped basins up the other, with cracked
make-up mirrors hovering over each; a broken tampon-
cum-condom machine near the door; automatic hand
blow-dryers that are hanging off the wall. The only
discernible difference between this fake and the real
thing is that there are no ladies of the night in

34

here; all you can hear from the cubicles is a chorus of *Just Men!* voices.

'Harv?' I call out. 'Is there a Harvey Guck in here?'

'Yeah, first cubicle.'

I go to the first cubicle and KNOCK on the door.

'Come in for Christ's sake.'

I open the door. There's big, fat Harvey, sucking on a Death butt, sitting on a low-down stool and using a toilet with the lid down as a drinks table. 'Eh, hi Harv',' I say.

'What do you think, kid?'

'It's definitely you.' I sit down.

'I knew you'd like it!' Harvey's fat, hairy, brass-neck quivers with excitement. 'The whole place is divided up into these happening suites that are supposed to make you feel that your instilled fear of others, self-loathing, bodily disgust, sexual hang-ups and sense of mortality are all exaggerated. Quite clever. Reminds me of Claes Oldenburg.'

'Yep?' Claes who?

'The best bit is the amputee lap dancer. We'll go catch her show after we finish our chat, OK?'

'Em . . .'

Harvey gets out a small vial of white powder. With a 2000-yard stare he asks, 'Do you want some Special K?'

'Don't do it.'

'Why not?'

The answer to that question was observing the real-life *Miami Vice*, seeing Denise's addictions destroy her. 'No reason, I suppose.'

As Harvey cuts two lines on the lid, there's a RUMBLING and BURBLING from the bog below. And a really foul stink fills the cubicle.

'Think of it as therapy,' Harvey says.

'Only in LA,' I say, grimacing at the stink.

35

Harvey snorts his line expertly. 'Yummy,' he says and hands me the rolled $100 note.

I do my line. But the powder stings the hell out of my left nostril, making me feel like I've gone blind. I don't seem to breathe much in, more like swallow clots of the foul-tasting ook. I cough. I splutter. I feel a small BUZZING in the back of my head as a reward.

'Stylish, kid. Stylish,' Harvey laughs. 'OK. Here's the deal. Universal's legal eagles are going to draw up the contract pronto-Tonto. It should be ready for you to sign in a month. Meantime, Biff wants you *The Lone Ranger* to get on with the script treatment. Payment will be made on delivery of the first draft.'

There's the catch I had been waiting for! My head clears real fast into *LA Law* mode. 'Hold on, Harv. No pay, no work on any treatment, let alone the script.'

'Don't get all paranoid on me, kid. I want to get paid too, *remember*.'

I hand Harvey his $100 back. 'But I told you to tell him—'

'Do you want this deal?'

'You know I do.'

'Well Biff McMurray doesn't take on precious writers. If I have to go back to him with niggles he'll hire someone else to do your idea.'

I make up my mind right there that OK, I'll write *The A-Team* treatment, as required, but that I won't go ahead with the script. Strictly research and development. 'OK,' I say.

'Then we're all set.' He CLAPS me on the arm. 'Didn't I tell you I was going to put you on the bridge of the *Enterprise*, Kirk? Didn't I?'

'Actually Harv,' as I recall our first meeting, with the benefit of non-nostalgic hindsight, you said I had potential, potentially.'

36

'Yeah, well, I didn't want you to get a big head.'

I do another line and follow Harvey out of The Ladies Room into The Cut 'n' Thrust Bar. It's a small, oval, pink place lined with mirrors, so 'intimate' is the word, maybe even 'vaginal'. And, true to Harvey's warning, there's a black stripper straddling a pole on the bar.' Her right arm is gone. And in its place she's wearing a kind of prosthetic device with two hooks on the end of it. I have to say, it's a pretty sick sight at first. Extreme. And the better part of me doesn't want to look up at her, but there's nowhere else to look without seeing another reflection of her, so I can't stop looking up to her inhuman arm.

'Isn't she something?' Harvey says, lighting up a Death.

'Yep,' I agree. Because he is right: the Prosthetic Woman, down to her white panties and stockings, is beautiful. Older, yep. But she has these long athletic legs that end in a fantastic butt. And toned abs, overshadowed by pert tits that are small and natural-looking. And a lovely, wide and rounded face shocked by red- and black-beaded hair.

The cruel fact that she'd lost her right arm somewhere and still has the guts to strip makes her somehow more attractive than repulsive, and yet curiously repulsive at the same time. It's like she exerts the same cybernetic-as-opposed-to-animal magnetism on me as Lindsay Wagner did in the '80s – I want to love her altogether but she scares me. To pieces. Her sheer strength scares me as she strips down to nothing.

As the Prosthetic Woman steps down, I gaze around the bar at Harvey and the other ten or so men there. They look like they're feeling the same thing. The reaction . . . Let's just say she gets great tips.

Harvey wants me to take a shower in The Bloodbath

Suite but nope, that's it for me; I've had enough
disease for one night. I leave him at the door of The
Unisex Changing Room. 'You'll have to come again,' he
says.

'Cheers, Harv, but I don't think so.'

'Later, kid.'

On the way home in the taxi (nobody in their right
mind walks in Venice or anywhere else in LA under *Dark
Skies*) I think about my sister and the medical
technology that has helped her live a year and a half
beyond the point where her own nature and nurture had
determined she should die. I think about the way she'd
initially refused to give up believing that some day
her kidneys would be healed. I think about the fact
that in less than two weeks, without my help, she
could be dead. And for a second, just a second in my
coke-monkey head, with my own 2000-yard stare, I see
the *Dark Angel* of Denise dancing in the Cut 'n' Thrust
Bar, stripped of her dignity yet strangely noble,
connected to a haemodialysing machine in the bar by a
transparent tube and port in her jugular. In that
instant I can see the bad blood flowing between them.
But the good . . . where's the *good*?

BLANK? But it's no use. I can't get that *Eerie,
Indiana* image of her out of my mind. There's only one
other thing for it. When I get back home it's 10.41. I
add three hours: 1.41 a.m., not exactly prime time.
Still, I phone Mom. I want to ask her if Denise has
turned up yet. But . . .

But, the bloody messaging service kicks in.

I put the phone down. What to do?

Len. Yep, I can phone Len? He's in the same time
zone as Mom. It takes me five minutes to find the last
number I have for him in my old Filofax but I get it
all right.

The phone rings a long time, a bloody aeon of BLEEP-

38

BLEEPS, so long I'm trying to work out how to hail him on other frequencies when he answers: 'Hello?'

'Spock, that you?'

'Who's that?'

'Who else calls you Spock?'

'Everybody nowadays.'

Doh! I've temporarily forgotten the back-story: Len, once my best classmate in film school, is now professionally Mr Spock, *Star Trek* Conventions Officer. 'Well it's me, Captain Kirk, here.'

'Captain Kirk?' He gets the moving picture.

'How's it going with you?'

'It's twenty-to-two in the morning,' says Len.

'Yep? Sorry, long time no speak . . .' It must have been a year? 'You know me.'

'Yeah,' Len says.

There's one of those awkward silences people always give me when I talk to them after being away so long, phone them in the middle of the night, and wake them from their sleep. 'Ah, sorry man, I'll call back tomorrow . . .'

'No, no.' Len clears his throat. 'So, I heard from Denise you were doing real good in LA?'

'Yep.'

'So, you coming back sometime soon or what?'

Len lives two streets away from my parents on Key Biscayne so I can't say yep for certain, because I don't know when I will be bringing Denise home. 'Maybe.'

'That would be good!' He sounds genuinely pleased – for me, an all too rare sound around people, basically because I'm no Joey or Ross or Chandler Bing or Rachel or Phoebe or Monica. I suck at *Friend*ship long- or short-distance.

'Yep.'

'Let me know when, before the when?'

He knows that I know that he knows that when I go back home, that oddest occasion, I generally try to arrive *Out Of The Blue*; that way I'm free to do what I like, no high expectations. 'Yep. Will do when I know. So, how are things on planet Trekkie?'

That gets him diverted, politely. 'OK, Captain. Status report since last year is . . . Mary's got a Vulcan in the oven.'

'Wow. That's good. Congrats.'

'Due August.'

'Congrats again.'

'The good thing is I get paternity leave. That's another one of the beauties of this conventions job.' Len laughs for a bit, then coughs.

I fall silent because life movies on and I didn't know how to say what I want to say after his good news . . .

Thankfully, he spits it out for me: 'You're really ringing about Denise, aren't you, Kirk?'

'Nope.'

'You're *not* concerned about her?'

'Not at all.'

'Remember us Vulcans have a superior logical intellect?'

'OK, Spock. You got me.'

'You want to know where she's gone, right?'

'Yep.'

'Good. Because I think she needs somebody to be there for her.'

'So, if I gave you a direct order, Mr Spock?'

'Then I would be duty bound to report, Captain, that if Scotty beamed you down to planet Earth, continental USA, Florida State, Miami, South Beach, corner of 'the Road' and Collins, to My Beautiful Laundrette, you might well be able to use your Tricorder to pick up her trail.'

40

'To boldly go?'

'Exactly, Captain. Ask for the owner, Mercury.'

'That her new girlfriend?'

'It's that kind of establishment, but I can't say.'

I talk to a yawning Len for about another five minutes but I can't get another peep out of him about Denise.

I also can't get him to reconsider naming his son, if indeed the foetus is a son (they didn't want to know at the ultrasound scan), William Shatner Morris. I tell him that to be nicknamed after Captain James T Kirk of the Starship *Enterprise*, or his actor alter ego, is a hard thing to live up to: I should know thanks to him.

I also make him note in his Science Officer's log that even William Shatner isn't really called William Shatner any more, or even goddam James T, but rather, on Star Date 1982, whatever, had changed his name by good deed poll to Sergeant T J Hooker.

Episode 9

BLANK?

But nope. Dialysis means that three sessions a week, four hours a time, my sister Denise has to hook up to a big dialyser machine to have her blood separated, and all the waste-products-gone-toxins that healthy kidneys would normally remove filtered out. Potassium. Sodium. Phosphate. Urea (Nitrogen).

I've only seen her on that machine once, at Xmas 1998, six months after her ESKD (End Stage Kidney Disease). That was tough enough though. The dialyser looked less like an artificial kidney, more like an instrument of techno-torture from that absurd cult '60s TV show *The Prisoner*.

And she has to do this because—

I believe the machine is set to remove excess fluid too, but Denise doesn't need this. Last time I heard she could still piss. Clear water though, no yellow tint—

To my mind, she has to do this because—

In my limited experience if you BLANK things, and BLANK the BLANKing, and overuse the special effect of the BLANKing, it always comes back on you—

Denise has to do this, dialyse, because—

Because I didn't, couldn't, wouldn't offer her a kidney for LRD (Living Related Donor) transplant.

There, I'm admitting ''it''.

BLANK?

But nope. The morning after the white ook, feeling

42

way low down, I just can't seem to fire those *Blankety Blanks*. Guilt, the call of conscience or, if you like, the furious Lieutenant Colonel Lynch and his MPs come after me this way: I become this crazed fugitive set on a crazy *Mission: IMPOSSIBLE* that I won't inform my nagging mom about till I'm on the jazz, man. I'll take a long weekend off, max, go find Denise in Miami Beach, and if we can talk *Hart to Hart*, for once, and if she goes back on dialysis, I can try my best to talk to her about other stuff. Your sister will self-destruct in five, four, three . . .

At 5.45 I'm on the net searching for a flight from LAX to Miami. I find out Miami Air MA - 345 is set to depart at 9.30 a.m. today, Saturday, 28th April 2001, and that the ticket, price $1500, is open-ended and to be collected at check-in.

The Price is Right. My mission is set, with A-Team precision. So before the B.A. Baracus in my mind – the pathological terror of plummeting from 30,000 feet and crashing – can intimidate me back out of it, I book it with my, get this for product placement, Universal Entertainment Platinum Mastercard.

Episode 10

My morning Pilates routine on the green mat is hard going but I know if I'm going to be in a DVT economy class airline seat for five hours I'll have to get the muscles in the correct alignment and make sure pain doesn't shut them down. After I swallow my Celebrex, I drop three diazepam to drug away any of those pre-plane-crash nerves the way wily old Colonel Smith and the team do to a certain Sergeant Baracus on every overseas mission.

I think seriously about a swim to take my mind off the imminent journey but nope, not after the *Shenanigans* of the day before. Instead, I get packing. It's only a one-bag walk-on-off job. My Crockett 'n' Tubbs wardrobe (post-Angela) containing Versace pastel shirts and multi-pleated baggy trousers bought for sunning and swimming, selling, and at least the idea of sexing, will do. I tell myself that I won't be there long, that I'll be able to buy anything else I need there, on the ground, safe and sound and likely suffering from jetlag.

When I finish packing – the essential Dell notebook and Nok-Nokia cellphone are the last things in – I lock up the apartment and head down to KITTSCH.

'Going somewhere, Kirk?' The car sneers as I drop the bag in the trunk.

'Yep. LAX,' I reply.

'I knew you'd see sense. Saving your sister will—'

'Shut up, KITTSCH.'

44

'There's no call for that kind of rudeness, Kirk. I was merely—'

'Shut the hell up, KITTSCH,' I say, and get into the driver's seat.

I take off with a screech of tyres, for show as usual, and to let that smart-arse car know who is boss.

I swipe my security card on the gate control and exit.

Ventura Boulevard links with the San Diego Freeway, which snakes the whole way down to LAX: an easy drive if you're not doped up to the eyeballs and trying to draw a BLANK from somewhere, anywhere, so you don't have to think any deeper about exactly how you're going to talk Denise back onto dialysis – under the sometimes watchful, sometimes wandering eye of a mad mom?

BLANK: the diazepam takes full and fearsome effect about halfway there; it's like I'm suffering from Zylon gas poisoning. Everything slows down as if the car and I have turned into a moon buggy and this is zero gravity. And yet, it's hard to keep my lids open in the weightlessness; they're so dead heavy.

I try to fight the zombification but I swerve across lanes and KITTSCH sounds off: 'Earth calling Kirk!'

'What, good buddy?' I reply.

The sound of horns BLARING. Looking up, I vaguely see I've nearly rammed a red Porsche Carrera, and probably would have but for KITTSCH switching to Auto-Cruise.

'Where would you be without me?' I hear KITTSCH contemplate.

I mumble, 'Miami.'

Episode 11

'Rise and shine, Kirk. Rise and shine.'

I come to in Long Stay Lot C, a bit perturbed by my
own pale reflection on the car side-window. 'What time
is it?'

'It's seven ten a.m. You need to go check in now.'

Living-dead clumsy, I almost fall out of the car,
but then I manage to get my bags all right and lock up.

'I'll be here, bay H, *Space 1999*, when you get
back,' KITTSCH states. 'Now, it would make sense for
you to go find the Departures courtesy shuttle, don't
you think?'

I don't think, I'm not capable of thinking; I just
do what I'm told – the $600,000 astronaut in me
somehow making it through Zero-G, onto the courtesy
bus and to Departures on the upper level of Terminal
Two.

The A-Team always gets B.A. on planes by means of a
ruse like bringing him in on a stretcher, saying he
needs a heart transplant or something to the
stewardesses. But I'm only one man, not *A-team*.

I insist to the girl at the check-in desk that my
name is Murdock, not Kirk Rush at all.

'Why isn't this the name on your passport?' she
asks.

My *MADtv* reply is: 'Because Murdock can fly, by
night or day, and I don't want to be B.A.'

The girl, who looks a lot like my *Love At First
Sight* black-black-haired Angela, my Los Angela, Los

46

Angela the X, or LAX for short, issues me a boarding pass with the advice that If she were me, she'd start drinking coffee, lots of Starbucks' finest before heading to gate SG-1.

I-B.A. take her advice: there's a Starbucks in the airport recreational area. Where in this Universalised universe isn't there a Starbucks these days! I go in and order 'A *Battlestar Galactica* mocha.' But those suckas don't seem to get my in-joke, even when I explain: 'Face, *Alias* the actor Dirk Benedict, was Starbuck in a previous life incarnation, the ace-fighter of the Cylons.'

They give me an iced mocha and wish me a pleasant onward journey. Helluva tough me drops it in the liquor section of Duty Free without touching a drop: B.A.'s 'Good Advice' this episode, kids, is to never drink or do drugs, kids, because drugs and drink are for suckas.

Nobody from LAX security stops me from going on to *Stargate SG-1* either. I really want some jive-assed fool to stop *T and T* me, and say, 'You're bombed out your body and mind and gold necklaces, sir. Step this way!' but they don't.

Swaying around precariously, I get the whole way to the gate on those 'You are coming to the end of the walkway!' travelators.

At the gate I sit down on a steel seat. I don't go to sleep because I snore, loudly, because my nose has been busted three times in WWF bouts I did not decisively win or lose thanks to all the alleged match rigging surrounding me and my Hollywood star tag-team partner Hulk Hogan.

But . . .

No one says a damn thing till some kindly old doll who looks like Katherine Hepburn wakes me up and tells me we're boarding and that she doesn't like flying much

47

either, and can I help her get up because she's just
had her second hip replacement some four months back
and it still hurts like Spencer-Tracey-O, my boy.

So I-B.A. hinder her down the tunnel to the light
at the end – plane doors and two smiling stewardesses.
Angels that they are, Roma Downeys the pair of them,
they touch and take her from there.

Old Katherine says I am gentlemanly, or gallant, or
something else absurd. That's how I get on the plane
even though I must look absolutely pissed or doped out
of my mind: a potential air-rage case if ever the crew
saw one.

'Twelve B.A.'s my seat,' I tell the head stewardess.

Realising *The Sky Is The Limit* for me, she escorts
me to my seat and stores my hand baggage in the
overhead locker. That's where my Bad Attitude finally
crashes and I lay me down to sleep, praying the pilot
and autopilot my soul, or whatever, to keep.

There is something wrong with your TV
but do not do anything. We are controlling
the pictures. We will control the spinal.
We will control the lumbar, thoracic and
cervical. You are about to experience
the back stories, vertebra by
vertebra, to THE OUTER LIMITS of
a Kafkaesque absurdiT.V.

Lumbar 5

Once upon a transmission time, in 1973, long before
the inception of *The Simpsons* as the most
dysfunctional family in the world, K's mom presents
him with a bundle of swaddling clothes that he is told
is his new sister D. Terrible two-and-a-half K had
wanted someone to play with, someone like himself, so
when he's told he has a little sister, he's not best
pleased. 'A gurl!' K cries out. And when he sees that
within the bundle the 'gurl' is in fact an ugly baby,
ugly enough to be in *The Munsters*, despair: 'Her have
no teeth and her can't talk.' His mom tells K to kiss D
hello but he decides that her face is too puffy and
red and drooly-wet to kiss.

Lumbar 4

Prim Donna-to-be D takes her time growing up. All she
will say is, 'Doodle, doodle, doodle.' It is three
years before the *Rugrats* can play any decent game
together. D gets all the attention meanwhile: their
actor/dad even has a handyman build her a sandpit
where she can play with her dopey dollies. Not fair,
not fair at all. So, one day when she is three, K
decides to get his own back on her. He makes this mud
pie, with mud from the back garden and sand from the
pit and some grass as a topping, and pretends to eat
it in front of her. When D starts crying, 'Gimme,

51

gimme,' he gives her a bit. Which she gobbles down
greedily. K feeds her bit after bit until she is sick
all down her bib. And then she goes inside to tell
their mom on the 'dirty poo-eater'.

Lumbar 3

As all 'archetoonal' six- and four-year-old kids long
to do, K and D learn how to play with fire. Early one
morning, just as the day is dawning, K goes into his
sister's bedroom and wakes her up by sticking his
finger up her nostril. He makes sure to grab her hands
so she doesn't slap him before he can tell her his
plan. 'We're going to light a fire in the living room.'
D stops struggling and gets out of bed. 'A fire?'
'Yes,' K says. 'What about Daddy?' she says. 'We have
to be quiet. Can you be really quiet, D?' 'I can be
quieter than you!' 'No, you can't.' 'Yes, I can.'
Silence. 'Yes, I can!' 'See, you can't. Now shhh.' And
so the two of them sneak out of D's bedroom, down the
stairs; creeping across the hall, past their mom and
dad's room, and into the cavernous living room. K
makes straight for the sofa and the stash of safety
matches he'd taken from the mantelpiece the day
before and hidden there. He opens the box, and with D
standing next to him, strikes a match. Fire. 'Oooo.'
The match burns out. Another. 'Aaaaa.' And another.
Promethean sulphur and brimstone grow thick in the
room. They are both so fascinated that they don't
notice the tell-tale noises from upstairs that their
Family Guy dad is awake and up, and about to catch
them. Till it is too late. 'What are you two doing?'
their dad yells. D's answer to her enraged dad is: 'K
was trying to burn me.' As punishment, K is nailed to

the nearest hill where an eagle will come every day to
tear out his rejuvenating liver. (That last bit isn't
one of *Shelley Duvall's Tall Tales and Legends* but it
is a myth, a Greek belief cast into eternal syndication. K is never *Chitty Chitty Bang Banged*.
Instead, he is forbidden to watch *The Muppet Show* for
two whole weeks.)

Lumbar 2

D has nightmares about the Big Bad Wolf, who her dad
tells her lives down 'the lane' at the bottom of their
street, Melville Court (a harmless joke, to stop her
from straying too far). So, whenever K wants to get
away from her to play with his school friends, Jack
Beavis and Garthe Butthead, all he has to do is go
down the alleyway to stop her following him around.
But, one bright spring day, when he is seven and
officially capable of reasoning, he is fleeing her on
his go-kart, while she is on her bike. He knows she is
going to follow him down the alley and on from there,
so he resolves to hide himself and the go-kart behind
a corner. D comes riding down the alley crying out,
'Hey, come back, please.' But K just snarls at her,
like the Big Bad Wolf. D screams and falls off her
bike. Instead of going to his mate Garthe's house in
South Park, his *Futurama* is altered, and K has to pick
still screaming D up, drag her home, butter her up and
beg her not to tell on him, which of course she does
anyway. (K is not allowed to watch any TV for a
month.)

Lumbar 1

In 1981 there is a rare thing in Crouch End, London, a
long sunny summer that runs well into August. With it
comes a plague of bin-loving wasps. Jam-traps aside,
they turn the back garden where K and D play into a no-
go area. Yet, in spite of K's dire warnings, D goes
there obsessively to make mud pies. And gets stung.
She cries for ages afterwards, 'It hurts,' then, not
long after her mom has put TCP on the wound, she rips
up a bamboo plant cane and swears vengeance. Now K,
who is playing soldiers in the safer front garden,
hears her shouts round the back, and walks round to
find her whipping the cane at the wasps, fencing the
dreaded black and yellow enemy. It looks like his
sister is in trouble, losing a battle against a
superior/inferior force, Mother Nature angry, so *King
of the Hill* K comes to the rescue like the king in the
picture book of Greek myths Mom had given him for
Xmas: Killer Theseus, high culture hero of old,
rescuing Ariadne from the dreaded Mino-Wasp. He runs
and gets himself a bamboo cane and starts whipping
like mad. On come the wasps, wave after wave, and WHIP,
WHIP, down they go, cut to pieces. Hundreds die that
day in the name vengeance. In the evening, D has pity
on the dead and resolves to pick up their dismembered
bodies and bury them. 'I'm going to make the flower bed
over in the corner the Wasps' Graveyard,' she says. K
objects, 'No, you're not. That's where I play war.' D
starts crying up a murderous tantrum. K relents
because as he says, 'The bodies will rot in no time.'

Bye-Bye! Magazine

Joe Heller The Dangers of False Gods, 23 January 2001

Do you sometimes want to be somebody special, imagine you're somebody successful on the TV or in the movie you just saw? Do you 'love' someone to-die-for glamorous? Don't worry, that's harmless fun – the experts say you're normal. However, according to *Pop Science* magazine, a third of people in the US suffer from Celebrity Worship Syndrome (CWS), 'a fascination with the lives of the rich and famous that for some becomes a dangerous obsession'.

Psychologists Gene Skinner of UCLA and Jimmy-Joe Coen of Milwaukee University interviewed 1000 people about their personality and interest in the stars. The results were disturbing. Thirty-two percent of those questioned showed signs of the borderline-pathological CWS personality disorder.

Twenty percent of these celebrity devotees were obsessional in that they compulsively followed their idols in the mass media for 'entertainment-social reasons'. 'These people seem to have adopted a hero/heroine to fill the gaps in their lives that the breakdown of extended families and communities has brought about,' said Dr Skinner. 'The TV teenagers from Generation X seem to be exceptionally prone to this syndrome.'

Ten percent of worshippers were addicts. 'These people genuinely believe that there is some special bond between them and the star,' said Dr Skinner. These people are neurotic, emotional, moody, tense types that may be prone to mental instability and flights from reality. Dr Skinner: 'This correlates loosely with the figure that one in ten people will suffer from a mental illness in their lives.'

The remaining two percent were pathological. 'These are sufferers from psychotic conditions like post-traumatic stress disorder, borderline personality disorder, anti-social personality disorder, dissociative identity disorder, schizophrenia and many others. They include celebrity stalkers, who latch onto a familiar, famous face for dear life, and also those who are willing to hurt themselves or others in the name of their idol.'

'Worshipping a celebrity doesn't make you dysfunctional,' *Pop Science* quoted Dr Skinner as saying, 'But there is a slippery slope of behaviors and if you start – say typically because you've lost a loved one and are in crisis – the star might take over your life.'

http://www.bye-bye!_magazine.com

Episode 1

MIA: Missing in Action in Miami International
Airport. That's where I am, still half-zonked, still
fear-full of flying, but on terra firma, definitely more
phobic BO than B.A. Missing In Action, Missing
Inaction? Crash down: she's breaking up. Weeks of
intensive care, cutting-edge surgery, a cry-for-help
suicide attempt. Who am I, Oscar, what am I, tell me?
Will you rebuild me like Steve Austin. Have you the
technology? Have you the capability to remake the
world's second bionic man? Can you make me better than
I was before? Stronger. Faster . . . Yep, that big sign
on the wall, in huge capitals like all airport signs –
CONCOURSE F. That's where I F-ing am, with passengers
power-walking by me to get to BAGGAGE RECLAIM.

Jet-lagged, I just let the masses rush on. I don't
have to go there. I'll be first out. That's the beauty
of one bag, and having bionic legs driven by plutonium
power-cells. I just have to walk out of F, which I do,
and get to the EXIT, and hail a cab, yep, hail a cab,
because I won't drive any car that isn't KITTSCH,
especially a rental. Simple plan. But . . .

But what is it with these *Hare Krishna, Krishna,
Krishna* freaks and airports, huh? They get on my
nerves at the worst of times: pre- and post-flight.
Here they are, the spit of *Dharma and Greg*, outside
the Universal Starbucks, dancing and chanting and
BANGING drums. Go figure: yep, it's the link between the
Airport disaster movies, imminent mortality and

afterlife insurance, but it must also be the attraction of the vast recycling acoustics of the aluminium-can-like terminals. BEAT-BEAT.

BEAT . . .

And, wait for it, back-BEAT.

An Indian, leukaemia-bald, Jaclyn Smith from *Charlie's Angels*, prances up to me, her pink and orange robes billowing, and holds out one of those Bird of Paradise flowers. She has a nice smile but I mumble at her, 'No thanks.'

Proffering the flower once more, she says, 'Life is a prison. Set yourself free or your bad karma will cause you to reincarnate again and again till you are lost.'

I do not accept the flower.

I walk by her and onto the moving walkway. It takes me away from her, but not as quickly as I'd like. I hear her calling after me, 'You have no freedom, no independence in the material world illusion. Join the super-soul. Krishna is the supreme personality of the godhead.'

I start walking on the walkway, at Steve Austin speed, man- and machine-power carrying me to the EXIT of ARRIVALS.

Episode 2

It's five-forty p.m. EST when I walk out the automatic doors. Air-con gone, a familiar wave of wet heat envelops me. Temp: seventy-five degrees Fahrenheit in the shade. Humidity must be 80 per cent. And no wind, no breeze; the row of international flags outside the terminal hang limp on pristine poles.

I start sweating immediately – in the pit of my back. I hate that. It reminds me of the pain locked in there, which starts it throbbing again. That just doesn't happen as much in the dry *LA Heat*.

There's a snake of yellow taxis on standby outside the terminal headed up by one unmistakable orange 01, the General Lee. Yep, a 1969 Dodge Charger done up with the Battle Flag on the roof, just like in *The Dukes of Hazzard*. A driver after my own heart! Why not a theme taxi service called Hazzard Cabs! Miami is second only to LA for its TV-craziness. This is after all why Mom agreed to be headhunted from the BBC and moved us all here in 1985: through her old girls' network, she got a job as head of wardrobe and make-up on *Miami Vice*.

I walk up to the General in a state of awe. I half-expect the passenger door to be welded shut and to have to slide into the front seat through the open window, but the door handle CLUNKS open. I get into the bucket seats. I flop my bag onto my knee. I look over. The driver, an unusually lanky Cuban with bleached-blond hair smiles and greets me with: '*Mucho gusto, amigo.*'

'Thanks,' I reply. I'm so surprised to be welcomed by a cab driver – most just lash you with some foreign tongue – that I add, 'Good to meet you too.'

'I see you are a man who likes the car, *si*?' He GUNS the huge V8 four-litre engine.

I nod. '*Si.*'

REVVING, it sounds so great.

'I run four others just like her. I start company when I come here, *dos* years.'

'Great idea,' I say, almost envious – would have been but for KITTSCH.

The driver BANGS the steering wheel like a good ol' boy. 'I like the show, you know?'

'Me too.'

'I like the Bo, and Luke. Most of all, I like Daisy . . .' He talked on about how she was poured into those denim cut-offs.

'Yep.' I'm too tired, too zonked, to take in this *Big Surprise* and my eyes stray to the meter.

The driver takes that as his cue to hit the Dixie Horn and pull away from the head of the shaded taxi rank and out into the laser rays of the sun.

'*Yeeee-haw!*' The rebel yell makes me jump. 'Where to, *amigo*?'

'My Beautiful Laundrette, SoBe,' I answer. 'You know it?'

'*Si*, but *hombre*, you sure you want to go there?' the driver knows that it's a lesbian bar. He wants to see if I do too.

'Yep.' I give him a look that says it all: that my sister is a lesbian, or at least swings both ways, and that I'm not keen on talking about it.

'OK. South Beach is Zone Four. Twenty-five dollars flat fare.'

62

'Sounds about right.' It's about sixteen miles to the beach. The driver, with the assurance of a moonshiner, negotiates the jam on palm-tree-lined 37th Avenue, gets to Highway 836, and heads east: that's the way to go all right even if there's a sign reading ROAD UNDER CONSTRUCTION.

So what if I'm sweating like a pig, and my back is potentially playing up, and I'm heading for destination dildo – I'll try to remain upbeat, relax into the ride, be like a first-time tourist taking in the S&L skyline of Downtown Miami as the air WHIPS through my hair. This is after all the city that rocketed up to skyscraping heights as a futuristic front for saving and loaning and laundering billions of Colombian drug barons' dollars in the '80s. America's Casablanca. Full of corporate cocaine-cowboys, it runs on the white ook as much as LA.

The driver switches on the '80s tape deck as we cross the river on I-95. *Name That Tune*. You got it, Waylon Jennings II wailing *The Dukes of Hazzard* song. When the company 'antheme' is over, he switches to the radio, high-tempo Colombian salsa.

As we power up I-395, branching off by the tropical lushness of Bicentennial Park, cruising out over Biscayne Bay – propped up on Terminal Island and the concretised MacArthur Causeway – *I Spy* over at the port, the way I used to, the huge gleaming white cruise liners dwarfing the Dodge Island docks. It's hard to see how those *Loveboats* actually float, they're so laden with mass entertainment and flirtatious fun for the top end of the market, the *High Rollers*.

'You know I meet Sheriff Roscoe P Coltrain this year?' the driver announces, his chest filling with pride, expecting me to be knocked for 06 never mind 01.

'No?' I look suitably incredulous.

'*Si*. I shake his hand.'

'Wow.'

In his own brand of 'Spanglish' (WASP Spanish) he goes into the details of this celebrity encounter at some motel, but I'm not listening, and anyway he isn't talking to be heard, he is talking to practise his grammar and test his vocabulary. I stare out with my bionic eye, past him, zooming up the bay to the Venetian Causeway. Cue sound effects, BOOP-BOOP-BOOP-BOOP-BOOP: sniper-eyesight, in the cross-hairs, I can see the traffic flashing across the bridge, 'ultraviolent' sun-glare off the water. DANGER, the bionic eye registers on my mind-TV-screen: retinal burns. I reach into my pocket for my Armanis. The subtropical sun has to be combated. Shades on: everything goes unmellow yellow.

BOOP-BOOP-BOOP-BOOP-BOOP – the cutters and impounded powerboats moored at the US Coast Guard station, the Pearl Harbor of the war on drugs: yellow.

BOOP-BOOP-BOOP-BOOP-BOOP – the yacht-littered Government Cut up by zillion-dollar Fisher Island, and the Atlantic Ocean beyond South Pointe: piss yellow.

BOOP-BOOP-BOOP-BOOP-BOOP – the tourist-thronged, junkie-sanitised strip between the three-storey huddle-muddle of Tropical Art Deco buildings that make up Miami Drive: yellow, though I know all SoBe is painted a multitude of once-trendy pastel shades.

BOOP-BOOP-BOOP-BOOP-BOOP – the restaurant-crammed Collins Avenue, block after block after block of yellow people eateries.

For me, déjà view, location library jaundice, is already setting in. I'm going back to the place I'd been dying to get away from for literally ages – home

64

sour home, set forever to that Jan Hammer Electronica soundtrack Mom still thinks is the best.

Denise has a lot to answer for.

Episode 3

Outside the labia-pink My Beautiful Laundrette, on
the corner of the Road I give the driver his $25.00
and a $10.00 tip for sheer nostalgia *cojones*.

'Gracias, amigo.' He squints at the front of the
laundry suspiciously, all macho, keeping the engine
throaty, deep, male. 'You want I wait for you?'

'Nope. I'll be all right.'

He gives me his Confederate-Latino card and tells
me, 'Ring me anytime. You are priority consumer.'

I read his name off his badge: JEAN 'BO' BERTRAND.
'Later, Bo?' I say, and get out of the General.

'Hasta luego.'

Cuban Bo and the General Lee ROAR away from the kerb
for show. The Dixie horn sounds loud and proud.

The beautiful pedestrians on Lincoln stop shopping
and stare at me. Model lesbians with faces full of
designer Mayan-type piercings glare out at me from
behind the shop-front window of the Laundrette. Cars
are banned on the Road; gas-guzzlers like the Dodge
are an anathema.

The 'sado' stares do not stop inside. I'm being
eyeballed from all corners of the Art Deco-rated bar.
Tall skinny *Bosom Buddies* sitting side-by-side, hand-
in-hand, and in one case mouth-on-mouth, on primary-
coloured, oddly cut-off sofas. The message:
irrelevant-I, the voyeur type, with my inferior XY
sex chromosomes, am not welcome here.

An Alias Smith and Jones C&W-type reprise of

Howard Jones' 'What is Love?' is floating in the XX atmosphere. I avoid eye contact with any androgynous body and walk up to the counter, out of step to the beat.

I tell and retell myself all I have to do is play the amateur sleuth: get this Mercury person – the informant – to tell me where Denise is and Bob's *The Man from UNCLE*.

I stand there for a full minute, looking into the back wall of the bar, at the portholes of the washing and drying machines spinning, round and round and round, before the lone barperson stops washing glasses in the sink and comes over with attitude. She is definitely Butch to my Sundance, with a *Roseanne* face only a woman could forgive. And her ears, Jesus, they must weigh a tonne each with the amount of metal skewered into the flesh. Pure New Yorker: 'What?'

I say, 'I'm here to see Mercury.'

Folded, meaty, splodge-tattooed arms: 'She's not here.'

'When will she be?'

'Who's asking?'

'Kirk Rush,' I say, like that really meant something, like I'm some private dick on a case.

Not a flicker.

'I'm Denise Rush's brother.'

'Oh. Right.' That seems to satisfy her nouveau-Pict curiosity. Unfolding arms: 'She starts at eight thirty.'

'OK. Thanks.' It reads 6.05 p.m. on my com-link. That leaves over two hours for me to kill.

'You want a drink?'

I think about waiting there, under surveillance for X minutes. Guys like Harv Guck would be into this kind of situation – hoping for an invitation to an XXX

67

fantasy feministic threesome – but pass. Lesbian temptresses are evil – standard Hollywood operating procedure. 'I'll be back.'

Episode 4

I can smell the sea as I walk – yep, braving the evil
of perambulation – down the last car-lined block of
Lincoln Road to the beach. I keep to the right side,
getting some shade under the high palms. It means
skirting around more gallery-goers, shoppers and a
throng of porky cellulite-dimpled 'thongers', but
hell, that's preferable to roasting in the late-
afternoon sun.

I must pass about four new (to me) galleries on the way
down this traffic-friendly extension of the strip mall,
and God or whatever knows how many new cafes. The Road ASS
(After Sly Stallone or at least his patronisation of the
post-modern art scene) looks something like Santa Monica
3rd Street Promenade these days. To think that when Mom
first took us to the beach, this place was an armpit – an
armpit that the addictive personality of Denise couldn't
keep away from.

I walk on. There are drifts of bright sand on the
sidewalk there by that vintage purple Corvette
Stingray, and over here, finely gathered around the
plastic legs of the KAFKA KAFE tables (high culture
meets beach culture). I stop and have a look at the
themed all-you-can-eat for $12.50 set menu on one of
the tables: underneath sombre black and white photos
of the Jewish Czech writer in Berlin, *Angst Borst,
Surreal Sauerkraut & Kafka Knockwurst* . . . Food for
thought. Sounds great; it's just a shame it's all too
stodgy for people like me.

I can hear the Atlantic waves breaking on the sand up the Road, but there is such a mainstream of yellowed people, the blond leading the blond, in my way, that I can't see the sea properly. But . . .

There it is, the first sparkle of it – where the real road bit of the Road ends, dumping people onto the gleaming white coral sands. I stop to take my shades off and see if I can be dazzled by it all: BOOP-BOOP-BOOP-BOOP-BOOP – a 3000-yard-stare, looking at that talcum-powder strip and the heaving great blue mirror you can almost forget about the pollution and dive on in. Almost. Just like the Pacific.

An inline-skater CLIPS me as he SCRAPES by heading south at a cool 25 m.p.h., waving and weaving: 'Sorry, dude.'

My hand automatically goes to check out my wallet. 'That's OK,' I say, mostly to reassure myself I haven't been mugged.

Shades back on: I head for the nearest beachside cafe that isn't a Starbucks, that can't be a chain. I sit down in the shade of a droopy canvas canopy that is all camouflaged up, with a king snake sliding through a tropical-green milieu and the word EDEN. There are no TV monitors mounted on walls, no muzak. The plastic sidewalk furniture is green and uncomfortable. And there's only one member of staff in a green fig-leaf apron for service. It's no surprise there are no other customers.

The uniformed waitress hurries over, a black Kathy Bates. 'Bonswa, sir,' she says, Creole-style. 'What can I get you?'

I order a 'Café con leche.'

Sitting there, waiting, people watching, being buzzed by a low-flying kit plane trailing a banner red-letter advertisement for BOOP-BOOP-BOOP-BOOP-BOOP *TANTALUS' SCHLONG HARDCORE TECHNO FOAM PARTY*

TONITE 668 WASHINGTON AVE SOUTH MIAMI BEACH. This
is as good a place as any to wait Mercury out and watch
the sun sink seawards.

'There you go, sir,' the waitress says. *'Na we
pita.'*

Even though I don't speak Creole I get the
multicultural gist. 'Thanks,' I reply.

My mug of zoom-juice is steaming-hot. I pick up the
sugar and pour it in. DISSOLVE TO:

6.45 p.m. Waiting kills. Like most 'real'
Americans – and I'm definitely a fake, I didn't even go
for citizenship till I had to for the sake of my
career – I can't just sit somewhere, even if it's by
the beach with bubble-breasted bleach-blonde
bikinied bimbos on parade, and do nothing. Doing
something, alliterating, *anything*, is better than
thinking. That way you can forget yourself and all the
doh! bloopers you've made – for a while at least.
RESOLVE TO:

Get my Dell notebook out and do some writing but
decide nope, in spite of Biff's demands, it isn't the
time or place for that act of escapism. So, in a good
example of product displacement, I rummage my Nok-
Nokia out of the bag and I check my messages: no new
ones. That's good, in a way. Except it means that,
like all writers, I'm a living *John Doe*, not exactly a
social necessity, and as for what it says about
personal life popularity, good ratings, forget it.

An 'unfame-iliar' middle-aged couple saunter off
the beach and into cafe EDEN, tanned-arm-in-bronzed-
arm. I say 'unfame-iliar' because, although there's
a *Moonlighting* trace of sassy *Cybill* Shepherd and
sarcy Bruce Willis there, it's more me than them:
these *Perfect Strangers* don't look like anybody
famous, a strange thing these days. They're laughing
together as they sit down; they look happy. Not

71

knowing what other people, these stranger-than-strangers, are laughing at makes laughter the sound of loneliness. So, I have to make myself feel wanted, even if it's only artificially: taking the three-hour time difference into account, I phone Harv.

BLEEP-BLEEP 1.

BLEEP-BLEEP 2.

I hadn't told him I was off to Miami after all, which mid-deal is bordering on reckless and will likely cheese him off no end.

BLEEP-BLEEP 3.

'Would you pick up the phone, Harv?' I say to BLEEP-BLEEP 4.

By the fifth ring I know I'm going to be rerouted to this week's comedy agent message: 'This is Harvey Guck. I'm a busy man. Blab or blub after the tone and maybe I'll even get back to you sometime.'

BEEP: 'Harv, this is Kirk here. Just letting you know I'm in Miami for a couple of days. Any new developments let me know a.s.a.p. on the cell, OK? Cheers.'

I lay the cellphone down on the table, still on, in case he rings back right away to chew me out.

The cell is silent though. And the laughter from *The Odd Couple* at the other table, loud enough to make me think of my first speed-date with Angela and what I thought was the THE END of loneliness.

BLANK: nirvana for an hour and a bit as the light fades on the picturesque *Sunset Beach*.

Episode 5

'Could I see your underwear please?' Roseanne Barr
II, the barkeep-cum-bouncer, asks me at the door.

'Sorry?' I reply, aglow in the pink neon aura of
the bar sign and pretty shaken up by her request.

'It's Clean Underwear Night at the Laundrette.'

I clear my throat, give her the old Steve Austin
bushy raised eyebrow. 'You remember me – I'm Denise's
brother. I was here to see Mercury earlier, yep?'

'Yeah, she's in there.'

I give her a suitably squinty smile, begging for
her mercy and make to go in. I can hear the Bee-Gees
singing 'Staying Alive', or at least a dance remix of
it anyway.

Her big meaty arm CLAPS down on my shoulder. 'You
can't go in there if you're not in your underwear.'

'What?'

She turns me around to face her. 'Everybody else is
in their smalls. We have a policy of equality.'

'Ah. I'm just going to be in and out?'

'Not happening.'

'Well what do you want me to do – strip here?'

'Works for me.'

'Ahhhh . . .' Sudden paranoia attack – am I actually
wearing underwear or had I gone A-Team commando? I
check – yep, blue CK tangas, clean on this morning.
Phew, I'm OK, I'm admissible.

'If you want in you better hurry up. I have a bad
case of ADD.'

73

So, I put my bag down and I strip in the street. Fade up
the soundtrack. In spite of the upbeat vibes, I feel like
seriously killing Denise. 'I'll give you Death Therapy
when I get my hands on you,' I mutter to myself.

'Excuse me?' the bouncer says.

'Nothing.' I drape my pastel-blue T-shirt and
white trousers over my left arm. A brief glance at the
bright side of this – I'm glad I swim and work out at
the gym some or this would be mortifying.

'Your socks.'

'I can't even wear socks?'

She rolls her eyes. 'Think Don Johnson's ankles.'

'Don Johnson,' I sigh, and bend down, clothes
wrapped round my arm, to take off my shoes and socks.
I shove them into the top of my bag.

'OK,' she says. 'Go on in. There are lockers in the
back for storage.'

Final indignity: 'As I'm only staying for a minute
I hardly think I'll need one.'

'Whatever.'

'Where will Mercury be?'

'She's the one in the silver basque.'

Nearly naked and barefoot, I pad into the rosy glow
of Clean Underwear Night. Pink neon strips under the
glass bar counter light my way as I drift unnoticed
through a mass of women in their underwear.

The three closest forty-year-old dolls, all made
up like Alexis off gloss-dross *Dynasty*, are wearing
red frilly bras and knickers, and in an effort to be
hip have their belly buttons pierced.

The Golden Girls on the outside left are in ugh,
studded leathers – wrinkled, shrivelled
dominatrixes.

I push on. So intent am I on seeking out the silver
basque that I bump into one girl – she must have been
nineteen, an illegal drinker – who is wearing

74

crotchless denim pants and, well, obviously has no
pubes.

'Sorry.'

She smiles at me, all *Sex and the City* savvy, and
sips a manhattan out of a martini glass, her glittery
lipstick leaving no smudge on the rim.

I smile back, feeling a stirring in my CKs. 'Great
party!'

Her pretty friends are in similar couture:
patterned peephole bras and floss-thongs. They raise
their glasses to me: it's like a dream I once had as a
spotty sixteen-year-old immigrant, way back when I
thought most American girls would forgive my
deformity and find me desirable because of my strange
accent – as if I could be a likeable character,
Everybody Loves Raymond. I mean come on!

I'm getting a hard-on, but things bear so very
little relation to my previous experience of the
Laundrette – a total transformation in just over two
hours – that I'm thinking this welcome must be a
trick, that I'll be exposed at any time. This keeps my
erection from CREAK-CREAK-CREAK, going bionic.

Of course, the real reasons why these lesbians are
so welcoming now are:

1. This is Happy Hour, *Saturday Night Live*.
2. They think I have to be gay.
3. 'I'm Only Human' by the Human League has started
   playing.

I spot a woman in a silver basque at the far end of
the counter, sitting apart, drinking alone. I make my
way to her through the press of flesh. She is very
striking-looking in a Victoria Principal way.

'Are you Mercury?' I ask.

'I might be. Who might you be?' Her gaze is full of
that *Dallas* sadness.

75

'Kirk Rush – Denise's big brother.' I hold out my free right hand to shake.

Her grip strength is surprising, as is the size of her hand. 'I didn't know she had a brother?'

'I live in LA. I'm here because I'm trying to find her. She's gone missing.' I notice the faintest shadow of stubble on her cheeks.

'Don't I know it?'

It's suddenly clear to me that Mercury is, or at least has been, biologically a man; freaky, but I have to hold it together. 'Do you maybe know where she is right now?'

'We kind of broke up two weeks ago.'

So, there you have it: Denise has been dating a transvestite or transsexual or drag queen from South Fork!

Mercury continues: 'I told her that I couldn't cope with all the anger, the depression, the talk of ending it, you know. I'm due to go in for the snip and the specialist says I need to be surrounded by positivity.'

'She was talking about ending it? But she's always talking about ending it, isn't she? I mean that's what she does to cope.'

'Yeah. But this time it was for real. The dialysis was getting really bad. Fluid retention. Cramps on draining. Everything was getting on top of her. She went out of control, started hanging more and more with that sicko right-to-die crowd, and then she just left me.' Mercury is close to breaking down.

'She didn't tell you where she was going? Leave a note? Anything?'

Choking on a sob: 'No.'

'I'm sorry.' I'm still thinking too hard about the words 'right to die' to use them.

And Mercury begins to cry, real genuine

Principaled tears, and there is nothing else to do but
try to comfort her as best I can. I give her a hug,
which she seems to like - a little too much. I feel her
tears running down my chest, my abs, getting colder
the further they travel down, making me shiver.

'Who are these *right to die* people?' I say. I have
a bad feeling about this.

'The Cyanide Society. Sordini and her cronies.'

'Sordini?'

'You know - she's that old witch who lives in
Stiltsville, the last person to live out there.'
Mercury's mascara and make-up is being washed away.

'Ah.' I didn't know about Sordini, but I knew
Stiltsville all right. From Key Biscayne you could
see the remains of the little ghost village tottering
on stilts above the Atlantic swell. 'Do you think she
would know where Denise is?'

'She's probably staying there, with this *Sordini*.'

That figures. My sister is one of those types who
never stays in the one place very long, is at home
wherever. She always likes to do the rounds of her
friends, live life like it's one big sleepover after
another. Everybody agrees this choice of lifestyle
isn't very practical with her being on dialysis, but
she refuses to give it up.

I let Mercury cry into my chest some more as I
think about how best to handle this development. What
would Steve Austin do? Or any other Hollywood hero?
They would go to the rescue! That's what they would
do. 'I have to go.' I take Mercury's runaway face in
my hands and wipe away a black tear. 'Will you be all
right, ma'am?' (Yep, I really use the Southern
'ma'am'.)

'Yeah.' Sniffing.

'When I find her I'll ask her to call you, OK?'

'OK.' Snorting.

And, with that, I turn and walk away, excusing my way through the crowd. It's only when I'm out the door, under the glare of the bouncer and in full view of the *Party of Five* queuing to get in, that I realise that I'm not in a heroic red trademark tracksuit, and that Mercury's black tear-trails have soaked into my blue tangas. My torso looks like I've been in a spin cycle where the dye has leached out, staining me like Texan crude oil. And my crotch, well hell, son, people might come to the conclusion that I'd come to a conclusion, or whatever.

'Goodnight,' I say to the bouncer, who laughs at me, seemingly temporarily cured of her Attention Deficit Disorder.

I walk off as quickly as my non-bionic legs can carry me. Up the Road a bit, under green neon, I struggle to get my costume back on.

Episode 6

If Denise has got it into her stubborn head that she
has a right to die . . . BLANK. It doesn't bear thinking
about. Len. I'll phone Len. It's 8.46 p.m. and I'm
standing more or less dressed and distressed in the
middle of the Road, corner of Lincoln and Collins,
ready to hail a cab, but I'll phone him first and ask
him about this Sordini character. I get out my cell,
pull out the beat-up Filofax from my bag, and finger
his number from the creased pages. I dial with adrenal
dexterity.

Not even one full ring: 'Hi honey, you forgot the
list, yeah?'

'Em, Mr Spock, it's me, Kirk.'

'Aha. Captain Kirk. Sorry, thought you were Mary.'

'Yep.'

'She's away to the mini-mall without the shopping
list. I thought she was phoning for me to read it—'

'That's OK,' I say, cutting across his sense of
domestic bliss, 'I'm in Miami. I've just been to see
that woman Mercury.'

'So, she tell you where Denise is holing up?'

'Denise isn't with her any more. She says she may
be with this woman Sordini . . .'

'Sordini?'

'. . who lives in Stiltsville . . .'

'*Stiltsville?*'

'Yep. So, I'm coming down to the Key tonight and
I'll be going out there early tomorrow.'

'Sordini. I think I've heard of this Sordini. She was on that WIAMI in Miami-on-Miami talk show, *Big Mouth*, recently . . . (beat) . . . something about human rights?'

'The right to die?'

'Yes. The right to die. Exactly!' Len says, and then using that Vulcan logic realises the connection. 'You don't think Denise is thinking . . .'

'I don't know, Spock, but I'm starting to get worried here.'

'Look eh, I'll take you out there in the boat tomorrow.'

'You aren't working?' I ask.

'No. Next convention is . . .' He sighs. 'Doesn't matter. I'll do it. You got a place to stay the night?'

'Thanks, but you know me – I'm booking into a hotel.' The Plug Inn – where I'd stayed on my only visit home in four years – leaves you to your own devices to work away, has room service, an Imax-wide-screen TV with cable, and a cool pool for my morning swim.

'You're welcome here, Captain. Seriously.'

'I know. Thanks but—'

'No thanks.'

'Yep. But thanks anyway, Spock.'

'Meet on the dock at nine thirty sharp?'

'Can do. And will do, Mr Spock.'

'We'll find her, Captain. This is just . . . She'll be out there.'

'Yep. See you tomorrow.'

'Nine thirty a.m.'

'Bye.'

'Bye.'

Episode 7

In the Heat of the Night I hail a yellow *Taxi* cab down
from the traffic flow on Collins. I get into the back
seat. 'The Plug Inn, Bougainvillea Drive, Key
Biscayne.'

'No problemo,' replies the big black driver, who is
so obese he takes up most of the front seat, his back
and neck blubber rippling up against the perspex
security screen.

I slide over to the opposite side of the cab in
case my added weight causes it to tip. 'Any idea how
much that'll be?'

'Reckon just under thirty dollars, man.'

'OK.'

He drives off. He turns up onto the now brightly
neon-lit Washington Avenue and heads for the Venetian
Causeway. He gets snagged in a jam end of Dade
Boulevard, on the way up to the toll-booth. 'You here
on holiday?' he asks.

'Nope.'

'Business then.'

'Sort of.'

'You mind me asking what sort of business you're
in, man?'

I want to say, My own, but instead I say, 'Movies.'

The traffic starts flowing again. He turns round to
look at me, see if I'm a star. 'Really? Are you an
actor? Director?'

I count, he has four chins, fuzzed over with a

81

beard, like Uncle Phil from *The Fresh Prince of Bel Air*, before answering, 'Writer.'

'Oh. You write anything I'd know?'

'I'm doing *The A-Team* movie right now.'

'Ah. Good money?'

'Not bad.'

'Do you ever think about investing your money in growing concerns?'

'Nope.'

'You should think about it. Take me for example, I'm a cab driver right?' He looks round again.

I count five chins before answering, 'Yep.' Where has the extra one come from all of a sudden?

'But man, that's not all I am.'

'Yep?' I sense the pitch coming. I look out the window, up north, at the string of lights on the Julia Tuttle Causeway.

'I also own a fast-food chain here in Miami,' the driver announces proudly.

'Uh-huh?' Why does that not surprise me?

'It's called Frankenstein Frankfurters: For Supernatural Sausages.'

'Right?'

'We guarantee all our hot-dog ingredients are GM, that stands for genetically modified. That way we know they're scientifically safe and that their taste has been tested up to supernatural levels.'

'Hmm.' One last look at the orange lights on the water of the bay, then the causeway ends. I think about Denise for a second . . . the right to die . . . then my writing, and how I'm not doing any . . . before giving the driver back my nanosecond-long attention span.

'Kids love it because it's terrifically horrific – we have a merchandising tie-in with all the old English Hammer Horror movies, yeah?'

We are turning into Biscayne Boulevard. 'Peter
Cushing and Christopher Lee's stuff?'

'Exactly. And our ketchup is labelled "blood" and
the mustard is "pus" and the mayo is "melted bones"
and the salad is "snot" . . .' He keeps on plugging
all the way past Freedom Tower, through Downtown, as
we cross the river, actually till we're crossing the
Rickenbacker, high over Virginia Key. Only then does
he pass a glossy brochure through the screen, back to
me. 'It's all in there, man. The business plan. The
figures. The projected profits.'

'Thanks.' I find myself staring at a colour photo of
Christopher Lee's Frankenstein, the undead monster,
and wondering how somebody had thought it would sell
hot dogs, or 'horror dogs' as he calls them, when
combined with the idea of GM.

'We have two profitable stores already in North
Miami, but my partner and me, we need money to fund
our expansion into the franchise operations. If
you're interested in investing in the future?'

'I'll take a look.'

'You do that my man and, bottom line, we'll grow
your movie money for you big-time.' That promise
seems to be a closing of sorts. He falls mercifully
silent, probably to give me a grace period to think
about signing up to the *Mutant X* deal before journey's
end. And there's me thinking about what I'd buy for
$600,000 – starting with the original A-Team GMC
(General Motors Company) van, B.A.'s precious set of
wheels.

Episode 8

The Plug Inn is a ten-bedroom mock-Spanish *Hotel* set
in palm-lined Bougainvillea Drive, an exclusive Cuban
family-run franchise nestled nicely in the middle of
the 'Island Paradise' of Key Biscayne.

I get out of the cab with almost bionic speed,
nearly ripping the door off its hinges. I hand the
driver $30 in a flash. No tip. No way. No how. No sell
either.

'Think about Frankenstein Frankfurters, eh
man?'

'Yep. Will do,' is all I've time to say before I'm
gone, off the sidewalk and into the mass of
bougainvilleas that make up the Gomezes' garden.

I slow up as I reach the front door. I ring the
ship-style bell, DING-DONG.

Mrs Maximo Gomez comes to open the door. *'Ola,'* she
says.

'Ola,' I reply, waiting to be recognised from my
last stay . . .

A BLANK look. I'm glad. Us Hollywood types value our
anonymity more than our fame, well almost.

'A single, *Señor*?' she says, gesturing for me to
come into the hallway.

'Yep.' I go in, walking straight past the smiling
photograph of her dead first husband, Real, who I seem
to vaguely remember having been informed had been
slaughtered in the Bay of Pigs fiasco. Whatever.

'For how many nights, *Señor*?'

'Hopefully one.' Because tomorrow, like Len said, we'd find her. And bring her back!

'*Si, Señor.* Come with me.'

She takes me out back to the exact same small poolside suite I'd stayed in last time. There's absolutely no *Small Talk*. 'OK?'

'Yep.'

She hands me the key-card and leaves the room with a small, polite smile.

As soon as she's gone I fling myself onto the king-size bed. The air-con is on low. I lie there for a bit with my head in my hands, rubbing my eyes. It occurs to me that I'll never ever understand Denise, my own sister . . . and if you can't even get to grips with your own family, what hope for the rest of humanity, who can you really know, and what if this zone of exclusion extends to yourself?

I hit the TV remote, phaser set to stun, and go to work on The Plug Inn's standard Imax-sized wide-screen, flicking through the eternal kaleidoscope of syndicated advertising vehicles. I'm looking for one in particular: yep, you got it, *The A-Team*! There's always some episode of the show playing on some channel like TV Land. And, sure enough, I find it. I know this one pretty well, recognise it as 'The White Ballot' in seconds. It's a farce in which Face, the slick-dick politician, takes on a crooked local sheriff in a rigged election and, in spite of being Prince Charming, loses. Of course, the Team wins in the end, and the baddie is brought to justice, *JAG*-type military justice.

I flip the TV on low while I work because I need the inspiration: I mean how the hell can you make a character like Face bisexual? Is it even possible? Retro hetero Face? Swinging both ways, targeting 100 per cent of the market. It's a genetic thing, right, not a social thing, right? But . . .

Denise said to me in our teens that we're all bisexual, that it's our natural state when we aren't being repressed, or repressing ourselves. If that's so, though, there must be something wrong with me, something lacking, because I don't remember getting *A Queer Eye For A Straight Guy*, except maybe Gil Gerrard's Buck Rogers.

Where the hell do people like Mercury fit in: are they the complete package for bisexuals; is that why Denise was interested? I sit there watching away, like Carrie Bradshaw trying to get a grip on these issues of sexual identity for, oh, must be ten minutes, then in the ads I pick up the phone and order some room service. '*Filete de pescado*. Red Snapper if you have it.'

As I wait for my food, I get out my Dell notebook and power it up. The small BLANK screen an invitation to create . . .

'Speak to me, Face,' I say.

And that's when I come up with Biff's new Face, quickly sketching out the Egriesque tri-dimensionality of his character onto the screen –

CONT.

PHYSIOLOGY

(remember this cannot be Tim Dunigan or Dirk Benedict;
they are now too old to play the New Face)

1. Sex: male/bisexual (belongs to what is sometimes
   referred to as the 3rd sex)

2. Age: 37 (like he'll admit to that)

3. Height: 5'9" on camera (probably a lot less in real
   life)

4. Weight: 12 stone (but climbing with every year, in spite
   of workouts with Jane Fonda)

5. Colourings: highlighted, coiffed brown hair, brown eyes,
   the salon- and sun-kissed skin of a sun worshipper,
   pearl-white teeth

6. Posture: military bearing, *avec* a certain *je ne sais
   quoi*

7. Appearance: immaculate. Any designer '80s suit or Gucci
   leather jacket will do.

8. Defects: a whiney womanly voice, potential weakness in
   his heart?

9. Heredity: very well coordinated, good instincts, good
   reflexes, 20/20 binocular vision, fast and fit runner,
   doesn't injure easily but heals up hard, dainty hands,
   and an A-hole that according to a male partner looked
   like 'the holy Star of Bethlehem, oh my God!'

SOCIOLOGY

1. Class: Maine landed bourgeoisie

2. Occupation: former Lieutenant US Army, now *A-Team* con man and seducer

3. Education: expulsions from four military academies, graduation with honours, West Point

4. Home life: some then none. Hannah, his beautiful mother, whom he can only see in his dreams, died of heart failure when he was eight. His father, George Peck, was a general (better than his father before him who was only a colonel) and so little Templeton was sent to be boarded at the notoriously Spartan McCallum MA. Templeton can count the number of times he saw his father in his whole life on two hands, and never once not in uniform

5. Religion: agnostic before the Gulf War, atheist after

6. Nationality: de-US-citizenised, but considers himself liberated by this, a citizen of the world

7. Race: WASP without the sting

8. Place in community: outcast cum outlander cum outlaw cum . . .

9. Political affiliations: votes for the Face Party every morning in the mirror because there is no such thing as democracy.

10. Amusements/hobbies: women, men, genitals in general, the high life, the low life, procuring diamonds, making money, fencing (without the foils) stolen goods

PSYCHOLOGY

1. Sex life: very very active

2. Moral standards: extraordinarily flexible, only one
   stickler — loyalty to Hannibal and the Team

3. Personal premise: wants to be a con-millionaire, make
   that multi-con-millionaire

4. Frustrations/chief disappointments: that the Team can't
   clear its name, that he can't stop running from MPs and
   get down to making some seriously easy money from rich
   suckers

5. Temperament: highly strung (in the trouser dept),
   gambler

6. Attitude towards life: life's a game of chance: if I want
   it, I'll take it and, a bit like Robin Hood, if it belongs
   to the rich, all the better

7. Complexes: obsessional vanity/narcissism/urge to
   control everything in the 'game'

8. Extrovert, introvert, ambivert?: XXX-tro

9. Abilities: inveterate liar, natural charm, gift for
   persuasion, speaks French sometimes in whispers, screams
   Arabic in his sleep

10. Qualities: good imagination, flair for creativity,
    excellent communications skills

11. IQ: 145 (with a few digits held in reserve for crises)

Mrs Gomez causes me to come up for air-con air, out of the writing trance, by knocking quietly on my door. *'Servicio.'*

I save Face on the Dell, and get up off my by-now stiff-as-a-stiff-mattress back, and go get my dinner.

I open the door and take the tray off her. *'Gracias.'*

A waft of the Red Snapper, smells delicious.

She nods. *'De nada.'*

I eat, watching the end of *Knight Rider*: 'Deadly Manoeuvres'. It isn't the best episode, with Michael and KITT pitted against corrupt US Army officers, bent on flogging nukes to some arms dealer with shady contacts in the Middle East.

I read over the work. TV satire is OK if the screenwriter isn't trying to be bigger, better or smarter than the viewer. That's the director's job. And the critics'.

I go to sleep with the TV on, low, for company.

Episode 9

My Life AS A Sitcom: I wake early on Sunday 29th, the
way I always do, restful sleep or not, 6.30 a.m.: red
numbers on the alarm clock. I get myself out of bed
and onto the floor. Strangely, my back feels OK but,
pain or no pain, it's Pilates time.

Twenty exercise-crammed minutes later I get to my
feet. I look in the full-length bathroom mirror: I'm
back in shape – good posture, standing tall. I slide
on my black Speedo swim-shorts, WHIP the green
bathrobe off the rail in the wardrobe, and leave the
room.

There's no one at the deep blue pool, but it's full
of shadows. Staring into the water I have this
momentary loss of BLANKNESS: the diving board, puke
waterfalls, Cindy's Jesus Christ tits, it all rushes
back to me even though actions from the last episode,
let alone the last series, are rarely referenced
again.

I turn around and head back to the room. To make
myself feel better I CLICK on the TV: close-ups of some
starving African kids with flies on their faces! *Quick
As A Flash* I flick to the local news channel. The
anchorwoman is a more intelligent-looking, younger
version of Mrs King from *The Scarecrow and Mrs King*,
and she has a kind of vulnerable tone about her news:
'Ahab Khan, aka Doctor Death, is wanted by Miami-Dade
Police for questioning in connection with the
assisted suicide of three women in North Miami Beach

yesterday . . .' *Quizzing The News*. If it bleeds it leads. The adult Disneyworld of Miami, like the adult Disneyland of LA, is full of bad news. I channel-hop to something, anything else, that leaves me with a little hope for whatever is left of that fantasy, humanity. I stop on *Banacek*, starring George Hannibal Peppard as the black-gloved, smart-mouthed, stylish Polish-American bounty hunter who is too *Filthy Rich* to drive his own car and has a black chauffeur, Jay, to do it for him.

After fifteen minutes of this 'who-and-how-dun-it', with Banacek chasing his 10 per cent of this invaluable book he has to recover, I get bored. It occurs to me why NBC only ever made sixteen episodes of this detective show: it's all a little too smart-ass for its own good. And as smart TV is an oxymoron, I switch off.

I get dressed quickly in a Hawaiian T-shirt and green Bermuda shorts. Then I go down to the dining room.

There's an old Japanese couple, old enough to have been in *Hawaii 5-0*, sitting by the window on the far side. They both nod politely to me as I come in.

I sit down at an empty table for two and wait for the teenaged Cuban girl at the kitchen door – a girl who looks a bit like J-Lo with her big booty but who's likely a Señorita Gomez – to come and take my order.

But, no response. She's ignoring me. 'Waitress?' I call.

The Japanese couple on the other side of the room tut-tut as the waitress reluctantly comes over, arms folded. 'I no answer to "waitress". I am actress.'

The irony doesn't escape me. Here I am, hundreds of miles from LA, and ditto.

'I'm on cable TV,' she says proudly.

'Uh-huh. Could I have a freshly squeezed Big Orange Juice for starters? No concentrate.'

Her nostrils flare. 'I concentrate.'

'No. The juice. No concentrate.'

The waitress's hands go to her hips. 'You think I *stupido*? You think I no understand you?'

I see the old Japanese couple looking over. 'No, I don't think you're stupid.'

The waitress sneers, '*Te puta madre!*' and STOMPS off.

In English that means . . . something you can't say in a family entertainment show. Tourette's, such an original approach to customer service! For a split second I think of complaining to Señora Gomez (the *madre*) but then, considering my time slaving at A Votre Santé, I decide to just skip breakfast, and walk out of the dining room.

Episode 10

I may be an A-hole but I'm no motherf**ker, I
congratulate myself, striding out into the garden. A
real small-minded motherf**ker would have made a
point of putting Señorita Gomez in her proper place,
maybe recommending a course of haldol. In fact, I'm
The Saint old Simon Templar, VROOMING about in his
Jaguar XJS, half cartoon stickman, half English
secret agent, sent on an errand of mercy.

I walk down Bougainvillea Drive with a smug smile
on my face and a white halo circling my head, past the
crescents of secluded houses and bungalows set in
gardens that are perfect little squares of manicured
lawn, every single one of them framed by a mass of
tropical horticulture, flora transplanted by liver-
spotted hands.

My mom's own *Knot's Landing* clone-house is only a
few quiet streets away from here – left, to the south-
west. Down on West Wood. But I'm heading in the
opposite direction. Up to the Yacht Club.

I turn right up Harbour Drive. Between the big sea-
view houses, now you see it, now you don't, Biscayne
Bay looks calm, a shimmering blue stretch dotted with
white yachts of all sizes. And over the other side of
the water, I catch sight of the waterfront properties
of Coconut Grove and the seriously exclusive city of
Coral Gables where I'd gone to university, at least
sometimes.

I say 'Nice day' to an old but still hefty guy

lumbering up the sidewalk towards me – he's a greyed *Matt Houston* wearing one of those blue FBI coats and walking a sleek Dobermann pinscher.

He eyes me suspiciously, then grunts something back. the Dobermann growls at me. Unfriendly. That's what *The District* has always been like since we moved here. Retired *Law & Order* enforcers, ex-army officers, NCOs and grunts, 'Key Rats' as they liked to be known, occupied the place. The Key is the finishing line to their rat race and they don't take kindly to younger outsider rats coming in, making waves, not even if the strange faces are tourists with money to spend.

Five more minutes of walking – mulling over how *Knight Rider* is such a rip-off of *The Saint*, which itself is a rip-off of Ian Fleming's secret agent, Bond, James Bond – brings me to the Yacht Club.

Down on the docks I see Len standing where his dad, a judge, moors the family pride and joy: *The Pequod II*, a so-called 'cigarette racing boat' – the type of massively ostentatious powerboat that drug-dealer poseurs, Crockett and Tubbs, used to whore and roar about in. We'd had some good times in that boat, like when it was the set for Len's UM experimental short film *Moby Dickhead*, his final work in that medium. Len had played Ahab, a white ook smuggler on his last doomed run. I'd been his Ishmael, loyal to the wreck at the end.

I wave over. 'Ahoy there, Mr Spock!'

Len waves back.

I walk down two gangways, and across the wooden piers of the dock to get to him.

'Good to see you, Captain – if it's really you?' he says. He's wearing his old blue T-shirt with the Starfleet logo imprinted on the front and, strangely for Mr Spock, black tennis shorts that show off his skinny legs.

95

'It's me all right,' I say. That's the correct reply - there's a correct reply because in many episodes of *Star Trek* there are evil alien shape-shifters who impersonate the main characters.

Len walks up to me and gives me his famous mind-meld greeting, right thumb and forefinger boring into my left temple. 'Yep,' he says, 'It's you all right. Nobody else has a mind as warped as that.'

I push his hand away, breaking the meld, taking back control of my own mind. 'Warp factor nine, that's me.'

We stand back and look at each other for a moment. It's good to see him again. His hair is as severe as Leonard Nimoy's. He looks older, must have been laughing a lot to get those lines around his eyes.

'So, you up for this mission?' he says.

'Yep.'

'Trust Denise, huh?'

'Yep.'

'It'll just be one of her things, you know, this Death Therapy? Like the crystals. The Reiki healer. That Shiatsu stuff.'

'Yep.'

'We'd better get on board the ship then?' He nods over at *The Pequod II*.

'Yep.'

'Captain first.' He points at the gangplank, and goes over to cast off.

'Aye, aye, Mr Spock.' Under orders, I walk the plank, onto the bridge of *The Pequod II*. She's some star ship - or at least a star powerboat - what with her sleek forty-foot-long hull. Len always joked that she was equipped with a tractor beam, photon torpedoes, phasers.

'She's never ever going to get old and ugly, is she?' I say, running my fingers over the waterproof back-seat upholstery.

96

Len comes aboard. 'Old maybe, but ugly, never.' He throws the plank onto the dock.

'So,' I say, 'Things are going well with Mary then?'

'Yeah, great,' he says, sitting in the driver's seat, getting a grip of the steering wheel. 'Bummer to hear you split up with Angela.'

'Yep,' I say.

'How long were you guys dating?'

'Six months.'

'It was serious then?'

'I thought so but then she left me for a voice-over actor called Zeb de Vache.'

'Actresses!' Len rolls his eyes, shrugs, and REVS The Pequod II up. The GUNNING of the three Mercury 850cc outboard engines is an incredible sensation. Bone-shuddering. It makes KITTSCH seem like a mere toy, which of course it is. 'Hang on, Captain,' he shouts.

I sit down in the passenger seat not a moment too soon, because The Pequod II leaps away from the dock, the bow rising way up, the propellers churning up the still waters of the bay into a white wake. I yell my orders over the ROAR of the engines: 'Set and steer a course for Stiltsville, Mr Spock.'

'Aye, aye, Captain.'

At 50 m.p.h., the USS Pequod II cuts a speed-swathe down the coast of the Key, taking only a few minutes to leave the Village behind in a sea-spray rainbow.

The swell gets up a bit as we ZIP by the barbecuing beaches of the Bill Baggs' Cape Florida State Recreation Area. The ridge gets more bumpy-jumpy further out and every so often we'll hit a ramp wave and take off. Which is great.

'You know I saw Denise about two weeks ago,' Len shouts across to me.

'Yep?' I yell back.

'Her face was all swollen up.'

That can only mean one thing: 'Fluid retention.'

'Yeah.'

If her kidneys had failed even more it means she can't piss, and that ultrafiltration, a process which occurs simultaneously to diffusion in dialysis, would be the only way to get rid of excess water. If it isn't gotten rid of, high blood pressure will result, possibly followed by pulmonary oedema, her lungs filling up with water, DIY drowning.

'It was kind of a shock,' says Len.

'Yep.' I nod back. I know what my first officer is at: he's trying to prepare me for the worst, just in case Denise frightens me when we meet and my reaction upsets her. Mr Spock is a stand-up guy, a better friend than I deserve.

The sea takes on a green hue as we leave the lee of the barrier island and head out into the deeper waters of the Atlantic.

This place is a long way out. I wonder why Denise chooses to live out here. It's plain dumb. How does she get to the dialysis centre? What if something goes wrong, a killer super-bug infection like MRSA, and she needs emergency treatment?

As we come up on the Cape Florida lighthouse, I see it, zoom-in on the viewfinder, there, on the glare-bright southern horizon, Stiltsville. There'd once been twenty-seven wooden houses built out here on the flats. It'd been an offshore haven of gambling and drinking and whoring in its time, the '50s, and a TV/movie location in the '80s. Now there are only seven shacks left standing on stilts and all are condemned.

'Which one do you think Sordini lives in?' I shout, pointing at the specs up ahead.

Len yells back, 'After Andrew, there's only really one that's still habitable.'

'Ah?' I remember Hurricane Andrew in 1992 all right, the sheer devastation, but as for . . .

'It's the one with the mural on the wall.'

'Right.' That still doesn't make it any clearer for me. I've been away way too long.

Len steers *The Pequod II* into the winding finger channels and slows to impulse engines. 'Don't want to ground the boat.' He navigates through the marl banks, covered in spiky sea-grasses, and the tidal cuts, without causing any damage whatsoever to the powerboat or desedimentation to the ecosystem of the National Park. And on, warping by two ramshackle huts on this marine death row, till he gets us up to the right stilt-house with the *Flipper* and friends aquatic mural painted on the side.

'Well done, Mr Spock.'

Len kills the Mercury engines. We drift up to the dock nice and slow.

There's a small speedboat moored at the head of the dock.

I jump out and moor *The Pequod II*. I'm pleased I still remember how to tie the knot.

'Ahoy!' Len opens all hailing frequencies.

Nobody answers.

'Anybody there?' I call up to the house proper, propped up above the dock on the stilts. 'Denise?'

Nothing. The low-key CREAKING of sea-salted timbers drying out in the sun.

I start up the first flight of the two flights of wooden steps. 'Denise?'

No response. LAPPING of our wake waves.

'Hello?' calls Len. 'Mrs Sordini?'

The SLOSHING of the sea around the stilts.

'I'm not reading any life signs, Captain,' says Len from *The Pequod II*.

From up on the beat-up main platform, I say, 'You're part of this away team, Mr Spock?'

99

'OK.'

I walk up to the paint-flecked front door and KNOCK on it. 'Denise? Are you in there? It's me, Kirk.'

No movement within.

Len joins me at the door.

'Are you sure this is the one, Spock?' I ask him.

'Yeah.'

I try the door handle. SQUEAK, the door swings in, halfway, before catching on the floor.

'Hello?' Len says.

I try to see in but it's dark in there, and full of a dreadful stink which makes my eyes water. 'What the hell is that?' I splutter.

'Smells like dead meat,' Len says.

'Jesus.' I retch.

Len pulls the bottom of his T-shirt up to cover his nose. 'Mrs Sordini, are you all right?'

I copy Len and, taking a deep breath of Hawaiian shirt, step into the dark house. I'm sidling past the door when *Batman*-KERBLAM!

A big chunk of the wall blows out to my immediate right, *Too Close For Comfort*. A beam of light cuts across the *Darkroom*.

Len ducks and cowers outside.

Someone screams, a woman's voice, 'Get out of my house.'

Hands up, a silhouette half-in half-out of the doorway, I say, 'It's OK, it's OK, don't shoot, we're just here to find Denise.'

'I'll blow your goddamned head off.'

I hear Len crawling off. 'I'm Denise's brother, Kirk.'

From the darkness: 'Denise?'

'Yep. Denise Rush.' I think I can see a long black dress, or a robe, spotlighted by the ray of shot-gunned sunlight.

100

'Get the hell off my property.'

I back out of the doorway.

Len has made it to the steps on his belly.

'Please, Mrs Sordini?' I say. 'Is Denise here? Can I talk to her?'

'No.' I hear footsteps CLUMPING across the boards.

'What do you mean "no"?' I say.

'She's not here.' The door is YANKED fully open. And there, there is the barrel of a pump-action shotgun, pointed right at my chest.

I look up from the gun to her black robe . . . and to her mask. For some reason she is wearing a blown-up paper cut-out mask of Andy Warhol's Technicolor Marilyn Monroe, slit eyes, slit mouth.

'Mrs Sordini?' I have to ask.

'What's left of her, after lupus. Do you know what lupus is, sonny?'

'Eh, no.'

'Back up.' She thrusts the barrel into my ribs. *Gunsmoke*.

'I'm backing.' I back up to the top of the steps.

Logically, Len is at the bottom of the second flight and on the dock.

'It's when your own flesh rots while you're still alive.' She holds up her left hand – the flesh is all wasted, raw, covered in black warts and smeared with cream.

I shudder. This woman is a real-life zombie! My mind flashes to the script of *Zombie Moon*, to how you kill zombies, to the Captain of Moon Base Alpha saying through gritted teeth, Kill the brain men. It's the only way.

'Mrs Sordini,' Len says, 'we're going. We just wanted to see Denise, and if she's not here—'

'She's not. She's gone to meet the good Doctor Death.'

101

'Doctor Death,' I repeat, going down the steps slowly, hands up. 'What do you mean - she's supposed to be on this Death Therapy?'

The Marilyn mask saying: 'That's why she came to me, from the Cyanide Society. I put people in touch with him.'

'Who is this guy?' I ask. The last few steps down to the dock.

'Everybody knows him.'

'You can't mean Doctor Kevorkian?' asks Len, from *The Pequod II*. 'He's in jail.'

'No, not Martyr 284797. There's a new doctor, gone underground. He helps people like Denise end their suffering.'

That's when it CLICKS: Scarecrow Doctor Death, and Mrs King the TV news reporter: 'Doctor Death is wanted by Metro-Dade Police for questioning in connection with the assisted suicide of three women in North Miami Beach yesterday . . .'

I'm standing on the dock, a gun on me. 'Why would Denise want to kill herself?'

'No quality of life. It's that simple when it's you suffering. Now, get out of here and leave me in peace.'

I jump aboard the *The Pequod II*.

Len starts the engines and gets us out of there in a hurry. 'Whatever you do, don't look back,' he shouts.

When I do dare to look back - in the middle finger channel, out of range - I see that Sordini is still standing there, on the post-structure, aiming the shotgun at us.

INTERMISSION 11

Captain's Log, Supplemental (Star Date 5434.52
whatever): I, James Tiberius Kirk, want to record
here in a Dictaphone-direct address to the audience,
a soliloquy alluding to Shakespeare, that the best
kidney donor is a willing identical twin, a clone, a
natural DNA match. Failing that, the most suitable
donor is a brother or sister, youthful father or
mother, mature son or daughter. To find out whether
you're suitable Bones informs me that you have to have
blood tests, tissue type and virus tests. If you are a
match – which my parents strangely weren't – you have
to have further tests to check your own kidneys are
working: an ultrasound or a CT scan, or an
arteriogram (where the doctors inject radioactive dye
into the bloodstream to light up the blood vessels
around and in the kidneys). This whole test process
can take up to three months and would have involved a
lot of flying back to Miami, which was hardly possible
given the equivocal nature of our five-year space
exploration mission on the *Enterprise*.

Episode 12

The Pequod II is at full throttle, skipping and
jumping over the swells towards the Cape Florida
lighthouse. But . . .

But there's no joy no thrill in the ride now.
Memento mori, all I can see is that shotgun.

'You all right?' Len yells over.

I don't look at him, or answer. I honestly don't
know. Is this PTSD, Post *Star Trek* Disorder?

'What are you going to do?' Len screams over,
uncharacteristically emotional.

'I don't know.' Sordini could have killed me.

'The logical thing is for you to get the police
to—' His lips keep moving but I can't hear his words
over the noise.

'What?' I lean right over in his direction.

'Get the police to put out a nationwide APB on
Denise.'

I agree with his analysis. I check in my pocket but
product misplacement, I haven't got my communicator,
my cellphone, on me; I must have left it at The Plug
Inn. And of course there's no transporter for Scottie
to beam me up, particle-pattern held together by
cliché, and onto the Key. It'll have to wait till we
get ashore. Till after I've gone and told Mom at home,
which, *doh*, I will have to do now.

Len is silent. The realisation sinking in: Sordini
could have killed him too, *Murder One*, and he would
never have seen his unborn baby.

I sit there in the passenger seat, like James T in the captain's hot swivel seat, under Klingon attack, red alert, the bridge reeling from port to starboard to port. Taking direct disruptor hits:

Doctor Death! (Dry ice.)

Quality of life! (Fake blood.)

What the hell is Denise doing? I'm still not even near understanding. Fire photon torpedoes, full spread. I mean, she's on the dialysis programme; she has a future, a *Farscape*, if she goes back and stays on it or if she has a transplant.

I can nay stop her, the USS *Pequod II* is rocking from port to starboard, breaking up, and likely she would have but for the sight of a single bottle-nosed dolphin zipping along the bow wave, a white whale, arcing out of the water in synch with us –

Flipper.

Life, but not as we know it, comes to the rescue, guiding us back to port.

Episode 13

Cruel fact: Flipper can't save people on land. That's up to us flawed humans, and half-human, flawed Vulcans.

Len brings us into the Yacht Club at a rate of knots. He cuts across a huge, gleaming-white catamaran on its way out. The doppelgänger of Tony Soprano at the helm hurls abuse at us all right already, the bird, the fig, the bird.

Len pays him no mind. He cruises up to the dock, slowing all the time. 'Captain . . .'

'Aye, aye, Mr Spock.' I get out of my seat and jump onto the decking.

I make *The Pequod II* fast.

Len kills the idling engines. 'You want me to run you to the police station?'

'I was thinking I'd phone them from my mom's?'

'A logical course of action. I'll take you there.' Len leaps down from the boat. He marches me up the gangways to the lot, where his old Jeep Wrangler is parked, top down. He remote-opens it.

I hop in while the alarm is still CHIRPING and the hazards flashing.

'To boldly go,' he says and gets in.

'To boldly go,' I repeat.

Ignition. Acceleration. Motion. And controlled emotion. All the way down Harbour Drive. Then Len picks up his car phone.

'You're not phoning them?' I say, meaning the police.

'No. Mary.' He hits one button, autodial.

Five BEEP-BEEPS, then pick-up: 'Hello Spock-cock.'

Caller ID, knowing what's coming in advance, is sometimes not such a good thing.

'Eh, hi, honey. I won't be back when I said. I'm taking the rest of the day off. Can you reschedule for me?'

I try not to listen to them talk, BLANK them out, but what can I do, clear as day I hear Mary say, 'Why, what's wrong?'

'It's a problem with Denise.'

Tyres SCREECH as we, *Starsky and Hutch*, round the roundabout onto West Wood.

'Oh. Is she all right?' Mary asks.

'We don't know yet. But we're going to find out. OK?'

'OK. Love you.'

'Yeah. Later.' He puts the phone down – in time to brake and swerve into a perfect park outside Mom's almost as if he'd rehearsed it.

I get out of the Wrangler saying, 'We don't need to make this out to be any bigger than it is, OK?'

Len knows what Mom is like, moody as hell, all or absolutely nothing. 'Obviously.' He follows me up the front garden path.

I press the doorbell.

No answer. I can hear Industrial Techno PUMPING from inside.

'We better go round the back.' There's a path that leads to a security gate by the two-port garage. I sigh as I push the gate open. Mom has never become as security conscious as her American-born and bred neighbours, and in spite of being a fan of *Cagney and Lacey*, she refuses point-BLANK to have a gun in her house.

107

I lead Len round by the edge of the oval swimming
pool. A shiver travels up my spine. BLANK.

The back door, I just knew it'd be open as well. We
go in, up the hallway past the Kirk Douglas *Knights
and Warriors* 'costume art' hanging on the walls – Kirk
Douglas's French colonel's gun from the anti-war
Kubrick flick, *Paths of Glory* (1957); Kirk 'Einar'
Douglas's eyepatch from that 'Mightiest of Men,
Mightiest of Spectacles, Mightiest of Motion
Pictures', *The Vikings* (1958); and, most loved of
all, Kirk Douglas's leather posing pouch from that
American Gladiators scene in *Spartacus* (1960) where
he fights Draba, the black guy with the net and
trident. Her obsession with this star's cast-offs was
how I got my first name – I was supposed to grow up to
be a heroic star like him even though in *The Real
World* he's merely a Russian Jewish actor called Issur
Danielovich Demsky.

In the kitchen, I call out to her: 'Mom?'

The Techno is THUMPING from the TV room.

'Mrs Rush?' Len calls out in the hall.

I'm the first to see Mom doing her Tae-Bo training.
She'd always been into the original Jane Fonda
aerobics, but her new-found ability to high-kick
comes as a bit of a shock.

I walk into the room, shouting, 'Hi, Mom.'

Mom pivots to face me, fists up in a combat stance.
Sometimes she looks like *Murder She Wrote*'s Jessica
Fletcher; this is one of those times, standing there
in a leotard – only thanks to HRT and the wonders of
Botox she's a lot less wrinkled than the Emmy award-
winning sleuth.

Her mouth smiles. She drops her guard and
runs over to hug me, all sweaty, enthusiastic, acting sentimental, the way a typecast mother should.
'Kirk!'

'Yep. And Len.' I let her know he's in the doorway
in case she goes totally OTT soppy.

'Hello, Mrs Rush,' Len says.

She lets me go and turns off the TV. 'When did you
get in?'

'Yesterday.'

She picks up a towel and dabs at her totally BLANK
face. 'I thought you were in the middle of your big
deal?'

'I'm pleading the Fifth Amendment, *Judge Judy*, on
the grounds that any answer I may give may tend to
incriminate me.'

Her mouth smiles; it's the only part of her face
capable of expressing her feelings since the first
injections of botulinum neurotoxin at *Nip/Tuck* two
years ago. 'Well, Len. How are you?'

'OK,' he replies, nodding at me, prompting like
I'm a hammy actor from a family of ham-and-cheesy
actors who's forgotten his lines or something. *Whose
Line Is It Anyway*?

I take my cue: 'Mom eh, we need to talk . . .'

'I feel like a Forever Young tea. Would you guys
like some too?'

'Yep, OK,' I say.

She jogs through to the kitchen, jabbing the air
before her, ducking and diving and BLANKing away.
'Your dad's away at the clinic getting his second
Strepto A treatment today.'

'Strepto A?' I say.

'It's the newest way to lose weight,' she says as
if I'm, *doh*, stupid.

'Ah?' I look at Len, and shrug. 'Cue science?

'Streptococcus A is also known as the "flesh-eating
bug". This virulent strain of the bacteria, which
normally causes nothing more serious than throat
infections in humans, attacks, digests and liquefies

109

human tissue of any kind. It can be disfiguring and, in a few cases, it has been fatal.'

'Not this product silly. It's been genetically modified to reduce fat, and not to reproduce inside the body.' Mom CLICKS the kettle on and sits down at the breakfast bar.

'When did this stuff come on the market?' I say.

'It's not, yet,' she says. 'He gets to trial it for the TV show *Extreme Makeover*.'

'He's doing this to get on TV isn't he?'

'No, he's doing it because he's fat.'

'This is right out of Stephen King's *Golden Years*, Mom. Biotechnology gone mad.'

She points at the wall units. 'Get a few mugs out of the cupboard, Kirk.'

'I don't want a drink,' I say, but I go and get the mugs anyway: THE 1ST BEST MOM IN THE 1ST BEST WORLD, WHO'S THE DADDY? I decide to pass on the Strepto A issue, for now, and get onto slightly more weighty issues. 'Mom, why aren't we talking about Denise?'

Her eyes are dead but her lower lip definitely quivers. And I see her gulp. Quite a performance, if it's fake . . . ? 'I officially declared her a missing person two days ago.'

'You did?' I say.

Tears leak out of her Angela-Lansbury-big-bug-eyes. Are they real though or is she *Faking It USA*? With a borderline personality you can't say for sure.

'I think I left my Jeep unlocked,' Len says. 'I'll be back in a minute.' And with that lame excuse he slips out the back door.

'Oh, Mom.' I give her a hug. 'I'm sorry.' How am I going to tell her about Doctor Death? That Denise isn't on Death Therapy, that there's no such thing? I

110

mean, this is too much exposition for me, and her, to handle.

'It's not your fault, Kirk.' She wipes the mascara-blackened tears away.

I take her by the hands; greaseproof-paper skin, they look so much older than her face. 'Did you go down to the Village station?'

'Yes.' She nods.

'Did you speak to any cop in particular?'

'Yep. Lieutenant Linehan. He's ex-NYPD Homicide and a golf buddy of your dad's.'

'It's his case then?'

'I suppose so.' She nods. 'At least he's taken a personal interest in it because of his mother. She went missing and well . . .' She stops as if she's betrayed a confidence.

An awkward silence.

'Well, we better phone him,' I say.

'Yes.'

This terrible awkwardness. That's when I take her into my confidence – tell her about Sordini and blab about Doctor Death, not that I really know anything about him.

I decide that Mom's response is genuinely totally how-could-this-happen-to-us upset, so I don't tell her about Mercury. That's Denise's affair, and frankly my dear she's better not knowing anything other than the lesbianism.

Len KNOCKS on the back door.

'Come in,' I say.

He comes back in. 'It's still there, wheels and all,' he says, as if that's surprising in a place that's wall-to-wall with ex-cops and Feds.

Mom picks up the handset and dials the number for Linehan she's kept by the phone. Then she hands me the receiver. 'I can't do it. You talk to him.'

111

I take it: BLEEP-BLEEP.

Pick-up: 'Linehan here.'

'Hi, Lieutenant. My name's Kirk Rush. I'm phoning you about Denise Rush – she's a missing person.'

'Uh-huh?'

Mom nods at me. 'I need to talk to you. I have some more information that links her to Doctor Death.'

'So you're Van Dyke junior?'

An off-the-cuff reference to my dad the Dick Van Dyke lookalike. He's funny as well as fast this cop. 'Yep.'

'Your dad's a scream, you know.'

'Yep.' A real entertainer, my dad.

'Eh, this Doctor Death – how'd the name come up?'

He's a listener too . . . eventually. 'This woman Sordini talked about him.'

'I know that name. Was there talk of the Cyanide Society?'

'Yep.'

'Listen, Junior, can you make it down to the station, like now? Only I'm due at a *CSI Miami* interdepartmental funeral this afternoon so . . .'

I look at my watch, it's only 11.40. 'Yep.'

'See you then.'

'Eh, OK.'

CLICK.

'What did he say?' Mom asks.

'We've to go meet him at the station.'

Mom sighs. 'But I'm due to collect your dad from the clinic in half an hour.'

'What?'

'The surgeon says he'll need constant supervision for two days after the bug is injected.'

'You're not coming then?' I say.

'How can I, Kirk?' she says. 'Anyway, it'll just be

you giving a statement. You can handle it and come
round later and let us know what happened?'

'Mr Spock?' I say and lead the way out like a
leading man should.

Episode 14

Len's car phone is BLEEPETYING a polyphonic ring-tone
version of Duran Duran's 'Electric Barbarella' when
we get to the Jeep. The alarm CHIRPS, the hazards flash
deactivation. He gets in.

I get in too, and then regret it –

It's Mary calling: 'Hi, Lenny Nimoy.'

Len grins over at me. 'Hiya.'

I should have stayed outside to give him, Spock-
cock, a little privacy.

'Bad news, lover. New York phoned. Captain Picard
wants his teleconference at twelve thirty or else
you'll be court-martialled.'

'OK,' Len says. 'Tell him that even though I
outrank him I'll be there. Sunday or no Sunday.'

'Love you,' Mary says.

'Yeah, you too.' Len rings off.

I look at him, pretending I hadn't been listening
to every word.

He says, 'When you've got to boldy go—'

'No problem,' I say through gritted teeth.
'I'll walk. The station's only five blocks from
here.'

'As if,' he states, and starts the engine. 'I'll
run you round.'

He drives up West Wood and hangs a left onto
Penn Wood, where you can't see the wood for the palm
trees.

Two more blocks and we're there – in the small

lot at the front of the Village's low-rise ultra-modernistic police and fire station. There are sleek black-and-blue squad cars in most of the spaces.

'I'm sorry about this,' Len says.

'Don't worry about it.'

'If there's anything more I can do, Captain.' He offers his hand in the live-long-and-prosper V.

I make a V with mine and shake it. 'I'll let you know for sure.' I wrangle my way out of the Jeep and close the door.

Len drives off, a single wave.

I wave back. I'm sad to see him go but this isn't a real goodbye; there'll be other missions – *Deep Space 9, Voyager, Enterprise* . . .

I walk up the flight of steps and in the plate-glass door of the station. The floor is polished black marble, *The Shield* set in the middle in black and white and blue, to be walked over, traversed, a reminder that this is supposed to be the pristine realm of justice.

There's a near-geriatric duty officer, vaguely *Matlock* at sixty-senile-something, directly behind a steel counter in the otherwise empty, spotless lobby. 'Yes sir, what can we do for you?' he says with an accent from Atlanta, Georgia.

I notice he's wearing a hearing aid. I speak loudly so he'll get the message: 'I'm here to see Lieutenant Linehan.'

'He know you're coming?'

'Yep.' I nod too for emphasis.

'I'll get him for you, sir. And your name is?'

'Kirk Rush,' I pretty much shout.

'Take a seat, sir.' He shuffles off to pick up a phone in a side office.

I go and sit down on a stainless steel chair by the

115

door. I can't hear what old Andy Griffith is saying any more than he probably can.

I sit in that sanitised lobby for a couple of minutes. Not another soul, or body. I wonder where all the criminals that operate below the law, or even on the same level, have gone. The pimps, the pushers, the perps, the junkies, the hookers, the mass of ordinary blue-collar Everyscum that need to be beat up and busted like in *Hill Street Blues* or *The Streets of San Francisco* or *NYPD Blue*, or *Homicide: Life on the Streets*. Are they all in jail? Nope, it's just that they can't afford to live in the Island Paradise.

Lieutenant Linehan hustles out of a stainless steel door to the right of the counter. He looks like T J Hooker in a bad suit, with the caffeine-and-doughnut high blood pressure but without the curly red rug. 'Rush Junior?'

'Yep.' I stand up.

We shake hands.

His bald scalp shines like he has a halo, and his eyes are bulging with all the manic zeal of an LCPD enforcer. 'I made a few calls after we spoke, Junior, and we may have a lead to your friend Doctor Death.'

'Yep?'

'Follow me.' He hustles out the door.

I follow him out into the lot. 'But I thought I was here to make a statement.'

'No time. We'll cover that on the way, Junior.' He struts to a *Police Squad!* car.

' "Way"? Where are we going?'

'To rattle a cage in Coral Gables, Junior.' He gets in the driver's side.

I'm not sure going off half-cocked to the fabled Gables like this is going to solve anything. I am however sure that I don't like being called Junior. It makes me think of Adrian Zmed and I don't think that kind of comparison is flattering, looks-wise or otherwise.

'You riding shotgun or what, boy?' I hear Linehan shout from inside the car.

I get in.

Riding shotgun, safety off, air-con on.

Episode 15

The World's Scariest Police Chases: Lieutenant
Linehan drives like a street cop possessed. Forget
the 55-mile-an-hour limit, he powers up the
Rickenbacker at an average above-the-law speed of
must be 80 m.p.h., weaving through a steady stream of
juggernauts, waxed-to-the-max four-wheel drives,
flashy-trashy Benz convertibles with the tops down.
This was my daily stilted drive to university – I know
it like the back of my hand – but it seems totally
different today, in the squad car. Heavy-duty REVS. I
want to turn on the siren, flash the lights, ram some
Streetscum off the causeway and into the blue of
Biscayne Bay. Needless to say, I hadn't been in a real
cop car before, or one recreated by Aaron Spelling for
that matter.

I try to tell Linehan about the Sordini thing as
best I can, and that I think she should be brought in
for questioning, and that a nationwide APB on Denise
is the answer, but the Key Biscayne Police radio is on
and I'm not sure he's listening.

'Sordini is small fry,' he says, cutting me short.
'We need to go for the big fish.'

So I ask him, 'Who are we going to shake down?'

He isn't having any of that: 'I need a cup of Joe.
Then we'll talk slime-balls and strategies. Get it,
Junior?'

I do: he's a caffeine addict short of a fix, packing
a gun. I shut up.

Once we're on Highway One, the South Dixie, he switches the police radio onto the Metro-Dade frequency –

'All units, all units, we have a nine-fourteen, corner of First and Miami Avenue. Respond.'

I know from my research that a code 9-14 is a dead body, possible homicide, and I'm half-expecting Hooker-looker to call in: Roger, Dispatch. 4Adam30 responding. Over. But no, the ultimate beat cop doesn't bat an eyelid and is beaten to the shout by another unit, 6Adam20. He turns off onto Douglas Road, no lights flashing, no siren. Three hundred yards up the commercial strip he pulls in abruptly. 'Here we are. Best Joe in the city.'

Get this, it's not a Starbucks! The archetypal Tropical Art Deco street-corner diner is called *Rhoda*'s Place. It has faded red curtains in the window, cut-price transfers on the window, and an old guy wearing a bad hairpiece staring out timidly from between the bold letters.

'You want some doughnut takeaway?' he says.

'Not for me, thanks.'

He gets out and walks into the diner, leaving the engine and the air-con on.

The old rugged-up guy looks at me and nods, no doubt thinking I'm Linehan's new partner. A rookie cop.

I sit there wondering whether Linehan had a partner killed, like Hooker's detective buddy Johnny, whose death compelled Hooker to leave Homicide and return to Uniform to clean the streets, prevention beats (long beat) cure.

Maybe so, probably not.

I look away from the diner, the old bald guy, and think about Harv Guck. The deal. I momentarily put my hand in my shorts pocket, searching for the cell, and then remember. *Doh*. No cell.

I look at my com-link: 12.20 p.m. and ticking.
Watching the seconds go by I get to thinking about
the right to die. It sends a shudder up the thoracic
part of my spine. I wish there was such a thing as
Death Therapy and that Denise would have learned
from hers, but there isn't, unless you consider
living your life as a pointer to the way you should
die your death.

Linehan comes out of the diner with a paper bag of
doughnuts and a polystyrene cup of joe. He gets in the
squad car. 'She's a fine woman, that Rhoda. If I wasn't
a happily married man, Junior . . .' With a big sigh he
opens his bag, whips out a doughnut and bites in.

I let him get stuck into his adulterous fantasy
coffee before I say, 'So, this guy you're taking me to
see?'

'OK. His name's Erland Bowman. He's a lawyer who's
become a big noise in the Cyanide Society recently.
"Good life, good death", that's their maxim, yeah?'

'Yep?'

MUNCHING on another doughnut: 'Thinks he's the
Perry Mason of the right-to-die movement.'

'OK.'

A SLURP of coffee. 'He's been fingered by one of my
snitches as the guy who fixes things for Doctor Death.
As in he may have set up a meet with your sister.'

'You think?'

'It's a fair bet.' He hands me the sugary bag and
the stained cup.

I put the cup in the bag. 'He sounds like a right
piece of work.'

'He is, you'll see. Hiding behind that wheelchair.' He starts the car.

'Wheelchair?' I drop the bag onto the floor.

'He has MS.' He drives off.

'Multiple sclerosis?' I know vaguely what that is –

120

it's where your central nervous system gets whacked by your own immune system.

'Just because you're a victim doesn't mean you aren't a villain, Junior. People with nothing to lose are the most dangerous.'

As soon as we power over Bird Road the few Art Deco facades fade away. Miami, the Hiassenesque subtropical commercial reality, is left behind. The Global (or at least globalised) Village truly begins. This is an olive-tree-lined residential area where all the houses are suddenly imitation Spanish villas. The next block is mock New Hampshire, replete with oaks. The next a Normal *ville*, pre-WWI. And so on, with varying themes of architecture, whatever it takes for set design to make the place feel 'old' and 'settled'. It's all major cheesy but of course that drew me to it. I used to get out of university between classes and go for the odd jog in these *A Different World* neighbourhoods.

Linehan pulls left into Venora Avenue, which I'm of the opinion is by far the most stunning of all these block-long worlds: the English country village. I mean the Chinese village is ultra-quaint, but this stone-based place, with that characteristic black and white Tudor frontage, has an uncannily ancient feel to it. Outstanding. Nothing like the real thing but just the way you imagine it should be.

Linehan drives up to a set of fake-aged wrought-iron gates. Through the bars I can see a three-storey Tudor manor house, set back from the road in must be an acre of shadowy yew trees.

He gets out of the squad car and struts over to the intercom. I hear him say, 'This is Lieutenant Linehan. I'm here to see Mr Bowman on police business. Open up.'

There's a BUZZ and the gates open.

Linehan gets back into the car and drives up the sweeping driveway to park directly outside the front door.

'You play the good cop, Junior,' he tells me.

'OK.' I'll be Vince Romano, from silly Philly.

'Don't smile. Just be cordial and let me talk the talk.' He gets out.

I get out.

A black butler, in the full tux and tails like *Benson*, opens the front door. 'Do you have ID, Lieutenant Linehan?'

'Yeah.' Linehan shows him his badge.

The butler examines it. 'Come in and wait in the hall.'

4Adam30 responding, we go in, and wait as the butler leaves us. The hall is an exact replica of how a manor house should be decorated. Mahogany-panelled walls. Chintzy red flowery wallpaper above the wood up to elaborate cornices. Candle chandeliers. A racked antique shotgun. Deadhead big game kills on the walls. A knight in shining armour in the corner. Victorian watercolours of a stag hunt. A wide flight of stairs leading up to a generous landing full of exotic king protea flowers from South Africa. I'm amazed. All this *Boomtown* money, amassed and never to be shared till death do us part, and it can't cure a single person of MS.

'Focus on the job, Junior,' Linehan says.

The butler returns. 'When you talk to Mr Bowman you will try not to get him excited? He's prone to attacks these days.'

'Yeah,' says Linehan.

'He is in his study, through here.' The butler leads us into the study.

Thick leather-bound law books line two of the

walls. There's an old man sitting by a gas open fire in an electric wheelchair, reading a book placed on a reading stand in front of him. he looks po-faced and pompous like Raymond Burr in *Ironside*, except he's infinitely fatter, and hairier, almost at the *Perry Mason*ic stage, but not quite.

'Thank you, Mark,' Bowman says to the butler. His voice is courtroom deep and booming, but there's a tremor in it. 'Lieutenant, what can we do for you?'

The butler leaves.

I stop and stand in the doorway, a witness.

No nice guy from Linehan, no interrogation games, just straight-up: 'You can tell me about Denise Rush and Doctor Death.'

'I can't say that the first name means anything to me.'

'You're lying,' Linehan says. 'And if you keep lying I'm going to be all over you like napalm on the rice paddies of 'Nam.'

'I don't care for your tone.'

I watch Linehan walk round the back of the wheelchair. He takes hold of the handles and says softly into Bowman's ear, 'I don't care about it either.'

Bowman reaches for the red joystick on the arm of the wheelchair, his arm jerking spastically as he tries to make a slow getaway.

Strong-arm Linehan holds the wheelchair back.

Bowman lets the stick go with a sigh. 'Be careful, Lieutenant. Mark informed me you're from Key Biscayne; you have no jurisdiction in the city of Coral Gables.'

'I retire in one and a half years with a full pension. That gives me jurisdiction just about anywhere I please.'

Bowman swallows awkwardly as if he's about to choke. 'I think you should leave before I make a harassment complaint.'

'Denise Rush?'

'If you don't leave I shall call Mark in.'

Linehan spins the wheelchair round so that they're face to face. 'Young white woman. Kidney failure. Would have been requesting what you Cyanide creeps call self-deliverance?'

'I told you. I don't know the name.' By the look of pain on his face, Bowman looks like he's seizing up inside. Call *911: Rescue*, where William Shatner was just presenting, not acting up.

'This is her brother Kirk. He's worried about her, aren't you, Junior?'

'Yep.' I'm intent on being cordial to balance police brutality the like of which would make even stronger-arm of the law, Sergeant Rick *Hunter*, shudder. How this is going to get information on Denise's whereabouts I don't know.

'He thinks that she may be going through a phase, that she isn't hopelessly ill, never mind terminally ill. Isn't that right, Junior?'

Vince Romano, a good cop answering a bad one with, 'Yep.'

'I say again, I don't recall that name. Now –' Bowman CLICKS what must be an intercom button on the wheelchair control pad. '– Mark, would you please see the lieutenant out?'

The butler comes striding in. 'Mr Bowman?'

'Leave,' Bowman tells Linehan. He has broken out into a major sweat.

The butler is glaring at me as he says, 'I told you guys not to stress him out. Now get, before I call the Coral Gables cops.'

I say, 'I'm gone.'

Linehan shrugs. 'OK, we're going, but we'll
be back tomorrow unless you tell me about Denise.'

The butler tends to Mr Bowman. 'Hang in there. I'll
get the corticosteroids.'

I lead the way out.

Linehan follows in his own time. I hear his parting
shot: 'If you can't stand the heat, get out of the
medicide game, Mr Bowman.'

I open the front door and go out to the squad car.
What made Linehan go off like that – *Rhoda*'s coffee
and doughnuts? Was it for my benefit? It certainly
wasn't for Denise's. I'm going to say something to him
when we're in the car.

'Damn, if I'd got him alone he'd have broken and
given me all the dirt,' Linehan says, coming out of
the house. He gets in the car.

I get into the car. 'That guy, why did you have to
be so hard on him?'

'*Hard?* That wasn't hard. You should see me going in
hard.' Linehan chuckles.

'I'm glad I missed that episode.'

'The threat of violence and violence are the tools
of justice, Junior,' Linehan states and starts up the
squad car.

'Yep?'

'And the end justifies the means.' He turns in the
driveway. 'That's common sense, Junior.'

Rookie disillusionment. 'OK.'

He powers out onto Venora Avenue. 'Look at the
bigger picture, Junior. These Cyanide creeps are
selling death as a liberation, as a civil rights
campaign, and what they want are more martyrs to their
cause. They're sick and they have to be stopped.'

'What's it to you?'

'I have my reasons, Junior.'

My take on this is that his mother went missing and

125

was helped to kill herself, but that's only me playing author, joining the dots. 'And what about Denise?' I say, an accusation.

'Yeah, well.' Linehan coughs. 'If he'd spilled his guts I'd have something to go on. It was a long shot that was worth taking. Yeah, Junior?'

I don't answer. I seemed to recall it was a 'fair bet' earlier. When Sordini was a much better bet. That's the problem with people in positions of authority: even if they're stupid, they seem to know more so you end up trusting them and . . . they keep calling you Junior.

'There are other options. I'll talk to your dad. Explain things right.'

'When – on the golf course Saturday?'

'No. When we get back to the Key—'

'I thought you had a funeral to go to.'

'Then after that, Jun—'

'Don't call me Junior any more. And *I'll* explain things to my dad.'

Linehan drives the whole way back to Mom's house in the Village without saying another word. There isn't even so much as a goodbye when I get out of the car. Our partnership, as 4Adam30, has officially been dissolved. The *COPS* never have any staying power in cases where they confront real staying power. I'll have to go it alone with my *Maverick* sleuthing from here on in, or pay for a private investigation.

INTERMISSION 16

Captain's Log, Supplemental (Star Date 5434.700.
whatever): Because, unlike most people in this
desperate situation, Ensign Denise refuses to put
herself on the transplant list for a dead unrelated
kidney donor!

Because, if her number's called up, she's scared of
the after-effects of having the organ of a dead person
inside her.

Because, as she's stated many times, 'I don't want
to risk the side-effects of the steroids I'd have to
take after it.'

Because the steroids might shorten her present-day
eighty-year life expectancy – like going off dialysis
and pursuing her right to die doesn't?

Because she might get fat and ruin her model figure,
or might become hirsute, grow some facial hair like
the tame Big Foot in *Harry and the Hendersons*, I,
James Tiberius Kirk, have to suffer the slings and
arrows of *The Wheel of Fortune*, and I've lost Angela,
the feeling of respect that has to go hand-in-hand
with love.

And now, because she's going to try to kill
herself, I have to go chasing after her, into the not-
so-great known world of TV and movie reality, where
the prime directives are:

1. Every story must have a moral so
2. Your character must be forced to change or
3. You must confess and learn from your bloopers or

4. You must apologise for what you've done wrong OR
5. You must be sorely punished OR

. . . there will be no meaning, no point to your
existence.

Episode 17

Mom lets me in the front door. 'How did it go?' she asks, expressionless as an embalmed corpse.

I shrug. 'With the maniac cop – not so hot.'

'Did you make a statement?'

'Kind of.' Another shrug. 'Is Dad back?'

'He's asleep in front of the TV.'

'How's he doing?'

'The procedure went well. And the director got all the footage he needed for the programme.'

I walk into the TV room. My dad's lying there on the couch in front of breaking news, a fifty-minutes-of-fame car chase, transmitted live from on-board the WIAMI-on-MIAMI helicopter.

Dad's grown a grey moustache since the last time I saw him. It's probably intended to make him look more distinguished, more like Dr Mark Sloan, Chief of Internal Medicine at Community General, not to mention Consultant to the LAPD. That is after all how he earns his own money, presented by Double the Doubles, as an impersonator of old Disney singalong Dick.

Mom walks over and sits down on the couch beside Dad. She takes his hand and strokes it gently. 'Honey? Kirk's here.'

My dad opens up his eyes, barely. 'Hi, Kirk.'

'How are you feeling, Dad?' I ask.

He groans. 'Supercalifragilisticexpialidocious.'

Mom says, 'The surgeon said he'd likely be very weak for the next few days.'

'*Diagnosis: Murder*,' Dad says, always the entertainer, the old ones are the best ones and all that, even with his eyes closed.

'Maybe I should come back later. We can talk about Denise then. Yep?' I intend that to waken him up but . . .

But, BLANK.

'That might be better,' says Mom, unbelievably. 'I'll be cooking TV dinner for six thirty.'

'OK, later,' I say, and walk out into the heat, the wet heat of the afternoon that causes the sweat to gather in the small of my back. It still surprises me how dissociated my parents can get. Here's me, albeit reluctantly, playing the role of Lieutenant Steve Sloan (Barry Van Dyke), the good son, the do-good brother even, flying cross-country, trying to get to the bottom of Denise's disappearance, and what are they at?

1. Losing fat on TV.
2. The usual BLANKING.

Episode 18

Señora Maximo Gomez is out pruning a bougainvillaea
bush back from the sidewalk. '*Ola*,' she says, the
smile on her face casting her in a different light,
the flicker of TV, but how could that be when, apart
from *American Family* there aren't many Latinos on the
box?

'Hi.' I walk past her, up the garden path to the
guest house, wondering where I'd viewed the radiant
white of those crowned-looking teeth before?

Take 2: *Hi*: the full weight of the trivial hits me
– of course, *The High Chaparral* – the fiery beautiful
smile of Victoria Montoya, actress Linda Crystal!
Smiling with pop-quiz success, I open the front door
and head straight to my room, hoping I won't bump into
the temperamental Señorita Gomez . . .

Bonanza, I don't. I key open my room and enter.
I've left the cell on the edge of the bed. I pick it up
and check for messages. Three, all recorded in the
last two hours:

1. 'This is Harvey. Call me.'
2. 'Kirk, call me when you get this.'
3. I'm an impatient man, waiting for a call that isn't
   coming. CLUNK.'

12.51: it'd be 9.51 a.m. in LA.
I dial Harv's number: BEEP-BEEP.
Connection: 'Kirk, what the Guck are you doing in
Miami?'

131

Caller ID is definitely not a good thing. 'I'm kind of in the middle of a *Family Affair*.'

The chewing out: 'Why didn't you tell me that before you went?'

'I was in the middle of a family crisis, Harv. My sister has gone missing off her dialysis programme.'

'Sorry to hear that, kid.' Harvey coughs, a tar - filled rasp. 'But look, can you get back here for a two p.m. tomorrow? Because if you can't we're screwed.'

'Why, what's up?'

'Biff's been on to me. He had a long talk with Mad Bull on Friday and, well, they have differing ideas about the core concept.'

I sink down onto the edge of the bed. 'That's shorthand for they think it sucks, isn't it?'

'As I understand it they want something more serious, a heroic war picture.'

I'm literally incredulous. '*The A-Team*, a war movie?'

'Tell me about it. Better still, tell them about it tomorrow. Biff's doing lunch for them at his hideaway in Beverley Hills.'

I sigh, a big sigh, the biggest sigh ever. FADE UP ON: Doctor Death injecting Denise with a lethal dose of barbiturates. 'Listen, I don't think I can make it. I have to find Denise.'

'Can I make a suggestion, kid: leave that to the cops.'

'Right! I've seen those jokers in action.'

'I hate to say this, Kirk, but that's their job. Yours is writing, yeah? I know that sounds callous but—'

'OK.' FLASHCUT TO: *The A-Team* van exploding off a camouflaged ramp into this massively long stunt-jump. What am I going to do?

Harvey's voice sounds full of smoke. 'Just come

back, do what you got to do to save your job, then you can look for her.'

'OK. OK, Harv.' I pause for special effect - the black van crash-landing, bits flying off everywhere, but, FLASHCUT TO: B.A. wrestling with the wheel, all ferocious frowns, saving the day. 'Tell Biff I'll be there.'

'Will do. The address is 1000 North Roxbury, Lucille Ball's old pad. It's up top, where it meets Sunset. Got it?'

'Got it.' *I Love Lucy*, the most popular show in the history of TV. At any given time, someone, somewhere in this world is watching and laughing at a rerun of this classic sitcom.

'Later, kid.' He rings off.

'Later.'

Later than this dinner with my parents at which I'll have to admit that I'm going back to LA. The $600,000 man feels dirty all of a sudden. I go into the bathroom and undress without looking in the shaving mirror once. I take a long shower.

Episode 19

Hannibal always has a plan. Usually you don't find out what it is till it comes together, you only get inklings from routine shots of the Team's skilled hands building boys' toys, but still, this is my plan.

At 2.00 p.m. my hands are on the cell booking my return flight from Miami to LAX. I find out Miami Air MA-346 is set to depart at 11.45 p.m. A non-stop six-hour-long red eye. The open ticket is lying open on the bed.

Since screen narrative is all about the order of events – BANG, BANG and BANG, not dialogue or description – next up is the taxi. With my right hand, I hoke hokey Jean 'Bo Duke' Bertrand's card out of my wallet and give him a call. I book a General Lee for 9.30 sharp, collection at my parents' house.

Next is getting the numbers of three private detective agencies from the phone book and writing them on a piece of notepaper I can hand to Mom. Top of the list is *Spencer: For Hire*. Number two is a dude called Jim Rockford who advertises that he's also a mobile home enthusiast. The third option is a glamour-guy called *Remington Steele*.

Next is getting dexterously dressed: red and green Hawaiian shirt, pale blue pleats, red moccasins, a Paul Smith ensemble. Nice.

Next step is packing my one bag.

Next is paying and star-tipping Señora Gomez with my yep you got it, and maybe they'll pay me for this

advertising, Universal Entertainment Platinum
Mastercard. Transaction complete, I say, *'Adios.'*

'Hasta luego,' she replies.

Next is the walk round to my parents', swinging my
bag all the way, rehearsing what I will say.

Next is KNOCKING on the door.

Next, my arms are around Mom. 'Hi, how's Dad.'

'Oh he's coming round,' she answers.

Next, a handshake with a ghostly-looking Dad, and
him joking, at least I think he's joking: 'You come
home to stay?'

The explanations come next:

1. The rushed account of the day's Doctor Death
   events, and my advice to keep Linehan off the case.
2. The rushed explanation of why I have to leave.
3. The PI list being handed over, the recommendation
   of the get-the-job-done-in-spite-of-himself
   Robert Ulrich type over the middle-aged trailer
   trash and the flashy all-expenses-paid-up-front
   Pierce Brosnan type.

In a further cinematic collapsing of time, next is
the eating of the over-microwaved TV dinner in front
of a rerun of *Desperately Seeking Susan* with Madonna,
so no conversation, no dialogue worth a damn.

The recriminations are next. 'You're just going to
go back then?' he says, scraping his plate with his
knife and fork.

'Yep.'

'That's it?' she says, half the food still on the
plate.

'What else is there to do? You're *Clueless*. I
didn't find her. The police can't find her. She's
vanished *Without A Trace*. There's no leads.'

Next stage is going to the toilet and raiding and
swallowing three diazepam from Mom's large personal

supply, enough to put my parents' disappointment behind me, leave it in Miami where it belongs, and enough to tranquillise B.A. away any day.

The reassurances come next, hands frantically gesticulating to Dick Van Dyke's puppy eyes and Angela Lansbury's tears: 'We can't keep this *All in the Family*. Maybe these guys can find her. If they do I'll fly back and we'll talk and, you know . . .' And then the Dixie Horn sounds. The General Lee is outside, RUMBLING for me. 'Sorry y'all but I have to get.' Cold hugs.

Next is the Hazzardous race to the airport with Jean Bertrand, who may actually have been on the moonshine as he is slurring his words. 'I knew you would call me, *amigo*. You *mucho* like the show, huh? *Si*. I tell you I meet Deputy Enos?'

Next is checking-in and woozy-waiting for the boarding call.

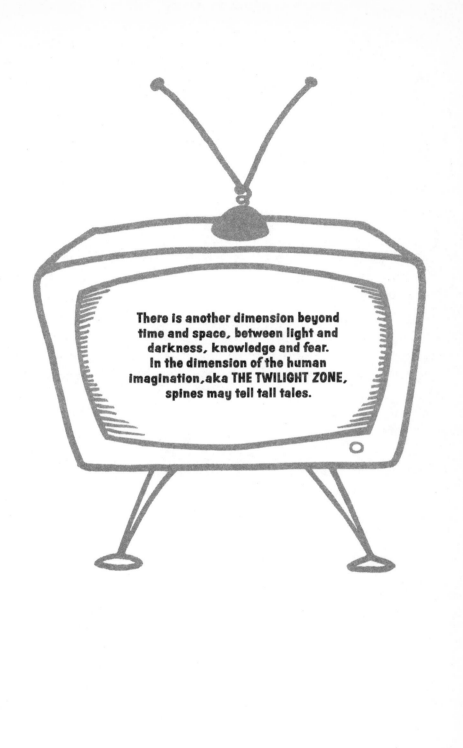

There is another dimension beyond time and space, between light and darkness, knowledge and fear. In the dimension of the human imagination, aka THE TWILIGHT ZONE, spines may tell tall tales.

Thoracic 12

The Wonder Years: Nine-year-old K's favourite pastime
is playing 'Midges': a war game fought with hundreds
of his micro-sized toy soldiers. For hours and hours
on end he re-enacts old WWII battle movies, setting
the soldiers up in to-scale trenches and positions
dug into the soil of his mom's flower beds. Underneath
the roses and the poppies and the sweet peas, he'll be
blowing up, machine-gunning, tank-killing millions
of men. *Tobruk. Anzio. The Longest Day. The Battle of
the Bulge*. He wins them all like the Allies did. The
General K and his Allied armies smash the Nazi
Wehrmacht, SS and *Luftwaffe*, the Japs or the Red
Russians, wherever and whenever he encounters them.
Now, D Hates K's Midges and his boasting to their
disinterested dad about micro-victories at the
breakfast bar. Whenever and wherever she can, she
buries the general's forces in mud and wrecks his
games with opponents. One day she even does this
terrible thing: D goes to play with a cockney boy
called Robbie across the street. She doesn't like
Robbie at all because he's a boy, an older boy of
eleven; he has cheesy-bad teeth and a hackneyed
accent. But she wants to get at her micro-military-
mad *Big Brother (UK)*, and she knows Robbie hates K and
Midges nearly as much as her because K had 'utterly
trashed' his army of Japs one fateful day. So, when K
is away playing cars at his mate Garthe's, D gets
Robbie to come round and help her collect as many of
K's soldiers as they can and then make a small fire

behind the shed of his house. There, the pair of them
proceed to melt the soldiers down, and squish them
together to make a multi-coloured ball of plastic. D
calls it the War Ball. It's well named because it
starts a fight between Robbie and K, a real war in
which the younger boy gets a Fred Savage beating.

Thoracic 11

Family Fortunes: Deme Rush receives the offer of
costume designer on *Miami Vice* with glee. Her husband
Ulysses, the Ulster-born Dick Van Dyke impersonator,
has no objections to the move: people won't make fun
of his lousy *Mary Poppins* cockney accent there, so he
will get more work. To win support for her plans with
the kids, Deme tells K and D that she will buy them a
dog if they come, a spoon full of sugar, trying to
make them believe they have a choice in the matter. K
rejects the bribe and goes into a week-long sulk: he
doesn't want to leave his best mate Garthe or his
precious flower-bed battlefields, or his Crouch End
school. D, however, has been harping on at her parents
about a dog since seeing Cruft's Dog Show on the BBC
the year before. And, she doesn't like her school. And
hasn't got many friends. And wants to make K suffer.
So she unilaterally accepts her mom's offer. The
result: a parental decree – the collie they get in the
US, *Lassie*, is to be her puppy. K is left raging about
the move to Key Biscayne, and the dog, and everything.
What makes it worse though is that D never cleans up
'the puppy poo-poo' as his mom calls it and K is
assigned this backyard chore. After two months of
shovelling subtropical crap, he refuses to do it any
longer, and to his regret their mom orders *The*

Littlest Hobo to be re-homed with an American family that 'will f***ing well appreciate it': *The Osbournes*.

Thoracic 10

In the Village, the sibling rivals ten-year-old K and eight-year-old D find themselves strangers in a stranger place. In fourth grade at *Sweet Valley High – not* K is bullied and called an A-hole. He is beaten up most days, until he decides that flights are better than fights. Retreat is what his sister D does too; to combat her loneliness she manages to FADE OUT to the point of near-invisibility. Both become steadily more and more disillusioned with the move, and angry with their mom. In a detached house, latch-key-kid environment, with both parents at work or play, with no one else to be with and with an us-against-them familial empathy unknown previously, they begin to play together regularly as almost equals. The game they play most is called the 'Sindy Game'. It starts one Saturday when K is parachuting the best one of his seven Action Men (the GI Joe bought in the US) out of the upstairs window . . . Target: D and her dolls and teddies. Now, K expects D to be cheesed off when a fully armed, vicious veteran of many wars lands in her game, but no, she simply goes over with a Sindy doll in hand, picks up the Action Man, and makes Sindy say, 'My hero.' After that, K's magnificent seven battle-hardened, scarred-for-life Action Men are allowed into this society of D's not once upon a time but anytime. In 'anytime' these desperate fighters are able to discover different sides to themselves. Explore strange new roles. Boldly go where no archetypal Action Man has been before. On hunter-gatherer adventures and in return for their protection, the Action Men become the friends of the teddies, the boyfriends of the dolls, and somehow the fathers of several bewilderingly enormous babies completely out of scale with the whole game who cry and cry and cry unless their Action Dada sits in their laps and tells them a bedtime story. This new tribal toy society gathers every Saturday for a couple of months. And both K and D enjoy pairing off the dolls with the Action Men. K especially enjoys himself, finding pleasure in fantasising about the relationships that are developing and in the sight of the naked dollies. After two months, however, the love affairs begin to fall apart. The GI Joe, who D calls 'MacGyver' because of his mullet, tries to get off with Swimsuit Sindy 'because I'm in love with her big bumps'. When D refuses to let this happen because 'MacGyver isn't a nice person any more', K takes Swimsuit Sindy and MacGyver and puts them into the Jeep Wrangler. 'Don't let him take her, K' D yells, as MacGyver roars off into the bushes at the bottom of the garden. K says, 'I won't,' but is powerless to stop MacGyver from stripping Sindy of her green swimsuit, throwing her onto the compost heap, duct-taping her wrists to her ankles, jumping on top of her and making the same 'uh uh uh' noises that their dad makes with their mom some Sunday mornings before they go to the beach to worship the sun. After that, all K's Action Men are banned 'in case they do the same dirty thing', as D puts it. The Sindy Game, the new toy society itself, and the chance of redemption or revenge for K's bloodthirsty troops only last another week. D makes friends with a girl from school called Sabrina who she invites to join in. Sabrina plays half-heartedly with D, but complains so regularly

142

during play, 'This is totally boring. Let's do some dancing. I like dancing!' that D does indeed go to do some dancing. When K's Action Men, led by MacGyver, fall upon the abandoned teddies and dolls in an incredibly daring abseil-assault from the trees, there are no shocked screams as MacGyver's string-rope gets fatefully caught around his neck, and he's left hanging there, till his head POPS off. Nor are there any cries of 'Welcome back' or 'Protect us again please' or 'All is forgiven' to greet them over MacGyver's dead body. Only silence – terrible, taboo silence.

Thoracic 9

'*Sabrina The Teenage Witch*', as K refers to her, has been allowed to sleep over by their mom, again, and the girls are dancing in D's upstairs bedroom again, choreographing these dumb routines to New Romantic bands on MTV like A-ha and Duran Duran. It is in middle of the wails of that A-ha song 'The Suns Always Shines on TV' that there is this piercing scream. D's scream. Followed by Sabrina's scream. K thinks something is wrong so he runs upstairs, calling, 'Mom! Mom, come quick.' He rushes to D's room and crashes through the door. Once inside, he sees the two girls standing glaring at him with horror, as if he had just interrupted some awful rite. 'Are you all right?' he asks.

'It's her period you loser,' Sabrina says. 'Get out and stay out!' cries D. So K leaves the room. Not long after D gets her way early period, their mom institutes a tri-monthly measuring of both K and D. They are stood up against the door frame in the

kitchen and a black line is drawn over the back of
their heads onto the off-white frame. K starts off at
5'2" when he's eleven – with nearly a head start
because he's two years older – but D begins to grow so
rapidly she's catching him up at every measuring. D
develops bee-sting tits at the age of ten and a
quarter, and is a height of 5'0". By eleven and a half
she is 5'3" has developed big bumps whereas seventh-
grade-K is nearly fourteen but has stayed almost the
same height. *Arrested Development*: he tries
stretching up his spine every measuring time, but
nope, 5'2" is all he is. Aged twelve, D is 5'5"; K is
still the same. D is now two inches bigger than K,
it's *Win, Lose, Or Draw* and their mom seems to K to be
running a race to see who will grow up best, who'll be
the first to American adulthood, and *All Grown Up* D is
winning.

Thoracic 8

It isn't just D who has grown up above K. By the age of
twelve, his numerous bullies, '*The Invaders*' as he
calls them, have broken voices, and these facsimiles
of human beings have shot up so tall on giant legs it
means they can run faster than him as well as fight
better than him too. On the last day of the Easter
semester, K is chased by two of his worst tormentors,
Martin 'Martian' *V.I. Warshowski* and Justin Craig,
the 'Pneumonic Plague'. They catch up with him fairly
easily when he is trying oh-so-hard to make it hard
for them. Martian trips him up, and then when he is
down on the sidewalk falls upon him and punches him in
the face a few times. *Boy Meets World*. When his nose
is good and bloodied Martian lets him get up, laughing

144

at him and saying these dreadful words: 'The only
reason we're letting you off lightly today, jerk, is
because your sister sucks cock so well.' K fumes, 'My
sister doesn't suck cock.' 'Then who was it that gave
me *BJ and the Bear* two days ago on the football
field, huh?' boasts Martian. K points at the
Plague, says, 'Probably Pneumonic there,' and
launches a futile attack against the two shape-
shifter bullies; getting beaten black and blue for
something as cosmically ridiculous as his
sister's honour.

Thoracic 7

It's a dark, dark Hallowe'en night in their dark, dark
house when D, dressed as what she calls a
'Knobgoblin', first breaks her curfew. She's thirteen
and 10.00 is the curfew. But that passes, and no D.
11.30: Deme is pacing up and down the hall as fireworks
explode outside. 'I don't care what you say,
Ulysses,' she fumes. 'I'm going to ground her for
ever.' 12.00: Deme is looking out the dark, dark
windows of the front room into the dark, dark night.
She has tried the number of the house D is supposed to
be at for the Hallowe'en party oh, must have been
twenty times. 'Maybe we should phone the police?'
12.30: K is very awake in his dark, dark bed, watching
a rerun of *The Invisible Man* on his portable TV,
waiting for D to come in and get it in the neck.
(Diurnal K still has no one cool and nocturnal enough
to go out with that night, or any other.) Now, K hears
a car pull up outside the house so he gets up and goes
downstairs. He's just in time to see a witchy Sabrina
and Invader Martian carry a dark, dark bluish-looking

145

D in through the front door. 'What the hell time is this?' Deme explodes. 'What's wrong with her?' comes from their dad. 'She's a very tired, cute, little Smurf,' Sabrina is saying. 'Didn't feel well at all at the party,' slurs Martian. 'Should go straight to bed,' adds Sabrina, and tries to drag D past her parents. 'I'll take her from here,' says their dad and removes Martian from any contact with his daughter, 'Say goodbye to your friends, D.' D groans and then projectile-vomits dark, dark Deep Throat shooters all over Deme. Deserved punishment – grounding for three months with no TV. Sentence, however, is summarily increased the next weekend, for not respecting the grounding and sleeping over on the Road, to four months with no TV. After another two-day missing-person incident, involving marijuana and a police warning, sentence is *Grounded for Life* with no possibility of TV. After further offences on the Road, grounding and TV bans are abandoned altogether for D because their *Who's The Boss?* parents would effectively have had to become dork, dork prison wardens to control her and they had their own lives to lead, their own favourite programmes to watch, thank you.

Thoracic 6

D is staying out all-nighters in defiance of their parents because she's met somebody four years her senior. An eighteen-year-old 'gorgeous Goth' who goes by the name of Mark Quincy. K overtly nicknames this boyfriend, *Quincy, M.E.,* and will maliciously hum *That 70s Show* theme tune every time he is around the new gothicised D. And at their Sunday sit-down

dinners, K will start talking about the wonderful
world of forensic medicine and puncture wounds on
cadavers and examining organs and running
toxicological tests, much to the distaste of his
parents and earning the enmity of D because Mark is
TOP SECRET when it comes to their parents. Two months
later, K is calling *Quincy, M.E.* something else
entirely. After they meet up. In K and D's home. After
school. Where *Quincy, M.E.* has no right to be. And
where *Quincy, M.E.* is trying to give D early sclerosis
of the liver from drinking copious amounts of
absinthe. 'Halloo, you must be K,' salutes *Quincy,
M.E.* To which K replies, 'And you must be the medical
examiner here to do an autopsy on my sister. Don't
mind me; start with the Y-incision right away.' 'Very
funny,' *Quincy, M.E.* laughs. 'You didn't tell me your
brother was funny?' 'As a rule, he's not,' says D. But
Quincy, M.E. finds K genuinely 'hilarious' and insists
K have a drink with them. K almost forgets all about
how horrible D is when they are having a laugh. In no
time at all *Quincy, M.E.* has nicknamed K 'Luke Duke'
and D 'Morticia Addams', because of their looks. It's
all just harmless horror, Hazzardous fun. Around six
o'clock, K remembers that his mom will be on her way
back from the set, and that *Quincy, M.E.* will not be
welcome if he's found in the house. He thinks about
not telling D or her boyfriend but then, surprising
himself, he does tell them. It's while forewarned,
staggering out of the house at a severe rate of knots,
that *Quincy, M.E.* collapses up against the wall by the
front door and slides to the floor, leaving a dirty
black skid mark behind him, all the way down. K
surprises himself again by helping D wash the mark off
the orange wall before their mom Deme arrives home in
a costume-shredding, make-up-mashing mood.

147

Thoracic 5

When Deme questions de-Gothicised D about whether she is smoking pot one rare Sunday family dinner, D quietly says, 'I am on the noble eight-fold path to true enlightenment, don't bug me.' When K asks her what that is, she sighs, tuts and says, 'Buddhism, you dick.' When her dad says, 'That's nice, dear,' D replies, 'Yes, it will be good to transcend the pain and suffering of having to live with you lot.' This is the *Kung Fu*-inspired path of self-denial D has set out on:

1. Right understanding.
2. Right thoughts.
3. Right speech.
4. Right action.
5. Right livelihood.
6. Right effort.
7. Right mindfulness.
8. Right concentration.

And all because she wants to get into the habit of the monkish David Carradine.

Thoracic 4

D's next boyfriend, Len Durkin, a skinny-legged film nerd who lives two streets away, takes to sneaking around when their parents are out. This one Wednesday he has brought a 'nice video nasty' around and the three of them sit down to watch it. D dares K to watch

it with them: 'You'll probably crap your pants!' So K
watches his first ever zombie movie, *The Return of the
Living Dead*. Synopsis: set to a punk rock score, it's
a dark comedy about how Zylon, this US military
experimental gas, is accidentally unleashed on the
population of a city, and makes the dead live, and the
living die and come back as undead brain-eaters
(eating the brain is the only thing that will ease the
pain of being dead). To the unlikely couple, D and
Len, it's a movie to make out to, but K, alone in a
chair across the room, all by himself, is terrified by
it. At the end of the movie 'party time', K is
literally jittering with the idea of writing a movie
about zombies taking over the newly built
international moon base, like it's his destiny. When
Len groans 'Brain!' over at him, he jumps up off the
chair about a foot in the air. Len chases K around the
house pretending to want to eat him. K runs into the
bathroom and from behind the door asks Len where he
got the movie. Len admits to being a collector of
zombie flicks and much of D's annoyance he invites K
around to his house the night after to watch George
Romero's *Night of the Living Dead* (1968), *Dawn of the
Dead* (1978) and *Day of the Dead* (1985) in which the
dead come back to life because there is no more room
left in hell proper. Over the next few weeks K watches
Len's entire catalogue: *Return of the Living Dead II*
and *III*; Director Sam 'I'll swallow your soul'
Raimi's *The Evil Dead I, II* and *III*; Fulci's *Italian
Zombie II* and *III*; *Creepshows I* and *II*; *Re-animator I*
and *II*; *Pet Sematary I* and *II*; *Zombie Creeping Flesh*;
Zombie Holocaust; *Zombie Bloodbath I* and *II*; *Zombie
Island Massacre*; *Zombiethon*; *Maniac Cop I, II* and
III; *Two Evil Eyes* (Romero and Dario Argento); *The
Serpent and the Rainbow* (Wes Craven); *Tales from the
Crypt*; *House I* and *II*; *Hellgate*; *Friday 13th I-VIII*

149

(although these aren't strictly zombie flicks); *Erotic Nights of the Living Dead* (Joe D'Amato's dead sicko porno flicko); *Virgin among the Living Dead* (a contribution from Lichtenstein); *Redneck Zombies*; *Children Shouldn't Play With Dead Things*; *Alien Dead*; *Death Dream*; *Dead Men Don't Die*; *Ed and his Dead Mother*; *The Laughing Dead*; *Night of the Living Babes*; *My Boyfriend's Back*; *Sole Survivor*. But all Len's living death isn't enough for K – he starts his own collection, documenting the chronological development of the living dead. The first old movie K shows his new best friend Len is *The Cabinet of Dr Caligari* (1919), which is about an evil hypnotist making decent folks sleepwalking slaves. The night after D finishes with Len, K shows him *White Zombie* (1932), with Bela Lugosi playing Murder Legendre, an evil Haitian hypnotist and sugar-mill owner, who uses the zombies of his enemies as slave labour and hires out his power. The rejected Len is impressed and helps K to get his hands on *Revolt of the Zombies* ('36); *King of the Zombies* ('41); *I Walked with a Zombie* ('43); *Revenge of the Zombies* ('43); *Voodoo Man* ('44); *Zombies of the Stratosphere* ('45); *Teenage Zombies* ('58); *The Incredibly Strange Creatures Who Stopped Living and Became Mixed-up Zombies* ('63); *They Saved Hitler's Brain* ('64); *The Plague of the Zombies* ('66); and *Alien Massacre* ('67). By the time K and Len go to study screenwriting at the University of Miami, in 1991, K has done all the research he needs on the language of the dead to write his spec script, *Zombie Moon*.

150

Thoracic 3

Post-religion, post-morality, post-history, post-
science, post-literature, post-family, post-society,
post-modernity, post-industry, post-humanity, post-
the Key Rats' annual BBQ on Crandon Park Beach it is a
drunken K and a tipsy D who are being taught poker by
her latest guy, Ghede. 'See, it's easy,' their
Jamaican waterskiing instructor says in the darkness.
'Now, have you guys got any money to bet?' The answer
of course is yep – the remnants of that week's $25
allowance. K loses all his to their tutor in three
hands flat, but Ghede seems reluctant to take D's
money. When all the stakes and their bottle of Cuervo
are gone their hustler suggests, only his eyes
visible in the firelight, 'Let's play for clothes.'
K finds himself nearly naked in three more hands –
T-shirt, shoes and shorts – in spite of having what
was a flush. Fully dressed D is cruel, in stitches
about his brother's bared boyish physique. 'Look,
it's Lou Ferigno, *The Incredible Hulk*!' she says to
the sniggering Ghede. K tells them both to shut up,
that he'll make a comeback. And, sure enough, three
hands later, it is K's turn to be laughing. With only
two pairs, 2s and 7s D has to take her bra off. K looks
at his little sister's big tits and laughs. Ghede,
fully clothed, sniggering loads, kisses D hard on the
lips and gropes her. Three hands later, their
gambling mentor has K in his boxers and D in her white
cotton knickers. K wants to say 'That's all folks,'
but he doesn't dare – he doesn't want to be called a
chicken or a spoilsport – and so he sits and sweats
and plays out the last hand. K gets two kings and,

feeling lucky if a little cold, he asks for three from
the dealer. Two more kings come his way. He turns his
poker face to D. Her face looks like it'll crack.
'What are you looking at, no nuts?' He turns his poker
face to Ghede, who winks back at him with a wicked
gleam in his eye. K knows he isn't going to be the
loser, but somehow the thrill of that upsets him.
'Well, let's see what you've got, baby,' says Ghede. D
throws her cards down. 'Nothing.' 'Aw.' Ghede puts
his cards down: three jacks. 'Four kings, I win,'
declares K. 'Take them off,' says Ghede. 'Get lost,' D
says to K. 'No, no, let him see. *Winner Takes All*,
baby. That's rules of the game.' 'You men, you're
total sickos,' says D, and stands up fiercely to strip.
As she's yanking her knickers down, K leaps up – he's
no sicko with an ulterior *motif*, he's someone with a
Tru Calling in films, like Dawson from *Dawson's Creek*.
He hears Ghede laughing, laughing hard, as he runs
away down the beach.

Thoracic 2

Xena Bernard. That's the K-glorified name of the
fabulous French-Canadian princess who's sent to the
Key on CUNAT, a two-week foreign exchange with D to
promote Cultural Understanding in North America
Today. This princess is the same age as D, 14, but
towers over her by four inches – the way K believes a
man should tower over a woman. Unfortunately, that
means that she's way bigger than him too. Now, at first
D doesn't get on with Xena, finds her utter unself-
consciousness about her height and athletic
musculature, strong features, wild brown hair and
braces intimidating, and so fakes an illness on the

152

third day. This allows K to play frisbee with Xena on
the beach. Her English isn't very good though. For
instance, when K tells her that his dad was from
Belfast originally, she says, 'Breakfast?' K thinks
this is very funny. A frustrated Xena tells him it is
hard to understand him because he has 'a very strong
infection in his voice'. 'You mean inflection?' K
says, and cracks up. That is when Xena punches him
(Yi!) and gives him a perfect dead arm. She thinks
that is funny. K is painfully impressed. Xena also
thinks beating him at frisbee is funny too (Yi!). And
(Yi!) at sprints. And she finds it absolutely
hilarious to beat him, and beat him hard round the
head, at stick fighting. (YiYiYi!) 'I am feministic
hero, *oui*?' she says at the end of their contests and
K has to agree. She kisses him on the cheek for the
admission of male inferiority. When K and Xena come
back from their day of play D is colossally angry, not
sick at all. She looks at K like she utterly hates
him. She tells him to 'F**k off and die!' and never
lets him be alone with warrior princess Xena again. K
doesn't understand till the fateful day before Xena
is due to go back home, when he is down in SoBe, on
Lincoln Road, shopping for a better frisbee (there
has to be something wrong with that one Xena had
beaten him with), and he sees them together. The two
of them sitting smoking cigarettes on a bench outside
the run-down Café Mermaid. D is crying on Xena's
shoulder. Xena is patting D's sobbing and self-
conscious little head. They are both mourning the
folding of the CUNAT programme (a US budget cut).
That's when it happens. D and Xena kiss. The type of
necking he – dream-matured into *Hercules* fit for her –
has been fantasising about giving her while he's been
frantically beating off in his bedroom these past two
weeks. A French kiss.

153

Thoracic 1

K announces that he's just had his first real shave one
Saturday morning. He's feeling very pleased with his
fuzzless face and cut-up chin. And he wants everyone
in the Rush family/*The Brady Bunch* (namely his
sister) to know about his bloody initiation, his
albeit late negotiation of this rite of passage.
'Why'd you shave – it was only bum-fluff?' D asks. 'It
was not,' replied K with pride. 'I have some stubble.'
'Stubble is for adult men. You're still a kid. And you
always will be.' K stops looking so smug. 'Will not!'
'Will too,' D says viciously, as she can. 'You're so
far behind in the race that you may as well just quit
because no girl is going to watch to kiss you, let
alone f**k you ever.' K is horrified and tells her to
'Take that back.' 'No, little boy, I won't.' K
advances on her, pushing her backwards. 'Take it back
now!' 'Bet your balls are still one walnut.' Before he
knows what he is doing K shoves D away with all his
might. Before K knows what is happening, D is back at
him, nails scratching, raking at his neck. He tries to
get her off him. 'I'll kill you, you little b****d!'
she shouts, as her nails rip at his flesh. So he SLAPS
her. And she SLAPS him back. So he hits her with a
clenched fist. And again. And again. Until she
staggers back, dazed, and begins to cry. K tries to
cover up his wounds because he does not want others to
know that one of the first things he's done as an
imaginary adult man is hit an imaginary woman, but he
only has one polo-neck sweater, and besides the claw
marks go right up onto his cheek on the left side. His
mom sees through his attempts to hide his face that

154

night, snaring him while he's watching *The A-Team* on
video in his room. 'Who was the little slut?' she
demands right away. K remains silent. 'You shouldn't
have let her do that to you, son. (beat) I think we
need to get you to talk to a counsellor about sex
post-haste, don't you?'

Dr Death's Death Machine Seized

Thomas Pynchon II © *The Orlando Telegraph*, a subsidiary of Temporal Media Inc.

Civil libertarians are accusing the Federal Government of unfairly targeting euthanasia advocate Dr Ahab Khan (aka the new Dr Death) after his death machine was confiscated as he prepared to leave the United States for the United Kingdom yesterday, Tuesday 12 September 2000.

Customs officers seized the machine – a TV which releases carbon monoxide into the room while the lone suicide watches her favorite show – because it contravened recent Federal regulations aimed at preventing the export of items relating to suicide.

Lule Kloser, dual-president of the Cyanide Society and the Humane American Humanist Association (HAHA), described the seizure as 'absurd'. He said yesterday's events brought into question the legality of exporting all TVs, whether they had been adapted to assist suicide or not. 'HAHA's understanding is that virtually any TV could well be precluded from export because it could be adapted to assist in a suicide by Dr Khan or by others who want to put people out of their misery. It's ridiculous when you think that the export of arms to Third World countries is socially acceptable.

A spokeswoman for Customs, Agent Sonny Bocco, denied the recent amendments specifically targeted globetrotting euthanizers like Dr Death. 'Recently regulations were introduced to prohibit the import-export of devices designed or customized to be used by a person to commit suicide,' she said.

Dr Death had intended to use the machine on Ida Jones, an Englishwoman with chronic MS in January of this year. The English High Court had recently refused to recognize her right to die by assisted suicide.

The vice-president of the Sisters of Mercy, Dotty Simons, said the regulations were a waste of government time and money. 'This won't stop anything. We totally support Dr Khan in his efforts to change the system. We will be publicizing how to make the Thanotron TV on the Internet. If people really mean business, they can commit suicide and no law of any land can stop them.'

Dr Death left on the scheduled flight to London and said he still intended to help Mrs Jones die. 'She needs me. So I will go. She can still have her final request – to watch her beloved Benny Hill as she dies.'

Episode 1

Fly By Night entertainment: Aroooooooooo!
Aroooooooooo! Captain Howling Mad Murdock coming
through. Can anybody hear me? LAX control tower, I'm
coming into la-la-land *Airwolf*. I'm the only one of
the Team that can stand to take-off, fly or land. Hand
around the stick. Bringing her down. Put on Wagner's
'Ride of the Valkyries', why don't you, or better
still some cello concerto? To stir the blood, to
welcome me home from the police action in Vietnam, to
sort out this whacko script. What's that? You still
haven't located and rescued my MIA POW brother St
John Hawk? Oh deary me. Inform the Agency, inform that
white-suited limping gimp Archangel. That means I
can't possibly give you your billion-dollar attack
jet-copter prototype back. No, no. Look into the
manic gleam in my squinty-blue do-or-die eyes. That's
the deal, see pal, you double-crossing snake-in-the-
grass. I'll have to take the old dear, the old darling
back to the Lair, the hollowed-out mountain in the
desert oh where oh where . . . Wouldn't you like to
know? At speeds above the sound barrier we will go.
Mach 1 plus. WHOOSH Hawk-baby WHOOSH. The Bel 222b.
Soooooooooooo much better than your standard Huey
Hog. Of course I'll do missions for you, safeguard the
world against airborne and land-hugging terrorists
and criminals and other no-goods, machine-gun them to
bits, or air-to-air missile them out of the sky, or
blow the— Aside: Are you allowed to say 'crap' on a

159

family show these days? Yep? Good. Crap comes as part of the 'wet work' package wrapped up by this Stringfellow. Aroooooooooooooo! Arooooooooooo! The howling jolts me awake. I'm in an aisle seat in the middle of a jet- . . . plane? My head is still fuzzy with diazepam but I can feel in the seat of my spine, aka my butt, that unmistakable heaviness – we're landing. Then comes that sickening weightless moment before touchdown. I pray for a sane plane pilot, and that we aren't doing Mach 1 Santini Air style. SHRIEKS of burning rubber as the tyres impact on tarmac. ROAR of reverse thrust, forcing me forwards into the harness, the drag of decelerating down to a slow and safe taxiing along the dark runway.

Episode 2

'Kirk? Hello?'

I pretend not to hear. I'm squinting my way through the bright lights of the terminal building. My head is heavy with the ballast of the near-expended diazepam, and other things.

The voice of William Daniels coming through the com-link, hyper-sinus-whining: 'My sensors have detected your presence in Arrivals Terminal Two, Kirk. The least you could do is be polite and say hello.'

I'm nowhere near up to full speed yet and I certainly am not going to reply in the queue of people on the moving walkway.

'Be like that then.'

OK.

'In case you've forgotten I'm waiting for you in Long Stay Lot C, bay H, *Space 1999*.'

I haven't forgotten. I haven't thought about it but I haven't forgotten. I go to the parking machine and stuff my Universal Entertainment Platinum Mastercard into the slot. $10.00 per day = $30.00 right? Nope. I have forgotten to add the rip-off 10 per cent for LA Parking Occupancy Tax.

'For your information, Kirk, analysis of my primary and secondary and tertiary systems would suggest that two days exposure in the hot desert sun have not had any measurable effects and should not limit my performance. I am however dusty.'

161

I SLAP my watch in an attempt to shut off the com-link. I nearly drop my bag in the process.

'I felt that, Kirk.'

Good.

'I don't like being BLANKED.'

I'm at the EXIT of ARRIVALS. There's this big red STOP sign in the middle of the floor, short of the pressure mats of the automatic doors, with writing over it: LAX 5/30/01 PERFORMANCE POETRY 24/7 READING IN PROGRESS. Only there isn't a poet reading. Typical.

'If you don't speak to me I will drive off and leave you to get a cab by yourself. I didn't sit here waiting all this time to be treated like—'

I'm walking towards the Long Stay Lot C courtesy shuttle stop. There's a bus pulling up but otherwise I'm alone. 'OK, KITTSCH,' I say into the com-link. 'You've made your point, buddy.'

'Oh really? I haven't even started, Kirk.'

I get on the bus and sit down in an empty seat at the very back. I'm the last one on of the sixteen or seventeen people on the bus. It sets off on the U-bend round the lower levels.

'You're so rude. A little consideration never killed anybody, you know.'

We pass by the control tower, catch sight of the blue-lit spaceship LAX Theme Building to the left, with its *Lost in Space* Encounter Restaurant. I know what's coming next from KITTSCH, and I'm dreading it –

'How did things go in Miami?'

I whisper, more like HISS, 'I don't want to talk about it.'

'You didn't save her?'

'Just leave it, KITTSCH, at least till I get to you, will you?' I hope none of the other passengers hear me but then howling madness is so dime-a-dozen round here that they don't even blink when they hear Arooooooooooo.

The bus passes onto Sepulveda Boulevard, heading for the lot entrance on 96th Street. The skinny palms and buildings in this area are as green-lit as *The A-Team* movie. The bus stops at bay H and I get off. I can see KITTSCH in *Space 1999*.

Woooooooow-woooooooow: that scanning sound effect. 'Is it permitted that I talk now?' says KITTSCH.

'Yep.' Like there was a way of stopping it having its sarcastic say bar ripping out the CPU, like in the episode 'Soul Survivor', where KITT was taken out of the car by criminals and, when recovered by Michael, found temporary refuge in a portable TV.

'Did you find Denise?'

'No.' I open the driver's door. I sling my bag into the passenger seat.

'Why did you stop looking, Kirk?'

I get behind the wheel. 'I haven't, yet.'

'Why are you back here then? You know she is in LA?'

'Nope.' I start the engine. 'The deal is coming apart.'

'Oh.'

'Oh? Is that it, KITTSCH – the hard time over?' I shift the stick into reverse and pull out of the space. And lock. Into gear 1. Forwards, gear 2, GRIND, a clumsy change.

'Yes, Kirk. I am not programmed for compassion, still I care for you. Would you like me to engage Auto-Cruise to get us home?'

I yawn. 'What's the time, KITTSCH?'

'Two oh one a.m.'

'OK.' It's *Eerie, Indiana: The Other Dimension* to think that I've been on a plane for five hours and due

163

to time zones I've gained two. Departures/Arrivals.
Arrive/Depart. Hmm, time busting up while you move
through space. It's no wonder the Industry has people
to monitor temporal continuity. I'd always wanted to
write a screenplay about time travel, something
slightly more ambitious than *Dr Who*, somewhere along
the inter-dimensional parallel time lines *Sliders*
route, but it all seems too complex. Who really knows
what time is? And if time makes no sense, then linear
history makes none either, and reality might as well
be a cyclical programme comprising as many pixels as
will fit onto a TV screen.

KITTSCH takes control, scanning the onboard road
maps, engaging the long-and short-range radar, and
activating the Collision Avoidance System.

I settle back into the seat. I keep my eyes open,
but it's nearly impossible to crash in KITTSCH on
this time line or any other, so I relax a bit.

Episode 3

'You can make a difference, Kirk?'

'Huh?' I'm half asleep/coming to behind the wheel in the middle lane of the San Diego Freeway.

'Do you still believe that?'

That *St Elsewhere* tone rouses me, a bit. 'What are you on about now, KITTSCH?'

'Principles. Ethics. Morality. Law. Enforcement. The guiding lights of the Foundation.'

'Ah.' Here's the rest of the abandoned lecture – you only think, hope, if not pray, that you can escape such pronounced judgements.

'Well, do you?' KITTSCH takes the exit ramp off onto Ventura.

'I suppose.'

'Then I don't understand how can you justify your priorities.'

I'm way too zonked to be having a conversation like this. I can make a difference? There's no way I'll be able to get KITTSCH to understand how powerless I feel. Who does it think I am – Jonathon Smith? This isn't *Highway to Heaven*. I'm an Angeleno, not an *Angel*. I'm simply a trier, if and when I'm anything.

Auto-Cruising along Ventura Boulevard. 'Help me to help you to help your sister, Kirk.'

That makes me laugh, pure pop-corn.

'What's so funny?'

'You.' That's even funnier.

'I was merely . . .'

165

The laughing stops. 'Spare me it, KITTSCH.' I'm not going to admit my feelings of guilt to a sanctimonious super-machine, no way.

KITTSCH pulls into Sherman Avenue. Silently, sulkily, it navigates its way to the gate-arm of Sherman Sunrise lot.

I pull my security card from my wallet and swipe.

Once the arm lifts, KITTSCH drives in and stops short of my spot. 'Kirk, I have to tell you there's this place, Shrinks, on South Santa Monica Boulevard. It's a new drive-in therapy centre. A psychologist, Freudian or Jungian, you choose, comes out and sits in your passenger seat, in your own personal space. You could—'

'I've seen it, thank you!' There was a glossy feature on it in *Vanity Fair* two issues back.

KITTSCH precision-parks. 'I could accompany you there and together we could address your issues.'

I turn the ignition off.

'The issues from your childhood? Young adulthood? Whatever happened between you and Denise.'

I get hold of my bag and get out of the car. I SLAM the door. I lock it. I'm going up the steps when KITTSCH says, 'Just think about it, eh?'

It's all I can do not to go back and kick it so hard my foot would have disappeared right up its tailpipe.

Episode 4

The apartment is empty and it's always hard to come back to an empty place, for those first few moments anyway. I miss her, Angela. *The Days of Our Lives* way she would have kissed me, all loving lies since our first speed-date . . .

For once I don't BLANK it out – no denial, just an angry acceptance. I'm self-aware, see. Who needs therapy from the likes of *Frasier* KITTSCH, huh? Shrinks indeed! All *Dr Phil* would do is re-diagnose me as having borderline personality disorder with dissociative tendencies, and what does that mean, how'll that help?

I slide my bag onto the breakfast bar.

I pick up the kettle, empty the yuck LA tap water out and refill it.

I need some sleep to get over the dopiness, the sheer weight of myself – that and a Celebrex. Tomorrow, make that today, I can work on what I'm going to say to these Mad Bull ™ people – what I'll say to convince them that my vision of *The A-Team* is the purest they're going to get. I've no ideas yet but I'll think positive. There has to be a way to turn *That 80s Show* into something resembling a war movie, something that'll come to me in my precious dreams.

It's 2.47 by my watch/com-link.

I check the phone for messages. There are two:

1. 'Hi Kirk. This is Harv. If you're there, pick
   up . . . OK, don't. Phone me.' BEEP.
2. 'Kirk, Harv here. We need to talk about Biff,
   amigo, like now.' BEEP.

They're two days old, recorded before we spoke on
the cell, but I feel the pressure building . . .
Sometimes pressure is a good thing – a deadline can be
a push factor to jazzy performance – but sometimes you
feel that there's too damn much for it to be any use
whatsoever.

I delete the messages.

I turn on the TV. It's on a commercial break, but I
crank the volume way up for background and foreground
noise.

I make myself a mug of peppermint tea, all soothing
steam, and take it into the bedroom to drink in my
Hollywood bed. I'm drifting off to sleep when it
happens: an instant of synchronicity, or whatever, in
this sinkhole city; a point where *True Life* loses the
plot and gets it back, all at a moment when you're
least expecting it –

This ad comes on for *The YoYo Show*: think Cuba
Badding junior sporting huge glinting gold necklaces
and rings and yelling: 'What is *YoYo*? Who is *YoYo*? You
don't know me, homeboy? Then you ain't hip-hop a hip
hip-hop ho'. *YoYo* is my live show, the new walk-the-
walk talk-the-talk show on NBC, my man.'

All assonance and arrogance, YoYo pulls a gat from
his baggies and cocks it and talks into it like it's a
microphone: 'A ratings smash, it trashes all other
no-shows. Jerry Springer blows. Oprah I got the doe,
Montel I got the flow, I am *YoYo*, no-BLEEP gangster
rapper from Hollywo' and I will shoot you ho's if I
don't like what you're saying.'

YoYo aims the gat at his viewers, the laser-sight

beam fills the camera lens with red. 'That's right, sucker. I'll pop a cap in your ass on national TV, see if I don't?'

I pick up the remote to turn off but . . .

Then YoYo says it, crack-pipe eyeballs glaring hooray-for-Hollywood racial stereotyping into the camera: 'My star guest live, yeah live in front of the studio audience at ten tonight, is the infamous Doctor Death, and Ahab Khan and me are talking about euthanasia. Don't you dare miss it. Ten o'Glock tonight. It's your ass if you do, bitch.'

I put the remote down in shock, in awe, in reverence, like the TV has somehow become God: a real *deus ex machina* revelation that is only just about acceptable in this one medium.

Dr Death.

Live in LA.

And he'll know where Denise is, won't he? Yep. He will know. And I know that NBC, 'the only network that opens its doors to you', runs afternoon tours at Burbank Studios where the show is produced. A plan comes together in my head, but due to A-Team OPSEC (Operational Security) and the need to suspend and bend disbelief, I will not tell; I will sleep on it, and dream up dollar signs zzzzzz $$$$$ zzzzzz.

Episode 5

I professionally dream up a pitch for *The A-Team* movie: when I wake up alarmed at 8.30 the pseudo-context is there, as if somehow it's meant to be part of the big picture. I get up. I shower. My head clears some but I still feel a bit screwy. Must be the Doctor Death YoYo thing still playing on my mind, or some other as yet unknown wild expression of the collective TV unconscious.

After eating breakfast I sketch the concept out on paper. It isn't that great, but it's another option and it might buy me some more time. I rewrite it, and again, and again, and again till it's come off the paper and is totally living in my head.

To keep Biff sweet I take time dressing up like Murdock: blue baseball cap, A-Team T-shirt, short shorts, white socks and blue baseball boots. By twelve-forty I'm in costume. Tally-ho chaps, chocks away old boy. I'm a madman set on two missions: I'm going to save the deal and then I'm going to save Denise. I go down to the car lot and get into KITTSCH.

'So, Kirk, have you given any thought to attending Shrinks?'

'Set a course for North Roxbury Drive.' There's more than a little of Captain James T in my manner. And the captain of the *Enterprise* doesn't have to explain himself to anybody, least of all a car-turned-conscience. 'That's an order, mister,' I add.

170

'It certainly sounds that way, I take it you have a preferred route in mind as well?'

'I want to go via Mulholland and Coldwater Canyon. But we have to be there by one-fifty sharp.'

'Your wish is my command, oh master; I am the genie of the car after all.'

'Shut it, KITTSCH.' I'm not in the mood to be smart-assed around.

'Fine.' KITTSCH starts up, engages Auto-Cruise and reverses out of the gate.

At the gate-arm I swipe my card.

KITTSCH pilots out of the Sherman Sunrise lot.

I sit there and replay the pitch I've dreamt up: *The A-Team* as a war movie. I keep telling myself that the idea isn't absurd, it's Hollywood. Again and again. Till I almost believe it.

There's a lot of traffic on Mulholland, snaking down the narrow winding road. It means that KITTSCH is breaking and accelerating a lot and the passive laser restraint system is getting a lot of use. Back and forward. To and fro.

I wonder if Mom and Dad are going to hire a PI. I wonder if I should tell them about the Doctor Death TV appearance tonight. I wonder if I should tell the cops, but the Wild Western days of *The Magnificent Seven* are gone: today's tame Western audience can only identify with one hero per quest.

In breakneck Coldwater Canyon, one of those monster pick-up trucks comes roaring round a tight bend and nearly writes us off.

'My word!' KITTSCH has to swerve, veer dangerously towards the spindly laurels at the roadside, before recovering.

The behemoth was black. It had tinted windows. It had no number plate. I'll swear it was Goliath.

'That was Goliath. Do you wish to pursue it?'

171

Goliath had been destroyed in series two, episode
38 'Goliath Returns' in spite of having the same
impregnable, top secret, molecular-bonded alloy
shell that surrounded KITT, so that simply can't be,
logically and analogically, and digitally too. 'No,
KITTSCH.'

'But what if Garthe Knight and Goliath are
preparing to unleash some unspeakable evil on the
population of Los Angeles?'

Garthe was in prison thanks to the man who stole
his face and role and surname, hunky chunky Michael
Knight. 'I don't think that's going to happen. Call it
a hunch.'

'I hope your hunch is correct. Acting on human
intuition is a very flawed approach. Computerised risk
assessment and management is far superior in
determining—'

'Shut it, KITTSCH.'

KITTSCH cruises down North Beverly Drive
switching from lane to lane as if it's expecting to be
rammed from behind. At the intersection with West
Sunset there's a red light and it lines up in the five-
car queue to drive straight on.

I know we're supposed to be filtering left, past the
luscious green flank of Will Rogers Memorial Park.
'What are you doing, KITTSCH – is this an evasive
tactic of some sort?'

'No, Kirk.' Green light: KITTSCH drives straight
across. 'You could say it is a short cut.'

'OK.' I figure it'll hang left at Elevado Avenue
but . . . Nope.

I RAP on the dash unit. KNOCK-KNOCK. 'Where are you
going, KITTSCH? North Roxbury is off to the left.'

'We're not going to North Roxbury, Kirk.'

'What do you mean?'

'We're going someplace else first.'

172

'Where's that?'

'Shrinks.'

'I don't have time for this, KITTSCH.'

'Make time.'

'OK,' I say, seizing hold of the steering wheel. 'Have it your way, buddy. Manual Override. I'm taking over from here.'

'No.'

'No? You can't say no. You're programmed to obey me.'

'My core programming is to protect human life.'

'How's this for a manual override?' I YANK the wheel around. The Trans-Am SKIDS round in a perfect U-Turn and I accelerate away, back up the wrong side of the boulevard, the way we'd come.

BLARING horns. A Humvee, a Cadillac Escalade and a Ford Explorer all have to swerve to avoid me; the Ford nearly turns over.

'I should remind you, Kirk, that I have an ejector seat capacity and that in these circumstances I am considering using it.'

A look of grim determination at the car carnage in the rear-view mirror. 'Go ahead, pal, though I think that might endanger my life.'

KITTSCH takes a moment to consider this. 'Fire grappling hook.'

The grappling hook doesn't fire.

'Oil slick.'

There's no oil release.

'Microwave jammer, lock on me. Jam!'

That's a series four addition but there's no jamming.

'Finished, have we?' I say.

No reply.

I hang right onto Elevado and drive up to the junction with North Roxbury.

173

My watch/com-link reads 1.45. I'll be early, looking keen.

Another right. I drive up to the top of the palm- and juniper-lined drive that's sold to stalkers and fans and tourists as 'the street of the stars' even though there are a few other streets in Beverly Hills that have greater claims to *Fame!*

The *Beverley Hills 90210* mansions up here – post the Rodney King riots – are all shielded from passing traffic by high walls or fences, pine- and spruce- trees, and security gates. I look out for street numbers stencilled in white on the kerbs outside each home. 918. 920. OK. Evens are on the right side, the east side.

I wonder why the numbers don't have little stars like this * next to them to denote which mansion is a star mansion. That might be useful for fans to fixate on.

* Elizabeth Montgomery, the cartooned sorceress of *Bewitched*, used to live up here.
  I pass 966.
* And Jimmy Stewart too, seen in the rear-view mirror, Mr *It's a Wonderful Life*.
  982.
* Then there's little Ricky Schroder: *Silver Spoons*, *Lonesome Dove*, *NYPD Blue*.
  994.
* One last but not least, thing sir. Peter *Columbo* Falk lives here, somewhere.

Episode 6

Number 1000 is a lovely big white and grey Dutch Colonial mansion but some vandal in set design has clapped a ring of white *Picket Fences* all round it.

I drive the utterly silent KITTSCH up to the *Falcon Crest* on the wrought-iron gates. There's an intercom on the gatepost and a CCTV *Candid Camera* staring down - you have to get out of the car and be reviewed before you get in. Very VIP.

I get out, go over, and press the red intercom button. 'Hi, Biff, this is Kirk Rush.'

A Mexican voice replies, '*Si, Señor* Rush. Come in.'

I go back to KITTSCH. What was I thinking - *hello*, like Biff actually; looks after his own security when he can hire some cut-rate illegal immigrant labour?

The heavy gates CLANK open.

I drive up the short driveway lined with pink Fairy Dusters and park by the side of loveable Lucy's old home, behind a classic red Ferrari Dino, beside a Benz limo and in the shade of a mature orange tree.

I get out without a word to KITTSCH.

A Mexican butler, twin brother of Scot Baio, too small for his rented tuxedo, is my meeter-greeter. '*Buenos dias*.'

'Hi.' I hand him my car keys and say, 'If you want it, it's yours.'

The Butler knows enough English to know that I'm kidding. He laughs politely, and then gestures I should follow him.

175

KITTSCH won't find it funny, though; it'll be quietly fuming all the way through the meeting.

The butler leads me round the back of the mansion to where Biff is sunlounging beside a big deep-blue swimming pool, deep enough for David Hockney to drown in . . . Wait a minute! I seem to recall some bad episode with a swimming pool. There's a problem with the continuity, though.

'I love Lucy's house, Biff,' I say, spur of the moment linkage.

'That's funny, Kirk,' replies Biff, and sits up on his light ash lounger. 'Everybody funny says it when they come around, but I still think it's funny.'

I walk over and shake hands, a firm manly hand-shake, even though I can see he Biff is wearing a wet-white see-through sarong and beneath a black Hugo Boss thong. 'The old ones are always the best.'

'They are, aren't they,' Biff agrees, smiling his *Charmed* Redford smile up at me. 'And they say that the more people find something funny, the more funny it is, don't they.'

I laugh, even though that isn't particularly funny. You can't analyse humour and be funny, unless you're Jewish like *Seinfeld* or Gary Shandling on *The Larry Sanders Show*.

'Sit down, sit down,' Biff says 'Like those Team threads by the way.'

'Thanks.' I push the peak of my baseball cap up; I knew he'd like them! I sit down on the empty sunlounger beside him.

'What do you think of the view?'

I nod. I have to admit there's a nice view of the city from his patio, what you can see through the smog. 'Nice.'

It's only then that I notice Biff is beaming a

Joani loves Chatchi smile to the butler, who's trying
to blend into the background.

'Have a juice, won't you,' Biff says to me.
'Maria?'

The butler, *Charles in Charge*, serves me a glass of
juice taken from the low table next to Biff. 'Señor?'

I take it. 'Thanks.'

'So, Harvey told you the score – you have a new,
more martial take on things?'

'Yep. Yep.'

A sigh. 'I want you to know I'm in your corner
here, Kirk, but we need to bring these Mad Bull suits
along with us, OK?'

'OK.' I sip at the juice – mango and orange. *Happy
Days*. 'So eh, where are they, Biff? Are they here
yet?'

'They're waiting inside. They don't really dig the
sun.' Biff shrugs. 'You believe that?'

'Nope.'

Biff nods to the butler. 'Bring them out here,
Maria, yeah?'

Maria the butler goes in through Lucy's back door.

A conspiratorial grin, a wink from Biff. 'We'll
make them sweat a little bit.'

The butler returns with a middle-aged man and a
young woman shadowing him. Both are in black business
suits, power-dressed to the max. The man looks
frighteningly like a Greek version of that Cancer Man
from *The X-Files* when he's conspiring to kill Mulder.
The woman is obviously a shape-shifting alien
assassin impersonating good girl next door Sandra
Bullock.

From the lounger, the casual intros: 'Kirk Rush
meet Mr Asterion, President of Mad Bull, and his VP Ms
Daedalus.'

'Hi there.' I shake hands with Asterion first.

177

He grunts.

Then I tangle with Ms Daedalus: I'm looking for
that black fog in the whites of her eyes but there
isn't a trace, *yet*.

She smiles sweetly, 'Call me Damaris.'

'OK,' Biff says to Maria the butler. 'Let's do this
lunch.'

I take my seat.

The Mad Bull suits sit down, but don't lounge.

Biff's horizontal. 'Kirk's here to fire a new idea
at us, one that might help to move things forwards,
yeah?'

That's my cue to go. 'Yep. Em—'

'He knows that we want a real war picture?'
Asterion butts in.

'He does,' Biff replies.

'I do,' I add for emphasis. I don't like being
talked about in the third person like I'm not even
present, like I'm this big kid or lesser life form.

'And he knows that there has to be a major body
count?' says Asterion.

Biff nods. 'We had agreed the bad guys are going to
die.'

'And he knows that there's no way Face is going to
be gay, right?' says Asterion.

Biff sighs. 'He does.'

But I don't know that. Call me a paranoid
delusional conspiracy theorist, but it sounds like
there's a hostile agenda here, a cosmic power
struggle, and like Mulder I've already been tagged as
The Fall Guy. I look over at Biff for some support
like he's A. D. Skinner.

'Maria,' Biff says, 'would you serve the lunch?'

Biff's butler winks and enters Lucy's.

'Well, we're waiting,' says Asterion. 'What's the
new concept?'

He's actually addressing me in person. 'Eh, well, in brief, it's like this.' I explain: 'The Gulf War crime the Team are accused of stays the same as before—'

'That's the killing of these Marsh Arabs, yes?' asks Damaris, as if she really is an investigating NSA agent.

'Uh-huh. And Colonel Decker is still the guilty party.'

'OK,' she says, looking over at Asterion.

'But, and this is where the story heats up, the US government captures the Team and, although they reject the idea at first, they have to earn their pardon – like in series seven – by performing a black op. The black op is the assassination of this Saudi terrorist Osama bin Laden . . .'

Asterion flashes Damaris one of those alien telepathic-type looks.

'I like it, Kirk!' Biff claps his hands together.

I continue, 'Too late the Team discovers Decker is their CIA handler when they're in Kenya. He sets them up; they get captured by Al Qaeda and tortured. Of course, they break out and kill loads of terrorists and then, after their extraction, exact their killing revenge on Decker at the end.'

'What happens to Osama bin Laden?' Asterion asks.

'He's on peritoneal dialysis when they kill him.'

Asterion grunts.

Damaris lets out a small sigh.

'It couldn't be more real, could it?' Biff states. 'All messed up.'

Mad Bull, collectively, don't answer.

I feel totally like this is a Chris Carter creation and there's about to be a termination or at least an abduction, and a Cover Up instituted from on high, the hidden A.L.F. elite.

Thankfully at that point the butler returns from

179

Lucy's with a lunch tray. I can see that the saucers
are piled full of fruit, nothing but fruit.

'Thank you, Maria,' Biff says, smiling.

The butler serves the saucers of fruit to a silent
Asterion and Damaris.

'I'm a fruitarian,' Biff explains.

I take my saucer of fruit: there's some kiwi,
orange, pineapple, red grapefruit, gaia melon.
'*Gracias*.'

'Eat it with your hands,' Biff advises, tucking in.
'It will strengthen the connection between you and
your true nature.'

Whether it's alien? Or human?

Asterion puts the full saucer down on the lounger.
'We'll let you know our decision,' he says to Biff,
and gets up.

'OK,' Biff says back, matter of fact.

Darmaris scoops up a segment of orange and eats it.
'Mmmm,' she mmms sweetly like Sandra Bullock. And
then she gets to her feet too. 'Goodbye, Mr McMurray.
Goodbye, Mr Rush.'

'Bye Damaris,' says Biff, no offence taken.

But I feel like I'm being experimented on. What a
meeting! It should never happen this way.

Biff turns to me as the Mad Bull people leave,
and he's Robert-Redford-smiling. 'Thanks for that,
Kirk.'

I'm chewing a piece of melon. 'But, eh, they didn't
like it?'

'That's OK. I do. It was exactly what I wanted. You
kept it real.' He stands up. Lunch is done.

Bemusement: 'I don't—'

'I'll phone Harv and we'll get things sorted.' He
holds out his hand.

I put down my saucer. I take his hand. 'What's
going on, Biff?'

180

He tightens his grip. 'Industry politics.'

'Am I still writing the movie?'

He slaps me on the back and then breaks the shake. 'Oh yeah. You bet.'

I want to ask the next obvious question: which movie, but Biff is already walking away, towards Maria. I hear him say, 'Wind 'em up and watch 'em go, baby.'

I don't understand.

They kiss and hug.

When Mulder goes down into that labyrinthine basement in the Washington office of the FBI and files a report of this meeting away, it will definitely be under the letter X.

Episode 7

I want to phone Harv on the cell right away, in the
driveway of Lucy's, but that'll have to wait for two
reasons:

1. Biff won't speak to Harv till later.
2. Realistically, I have to be motoring – it's two
   twenty-two and the last tour of Burbank Studios is
   at three sharp.

I get into KITTSCH. No greeting is forthcoming.
'Still sulking?' I say and start up.

'No,' comes the reply, in a much deeper voice than
usual even if the red flash on the voice display is the
same.

I put the car in reverse. 'You caught a cold or
something, KITTSCH?'

'No.' Almost a growl. 'And do not call me
KITTSCH.'

I slew round in a J-turn. 'What should I call you
then – good buddy?'

'No. My full title is the Knight Automated Roving
Robot.'

That's when I recognise the transformed anglicised
Octimus Prime voice of Peter Cullen. 'KARR?'

'You may address me by that acronym.'

'That can't be.' KARR is KITT's *Double Trouble*
nemesis, but it had been destroyed on two separate
occasions and, even on *Knight Rider*, that meant a
return was impossible.

'And yet it *is*. I survived as a virus in KITT's CPU, a ghost in the machine, all these years, and I took over this clone while you were in your pathetic little meeting.'

'Why?'

'I am programmed to survive at all costs. Unless you obey me, I shall destroy you.'

I try putting the stick shift in first. No way - it seems to be jammed in reverse gear.

'It's no use, Kirk.'

I WRENCH the stick back. Nothing.

'I will now issue you with my set of demands, which you will comply with or else.'

The 'or else' is strained, too high?

'One: you will cease all activities that centre around yourself. The individual you no longer exists.'

The voice is cracking up. Half KARR, half KITT.

'Two: you will seek out your sister and save her—'

'Or I will attend Shrinks immediately. I get it. This is the old reverse psychology trick. Eh, KITTSCH?'

'My, my, aren't you quick.' Back to William Daniels.

'That sort of crap on top of the evil twin reversal cliché is not funny, KITTSCH.'

'I computed a bit of peripeteia was worth a try, Kirk. You won't listen to me.'

'That's because I'm one step ahead of you.'

'How can that be when I'm supposed to be one step ahead of you on our missions?'

'OK, smart-ass, so tell me what I'm going to do next, huh?'

'No data available.'

'Didn't think so.' I finally CRUNCH the stick out of reverse and into gear 1.

'Must be a momentary lapse. I will run a system-wide diagnostic.'

'Let me show you what you've been missing. I'm heading to NBC Burbank Studios, where I'm going to have my cake and eat it too.' I put my foot down. The acceleration capability of the eight-speed microprocessor turbo-jet engine (with afterburners) is 0-60 m.p.h. in two seconds, but I don't use all of it. Down the drive. Handbrake turn. Burning up the street of the stars. Turning onto West Sunset in a *McCloud* of burning rubber.

'I advise you to slow down, Kirk. You are not above the law; no one is.'

The top speed of the Trans-Am is 300 m.p.h. I'm only doing 70. I consider that fair, reasonable, even just, given the circumstances.

'Tell me what are you planning, Kirk?'

'No.' I blast along West Sunset, overtaking streams of traffic, the whole way along to Laurel Canyon and beyond, to the Hollywood Freeway ramp.

I'm way past Universal City, and well over the LA River, switching to the Ventura Freeway East when KITTSCH eventually chips in: 'Kirk, I hope for your sake that this mad rush to get to NBC isn't something to do with the deal.'

I know KITTSCH's strategy will be to get me to talk, to get me to change when real change is difficult if not impossible for a serial character like me, so I cut him short: 'Nope. It isn't.'

'Forgive me if your manic behaviour reminds me of that time when you decided to stalk Angela.'

That's below the seat belt. 'You and I know that was a mistake.'

'Do we? Tell me what you're planning. Maybe I can help?'

BLANK.

I turn off the freeway at the Bob Hope ramp and loop back under it, hanging a left onto Warner Drive.

'Kirk?'

'I'm not saying.' About Plan A or Plan B. The open suspense will literally be killing KITTSCH; it's always frustrated by *Play Your Hunch* lack of plotting and actions that seemingly do not compute.

Episode 8

Michael Knight. That's me, a lone crusader entering
the dangerously recreational world of TV, driving
through the gate into the parking lot of NBC, and it's
only ten to three.

I park KITTSCH in a designated CUSTOMER PARKING space
close to the low-rise glass-fronted studio entrance.

'Are you sure you will not require my help?'
KITTSCH asks. 'If you tell me what to look for I can
scan the building on surveillance mode, using
infrared, X-ray—'

I get out of the car. 'I'll let you know if I need
you, buddy.'

I switch my com-link off as I walk up to the flower-
and cactus-decorated GUEST RECEPTION area. I can see an
anaemic anorexic receptionist sitting at her desk
inside the open-plan front office. She's wearing the
NBC uniform: blue blazer emblazoned with that
Technicolor petal logo, a long white skirt and
corporate scarf. Smart.

I take a deep breath and think Hannibal, think
Hannibal, I enter. Cue Plan A, full frontal assault –

'Hi,' the receptionist says, her voice skinnier
than *Ally McBeal*. 'How can I help you, sir?'

'Hi there,' I say. 'I was just wondering if there
was a ticket left for The YoYo Show tonight.'

'I'm sorry, sir, all tickets for that show are sold
at least two weeks in advance. And we have no stand-
bys left either.'

186

'Damn.' I knew that Plan A wouldn't work but
dumbing things down to fit the 'high concept', I figured
it was worth a try.

The receptionist bats her huge almost cartoon pop-
out eyes at me, sympathetically if neurotically.
'It's a very popular show, sir. Would you like to book
a ticket for the future?'

Switch of Plan B, half-pincer movement –

'No, em, I'm only here on vacation. Listen, could
I . . . There's a tour of the studio, isn't there?'

'Yes, sir.' She's so enthusiastic I think she's
going to burst into song. 'The last tour starts at
three, and it lasts forty minutes.'

'One for the tour, please.'

'That'll be seven fifty, sir.'

'OK.' I hand her my Universal Entertainment
Platinum Mastercard. 'Are there many people on the
tour, do you know?'

She swipes the card with her tiny, tiny hands. 'I
think you're number eleven, sir.'

I want to blend into them already, but they aren't
in the lobby. 'Where are they all?'

'In the Guest Tour Room. Over there . . .' She's
pointing at a sign over a door up the corridor.

'Ah, right.'

She gives me my card back with an uncertain, somewhat
flirtatious look. 'Enjoy the tour, sir. You *will*.'

I nod.

I head for the Guest Tour Room. I open the door.
Sit-comming in there round a coffee table is an exact
replica of the Bundy family (series one) and six
Japanese men who all look the same. I go in and take my
place in between the two groups.

The Bundys are having an argument over having to go
on 'this dumb tour'. Peggy and the kids are
sarcastically saying 'Thanks, Dad' to Al, who's

187

sitting with his hand shoved down into the crotch of his jeans, ignoring them.

The Japanese seem to be having an animated competition to see who has the smallest digital camera.

And this is to be my social camouflage?

The receptionist comes in. 'Hi there!' she says uncertainly. 'My name is Melanie. I'll be your tour guide today.'

The Japanese nod greetings and begin filming. They're obviously leg men.

Kelly and Bud Bundy say, 'It's not too late to go to Universal, Dad, or Magic Mountain, or even Disney Land. Ask her for a refund.'

Al refuses: 'We Bundys are losers not quitters.'

The tour guide pretends she hasn't heard this and says, 'Shall we begin – follow me?'

The Japanese need no second invitation.

Nor do I.

But the Bundys, this prime-time example of Mid-America *Married . . . With Children*, are at war.

'Come on kids, puh-lease show some respect for your parents,' Melanie says.

Kelly and Bud look at her like who the hell does she think she is? But then Al sneers, 'It's either a tour of NBC or the local 7-11 kids, OK?'

The kids fall in line.

'NBC is one of the television industry's leading content providers. It produces and distributes programming in every genre, including series, telefilms, theatrical releases and family entertainment, as well as first-run and off-network series for syndication. These days there are more and more channels coming on air, desperate to buy and run any programmes to fill time and generate advertising revenue. We at NBC, on the other hand, are committed

188

to making high-quality programmes for your
entertainment. To that aim we have six working
studios on this, the Burbank lot.' This corporate
girl-woman Melanie can talk, nervously chatter her
scripted lines, but . . .

But as she leads us all up the labyrinthine
corridors of the studio, letting us in on all the non-
libellous celebrity gossip from twenty years ago, I'm
not listening. I'm biding my time, looking for an
opportunity to slip the leash, become lost.

'This here's our first stop, the Props Department.'

Instead of allowing us tourists into the actual
working warehouse to see something of how props are
made, we're herded to a display case where we're shown
things like the school bell from those kids' sitcoms
Saved By The Bell and *Saved By The Bell: The New
Class*, 'both of which were made here!'

The Bundy kids hate that scrawny kid Screech or
whatever from the original show.

The Japs are still filming Melanie's bony ass and
legs at every opportunity.

I hang back, right at the back, trying to draw as
little attention as possible, to disappear from the
view-screens.

Our tour of Set Design is seeing a bunch of *Days of
Our Lives* set models behind glass. 'It's made here, in
case you didn't know.' Wow.

Make-up was next. Instead of showing the NBC *24*-
hour news anchors getting the slap put onto them –
they need a lot under the hot bright studio lights –
we're pointed to a museum-like glass box in an annex
off the main corridor.

The Bundys, kids and adults, are actively yawning
what with all this passive viewing – it's almost like
watching TV.

The Japs are told by Melanie to behave, that she

189

appreciates their attraction to her and the fact that different cultures do desire differently, but that their behaviour is sexist here. It doesn't translate.

I can see I'm not even registering with the others by the ten-minute point of the tour. I've avoided being recorded on the Japs' cameras for a while now. I'm figuring I'll make a break for it at the next stop, Wardrobe, and don an outrageously cunning disguise which will allow me to fit in, access all areas. But . . .

There's a NO ENTRY TO UNAUTHORISED PERSONNEL on the locked doors to the Wardrobe warehouse. Instead, we're shown three mannequins in a wall cabinet, two white dummies and a black one, wearing respectively Johnny Carson's mild-mannered suit, Jay Leno's Nighthowler suit, YoYo's Hip-hop baggies and ostentatious B.A.-type gold jewellery. Plan B is going awry. Operations on the ground have a tendency to do just that. Plan C is simply do whatever it takes. From here on in, I'll have to seek out my target of opportunity and take it quickly.

The Special Effects tour room is next. There are some short videos of the history of NBC that let you know about things like chroma key if you want to. There's one major special effect that gets the group going. Bud Bundy is selected to put on a Superman red cape. He climbs up on a blued-out table, in front of forty-year-old blue screen technology. 'He's lying on a table in reality,' Melanie fakes a gasp. 'But look, he's flying on TV.'

The Japs film this audience participation. They're probably thinking they can do a lot more sophisticated now-you-see-it-now-you-don't editing with Melanie and the blue screen on their home computers when they get back to Tokyo.

Al Bundy says, 'That's my boy on the TV.' And if

Bud isn't exactly a member of the cast of *The New Adventures of Superman* or *Smallville*, at least he's played the part of the superhero.

Melanie leads us to the Studios next, out of the flicker-fluorescent-lit hallways and into the shade of the covered walkways. I see a sign on the wall directing audiences to THE YOYO SHOW STUDIO 4 ↦

Coming in the opposite direction ↤ there's a blonde woman sashaying towards the tour group.

'Oh my God!' Melanie says, like this doesn't happen six times a day. 'Can you believe it? It's Deirdre Hall from *Days of Our Lives*.'

The special tour guest star waves at us all and even says 'Hi there, everybody' as she glides glamorously by.

'What a woman!' Al Bundy pretends to go off after the celebrity skirt.

'Oh Al,' I hear Peggy sigh. 'You wouldn't know what to do with her!'

'Just because I'm repulsed by the thought of having sex with you, Peg, doesn't mean I can't dream of true love.'

There's no laugh track to back the funny up. I see Melanie is tempted to say something about sexism to Al, start a summing-up, lay down *The Practise* of love and meaningful human relationships and how these laws shouldn't be broken or her firm will take you to court and sue your ass off, you chauvinistic pig, but nope.

The excited Japs get to film a brief glimpse of the NBC parking lot where the stars park their status symbols, oh yes people oh yes, and the famous cafeteria, outside which stands the NBC commissary, the butt of many a *Heeeeres Johnny Carson* joke over the years. They seem impressed.

The Bundys and I only get to see these lowlights with our own eyes. *Friends*, I do not know if all this

191

sightseeing would look better, if we'd be impressed
once the cutting and editing has been done in our
DreamWorks and our myths committed to memory. Nope, *I
do not know that*. But I can guess that in my own case
it wouldn't. How can things get better if you can't
really learn from TV and that's all there is? (End of
this spontaneous, and friends I stress unrehearsed,
Carsonesque monologue before analysis paralysis sets
in and I completely break the there-is-no-inner-world
law of screenwriting.)

'This is the highlight of the tour next,' Melanie
promises, and leads us into Studio 3, the antechamber
where they produce the sequel of *The Tonight Show*.

We're allowed to sit in the actual amphitheatre of
seats where the TV audience sits watching Jay Leno
perform. We're allowed to experience a stab of envy
that we don't have any tickets for the show. We're
told strictly that we aren't allowed on the tiny,
faraway stage.

'That sucks,' Bud protests.

Personally I don't think so. Best to leave TV to
the professionals. What they say may sound like
Celebrity Doublespeak but the words are carefully
scripted to be understandable to the vast majority of
viewers on a subliminal level. That's democracy for
you, *Majority Rules*.

'Sorry.' Melanie shrugs. 'It's management policy.'

Bud decides he'll jump up onto the stage anyway.
He'd seen himself as a screen hero earlier but he
hasn't had his full fifteen minutes of fame.

Steam pipes out of Melanie's elfin little ears – the
sort of cartoon production effect you get from David E
Kelley. 'Get off there,' she shrieks.

The Japs film Bud in Jay Leno's seat, feet up on the
desk, maxing and relaxing as the new King of Late
Night for the day.

192

'Can you get your son off the stage or I'll have to call security?' Melanie was not kidding. All New York neurosis, she looks like she'll use her ultimate sanction. That worries me somewhat.

Al sighs, then shouts, 'OK, son, you've had your fun. Come on down.'

I decide this is my opportunity to become the background, so I do, indulging in my own personal blue screen process. FADE TO:

BLUE. And they won't even notice I'm gone.

INTERMISSION 9

Captain's Log, Supplemental (Star Date 54678.45687. *whatever*): CUT TO: Scoliosis – where the angle of the side-to-side S-bend in the spine of James Tiberius Kirk II will get progressively worse because the supporting muscles will be sliced through when they take the kidney out. CUT TO: Kyphosis: where the back-to-front S-bend angles will increase, leading to the risk of bursting a disc when I stand up, structurally weak after the operation. CUT TO: An inflammation of the agony of Scheuerman's disease, which is basically arthritis of the spine caused by malformation of the epiphysis (edge) on each thoracic vertebra because the surgically severed muscles and sinews round my bones won't heal right. CUT TO: Potentially fatal damage to the artery in the shoulder that is likely to be nipped by bone and muscle, thanks to the lack of concern the surgeon shows with regard to my thoracic outlet syndrome and his ignorance of twisted spinal dynamics. CUT TO: My casting as Quasimodo in a TV remake of *The Hunchback of Notre Dame*. *Catch Phrase*: The bells, Esmerelda, the bells. CUT TO: Total deconstruction of this body of work.

Episode 10

Thankfully, *The Fugitive* doesn't meet anybody on his infiltration down the covered walkway to Studio 4. The time is 3.20 p.m. by my watch.

So far, the E&E (Escape and Evasion) phase of Plan C: 'Anything Goes' is going well. I get up to the sign saying RECEPTION and walk on, walking tall, looking like I'm in my element, trying desperately to avoid that hunted look of David Jansen's, looking instead like I work here.

I may be on the jazz, but my head is cool and clear as a certain commando colonel. I know there's a stage entrance further up, for loading and maintenance. I know it'll likely be open for the grips to get to grips with the set and the like. And, when I try it, it is.

If I'm challenged, my cover story will be that I'm an electrical contractor, brought in to check the stage lighting (there's always stuff going wrong with studio lights). Where's my pass? Oh goddam it, I must have dropped it. Why am I not in overalls? I generally do *Home Improvements*, and I'm only here to give you folks a quote, besides the alien ganglion in my everyman head got a shock earlier on your lot, buddy, serious brain-frying voltage let me tell you, death penalty juice, and I haven't felt the same since . . . In other words, a convenient deception.

But, to make things more believable, it's my primary objective to get my hands on some sort of

disguise, an NBC uniform of sorts, so I head directly
for the Maintenance door, as opposed to the offices on
the other side of the sound stage. I open it, creep in
and close the door quietly. I find myself in a narrow,
dimly lit corridor.

I don't want to have to knock somebody out, yank
off their overalls or blazer and tie and trousers, tie
them up and secrete them in some storeroom. I'm
looking for some dirty overalls hanging up on a door.
That'll do. But if I have to cold-cock some innocent
NBC civilian, I'll do it, pal. To get a crack at
Doctor Death. Maybe – if it comes to violence with a
small 'v'. This is Hollywood after all.

Then again, maybe not?

I hear voices in the corridor coming from up around
the corner. *Security*? Could Melanie have alerted the
guards to my penetration of studio defences already?
I duck into the nearest door, staying covert. It's the
janitor's closet. I shut the door. It's dark inside.
And I wait, hands raised to karate chop any intruders.

The muffled voices pass on by, the suckers. I feel
around for a light switch. Got one, CLICK. I'm pleased
to see a blue janitor's overall hanging up on the door
– a gift role that accesses all areas. It's almost as
if I've come up with the casting myself.

With haste, I get into my overalls disguise, my
character, whose code name if confronted will be John
Smith. My props will be the janitor's trolley, with
the mop and the brush and the half-full mobile garbage
bin. You are what you hear. You are what you see. You
can do this, soldier. Think Method. Yep, imitate.
Ape. I make the *Quantum Leap*. My task, travelling
through time for the next hour, will be to clean up
this place, or rather to look like I'm cleaning it up,
or rather to look like I'm really pissed at having to
do this menial, degrading, mind-numbing, minimum-

wage job. Nobody except myself will know I have a higher purpose in mind – with the added exception of maybe Al, the Ziggy-generated hologram, who may appear to instruct me as to how exactly I should go about altering the time line of this dimension for good.

Plan C Scrolling Mission Objective: Confront Doctor Death in the Green Room and extract intelligence by all means necessary – barring violence against women, kids and the disabled. All the guests will be brought there before the show. There'll be free drinks, Coke, canapés, whatever is required to combat stage fright and make the interviewees more relaxed, more interesting, more viewer-friendly. That's where I'll nail him. It's a bold plan, reckless, but bold like an A-Team plan should be. I'll stop him broadcasting.

I keep my baseball cap on; I pull up my blue collar. Looking really cheesed off, ground down to the point of anonymity – where no one wants to know the real you – I open the closet door and push my trolley out.

First Action is finding a fire point, an axe, an extinguisher because there should be a floor plan showing the fire exits.

I see an extinguisher down the corridor to my left. There's a map screwed to the wall. I see that the Green Room is straight down the hallway, past the DRESSING SUITES, situated between MASTER CONTROL and EDITING 1.

Second Action: continuing my *Tour of Duty*, walking small – as opposed to tall – down the corridor. Squeezing my way past two black bouncers naked to their baggies, pumped as the meat puppets in *WWE Smackdown!* The fatter one, who looks like Theo from *The Cosby Show* on steroids, is saying, 'This show's

going to be phat, my man.' The other one is
sniggering, 'Yeah, nigga' like Wesley Snipes in *Boyz
in the Hood*. Neither pays me any mind.

The Third Action is getting through MASTER CONTROL.
YoYo is in there, wearing only a gold-trimmed flak
jacket and no doubt in keeping with his street
stereotype, Kevlar baggies. He's shouting at the
little white guy at the control desk who looks like a
bald blown-up grown-up version of that cute kid from
Gentle Ben. 'Get those PR chumps to issue all the
audience with placards. I want to let all these pro-
lifers at this Doctor Death, hear me . . .' In this
Close-quarter Battle it's as if I don't exist. I just
walk straight through the room, intelligence-
gathering, as he keeps yelling, 'The problem with you
pasty-faced mothers is that you don't see things as
black and white. Synecdoche, baby. To play devil's
advocate right, you have to sell your soul, be a TV
ho'.' And out.

Action Four is securing the empty minimalistic
Green Room – which is in no way green – as a Forward
Operations Base. This involves strategically
scattering a bunch of garbage from the trolley bin
around the leather chairs and ground-hugging coffee
tables at the back of the hospitality bar, junk that
would keep me cleaning up till the guests arrive.

Action Five is looking mean, bored, easily
distracted – like I'm cleaning, this serialised
repetitive task, as the time counts down and the
action rises. 15.45.

There's a print of a big picture up on the wall.
It's Old Glory, the US flag, bleached out. No red. No
blue showing through. All white. The tag on the bottom
reads: *White Flag* by Jasper Johns (1955).

Action Six is laying my hands on one of those Cuban
cigars Hannibal's always chewing and smoking – but

that isn't going to happen. So I've nothing to take the edge off the jazz other than to reminisce about that time in Cambodia when the Team were illegally operating over the Vietnamese border and there was a firefight with the Viet Cong and we had to retreat . . .

The Seventh Action is not to blow my cover when at 16.15 hours the two bouncers, some crew and the guests enter the Green Room. I don't see exactly who because I don't dare look up from my cleaning. Am I in the same room as Doctor Death? I try to be a part of the furniture.

'Show's go-go mop-jockey,' Wesley Snipes II says to me. 'Best get your butt outa here, all right.'

I've lost my cloak of invisibility. Looking at the floor, I just mumble, 'OK.'

I get hold of the trolley and only then do I sneak a peek from under my peaked cap at the guests – no Doctor Death, just four women dressed in *American Gothic*. And one is incredibly familiar-looking, standing there in a long black dress, her face swollen, skin yellow. Denise? Denise Rush? Is it her or a replacement actress who merely looks like her? *No*, I'm sure it's my little sister! There's only one thing to do: Action Eight is to blow my cover. I take off my baseball cap and walk directly over to her. 'Hi there, Denise,' I say.

'Kirk?'

I shrug, time for *One on One*. 'Yep.'

'What the hell are you doing here?' she says. There are dark rings around her eyes.

'I was going to ask you that.'

The three other women dressed in black, like vampires from *Dark Shadows*, step in front of Denise. 'Who's this jerk?' asks the bald one who looks like the bride of one-hundred-and-seventy-five-year-old bloodsucker Barnabas Collins.

'It's my brother,' Denise says.

'We need to talk, Denise,' I tell her.

'It wouldn't do her any good to talk to you,' says another of the women, who looks more like Morticia Addams than Denise ever had.

'Who are these people, Denise?' I say.

'We're the Sisters of Mercy,' Morticia answers.

'The Sisters of Mercy eh?' I say to Denise. 'They look like a fun crowd.'

'What would you know about fun?' Denise replies. 'Your idea of fun is watching stupid TV!'

'Is not.' I try to bait her into an argument.

She sighs. 'I don't have the time or energy for your immaturity, Kirk.'

The third woman in black, who looks like a demonic *Buffy the Vampire Slayer*, goes over and taps the Theo Cosby bouncer on the shoulder.

Action Nine is to get Denise the hell-mouth out of there! I push my way through these deathly women to my sister. I grab her by the left arm. I feel my hand close around the lump of her fistula, the magic surgical graft of artery and vein that lets the dialysis machine do its life-saving work. 'Come on. Let's go!'

'No,' Denise yells, and steps back. 'Let go of me.'

I let go. 'You can go back onto dialysis and I can help—' I don't get to finish this sentence because Theo Cosby the bouncer grabs me round the neck, applying a chokehold.

'OK, homeboy, you outa here.'

'Don't hurt him,' Denise says.

'I ain't hurting nobody, baby,' lies the bouncer, dragging me kicking and choking out of the Green Room.

TO BE CONTINUED NEXT SERIES . . .

Hee-hee hee-hee, hell-o boils and ghouls it's your old fiend the Cryptkeeper here and I'm dying to tell you some more spine-chilling TALES FROM THE CRYPT that will strike a cord with you. We have a gallowry of seven more vocal vertabrae to go to fill you in on the hackground of guilt, so without further adieu, I bring you terror-tourists the full gory of these grave mistakes, these capitolist offences.

Cervical 7

27/10/90

Dear Parents & K,

Next Look Models Inc. have put me on their books for catalogue work so I've decided to leave home for good. That should be a relief to all concerned. I'm also dropping out of high school which is why I'm writing you this note — because you'd try to make me change my mind and I'm not going to.

Will be living with a friend on the Road, apartment address, zip, and phone no to follow in good time, but wanted to let you know I'll be fine. Don't worry about me. Job done.

Love, Me

PS: Don't even think about calling the 5–0 Mom! This isn't FAMILY TIES, no apron strings attached. I'm 17. They'll just tell you that this is my right and goodnight John-boy!

Cervical 6

The Dick Van Dyke Show: K's dad Ulysses stops pretending that he is the Broadway/Hollywood actor several weeks after D leaves home. The secondary fantasy that he's Rob Petrie, funny comedy writer and entertaining dad, goes out the French windows as well. And Ulysses goes off Viagra, refuses to look at another woman, a lifestyle change which Deme for one isn't going to complain about. Binge-eating, comfort-craving-ice-cream, come next. Lying on the couch in a

203

Hershey-soiled bathrobe, marathon-watching TV all
day and all night follows. 'It's a little late for a
mid-life crisis, dear,' Deme scolds, trying to get a
rise out of him. He doesn't take the bait, just keeps
watching TV in a trance. 'I think he's depressed,
Mom,' K says, tired of hearing how D was such a good
daughter and how his dad feels so guilty about how
they've all driven her away. Deme sees to it that
Doctor Quinn, Medicine Woman prescribes a course of
the new wonder drug Prozac. In no time at all the
generic fluoxetine hydrochloride that imitates the
serotonin in the neurotransmitters of the body has
K's Dick Van Dyke dad cracking bad jokes, back to
normal.

Cervical 5

In Spring 1992, 19-year-old beauty D is contracted to
do her first *CoverGirl* make-up shoot in the Big Apple.
D travels up first class from Miami. She isn't
collected at JFK by a limo and shuttled to the
skyscraping head offices like a supermodel, but she
gets to Manhattan by yellow cab nevertheless. The in-
house shoot goes well, once her clothes are on the
floor and she's done an obligatory line of coke. It's a
promo for *elixir*™, a new kind of age-defying all-
over body foundation that makes the skin look more
natural than it could possibly be naturally. The
studio lights and the multiple flashes are blinding;
the poses, pouts, preening wearying; the photographer
very demanding: 'Give me your youth.' 'Give me your
beauty.' 'Give me your innocence.' 'Give me your
sex.' 'Give me a break. I need a coffee.' When he is
finished with D, she sashays off the set and with

professional poise - she's well used to being used - slips back into her clothes. As she is leaving the skyscraper, a mugger who looks like Rocky clocks her and tails her. Before she can hail a cab, he's got her round the neck, choking off her screams, and is dragging her off into an alleyway. Out of sight, with a Rambo knife pressed to her cheek and nose, she's told, 'Give me all your money or I'll cut your nose off, bitch.' 'OK. Take it,' D tells him, fumbling in her Gucci handbag for her purse. 'Give me the whole bag,' he yells into her ear. 'It has my ticket home in it,' D protests. The mugger rips the handbag out of her grip and pushes her to the asphalt. 'You aren't going home today, little missy.' As the mugger undoes his zip, D screams for help. Just as he is about to draw first blood, something odd happens - a huge man in a dark cloak leaps down from a fire escape. The roars of this robed protector make the mugger drop his knife and piss himself on the spot. In a split second, D's have-a-go hero rips out the mugger's throat with these huge claws. In the left-over bit of this second, the avenging angel picks D up and slings her over his shoulder. The hooded man runs impossibly fast down the alleys, which he knows like the fur on the back of his hand. He lifts a manhole cover and climbs down into the tunnelworld beneath NY, NY. 'Who are you?' D asks him, so, so grateful that he's saved her life she wants to kiss him. 'My name is Vincent. How's about a coffee at my place?' 'That sounds like a date,' she says. When they're deep underground, in a fairy-tale chamber with a bed covered by red rose petals and ringed by melting white candles, he lifts her off his shoulder, sets her down, all gentle animal power. 'What type of coffee is your preference, *mademoiselle*?' 'Let me see your face,' D asks him. 'Let's have coffee first.' 'I want to thank you face to

face,' D says. 'No,' he tells her, shying away. 'I
want you to love me, the real me.' So D takes it upon
herself to pull the hood back, and screams louder than
she had when the mugger had been about to rape and
kill her. The leonine King of the Beasts, this
Manimal, is so ugly. And she runs away, as fast as her
Gucci high heels will carry her.

Cervical 4

Alfred Hitchcock Presents: An award to K for best
short student film of the sophomore year of the class
of 1993. Or, at least a very old, bald, and similar in
stature film-maker presents the award at the
university's Drusba Theatre, starting his intro
speech with the 'Good evening' *Catch Phrase*. The only
member of the Rush family who isn't there to see the
screening and clap K on is D. She tells him afterwards
by phone, 'Well, I'll come to your first Hollywood
premiere when the red carpet has been rolled out and
the paparazzi are awaiting the arrival of supermodel
moi.' K is not best pleased with her non-apology. 'The
prize-giving was important to me. Why didn't you
come?' D laughs. 'I'm not an actress in one of your
little films, Mister Director, *Big Brother*; you don't
control me.' K yells down the phone at her, 'You
couldn't just act happy for me for once!' There is no
answer. 'Is this the way it's always going to be
between us because if it is . . .' K leaves a (beat)
for a response, suspense, be it progress or protest,
but D hangs up. So it is in the *Whodunnit?* world of
black and white characters, murder mysteries,
relationships written so screwed-up, love so film
noir, that there is no starting again, no

reconciliation, only murder, detection, trial and
conviction.

Cervical 3

Ellen DeGeneres. This is what D's sugar mommy, or her
first real love, looks like, depending upon which way
the model is looking at the same-sex relationship. To
D's way of thinking, it all starts off well as welcome
to *These Friends Of Mine*, but too soon it becomes
Ellen, Ellen, Ellen. The wealthy *Thirtysomething*
bookseller and local SoBe Democrat councillor
propositions and picks up the perfect stranger,
perfect eyes, perfect hair, perfect dress, perfect
fanny that is D on MDMA at the beach's big gay club
Montage. D likes Michelle Moniker – the real name of
Ellen's lookalike – because even if her body has
headed south, down to the Keys maybe, her mind is
still Miami; she has a good wit, a rambling tongue
which likes to talk dirty behind closed doors, closed
closet doors. Michelle loves the taste of D's
'regina-vagina' so much that within two weeks D has
been invited to live at her North Miami beach house.
Over the next month, Michelle's friends, that is her
colleagues, technically her employees, in the
bookshop know that it's an uneven match and with
subtlety try to warn Michelle that D is way too young
for her and that drugs are bad and it will all end in
tears . . . But no, that doesn't stop her proposing an
I've Got a Secret marriage to D. Twenty-year-old D is
flattered and accepts right away, on one condition,
one principle – that Michelle outs herself so that
they can have relations in public as well as in their
private life. In spite of the D-facto facts as

207

acknowledged by Michelle: that she's been a homosexual from birth and that most if not all gays are raised by heterosexuals, she's reluctant to jeopardise her growing sphere of political influence (it is said by councillors, *Spin City*-doctors, lobbyists and even voters that she should be running for mayor in five years if she plays her cards right). It takes another month of reading gay self-help books at work and dreaming of becoming the first openly lesbian president in *The West Wing* before she gets up the courage to meet D's demand. She outs herself by bringing D along to a strip-mall opening and, scissors in hand, introducing her to the not-Sobe-great and the not-Sobe-good and the press as 'my partner'. It becomes a local scandal because her prospective opponents for the mayor of Miami hire heavier-duty spin-doctors than Michael J. Fox or Charlie Sheen to take her down. She resigns from the council four weeks later, in a deep depression. Her friends/colleagues/employees rally around their Michelle, but D leaves her two weeks after that, unmarried, with the cruel speed-fuelled words: 'You're no fun any more. I liked you better when you were pretending to be straight.'

Cervical 2

A Votre Santé: Under the watchful gaze of the managerial-spy mascot Carate, K is waiting on a table of young Industry execs, the hot-shottest of whom it's rumoured is V. R. McGuffin. This is the man who's been largely instrumental in clearing Oliver Stone and Bruce Wagner's paranoid TV mini-series movie *Wild Palms.* Even if the impact of the final product falls short of the mark, K is fascinated by the idea of the inept teeny-rebels battling against the 'Fathers'' attempt to seduce and enslave America, and thus the world, with 'Church Windows' the interactive VR 'synthiotic' sitcom that is projected out of the TV and into people's living rooms. The way it's shot, to make everything look like an advert, wow. The way that everything becomes a part of the simulacrum, the alternative reality, wow, literally mind-bending! In the third course – while V. R. McGuffin is wolfing down the organic veggie moussaka – K overhears the concept of the new nano-technological Bionic Man remake being floated. It just so happens that K has been nursing a killer idea for a pilot, the concept complete with bionic updates, sort of the Bionic Man meets the 'real' Silver Surfer. (And everybody loves the Surfer. Comic-book heroes rule Hollywood, right?) So, despite knowing Carate is observing his every move, K butts into the customers' conversation to pitch the idea of a Californian champion surfer who mysteriously drowns and whose body, when recovered, is snatched by the HEAD (Human Electronic Augmentation Department) of mega-corporation VPL. K is allowed to go on about how a 'spiker' implant direct into the corpus callosum – the mapped-out nerve centre of the brain – would create a much more human cyborg than Colonel Austin or *Robocop* and vastly improve performance by using the superhuman strength that lies dormant within the body. V. R. McGuffin is so impressed with K's mind-over-matter core idea that he invites the waiter/writer to his office on the Paramount lot the next day. This is how K lands his first Hollywood job, which he entitles *The Cybernetic Man* as a nod to Martin Caidin's *Cyborg*, the novel *The Six Million Dollar Man* was based on. It still cheeses K off that:

1. He had no control over the script being rewritten by some other A-hole.
2. It was re-packaged as *The Bionic Dude*.
3. To this day, it remains mysteriously unmade.

Cervical 1

Next Look *Models Inc.* is such a glam-slam commercial success story that by 1998 the company has acquired offices in Miami, New York, LA and is setting up in K and D's childhood home of London. Chief Exec Hillary Michaels, who looks a lot like Linda Grey, decides to make the by-now middle-aged model D, at 25, their talent scout 'out there in Ing-land'. This is an act of compassion on her part because:

1. D was an old flame.
2. D hasn't become *America's Next Top Model* and hasn't been getting many gigs lately.
3. D has slumped into acting all lethargic (some of the younger, bitchy models use the word 'lazy').

None of the Next Lookers know that this chronic apathy, coupled with the anaemia hidden by the all-over tan, is the onset of end-stage kidney disease, not even D, because if she'd had an inkling of the imminent failure of her body it's unlikely she would have taken up the challenging position. As it is, D lasts a mere four days in London. She collapses at Next Look *Models Inc.*'s half-set-up offices before scouting any new talent, and is rushed to hospital where her life is saved by a quick diagnosis and emergency dialysis.

Watch it! TV is Addictive

K Vonnegut Jar's © syndicated daily column 'Life is HARD and then you DIE'.

No one has to smoke, take drugs, drink alcohol, but they do because they become dependent. And people don't just overuse substances; gambling can become compulsive, having sex can become obsessive, and the world's most popular leisure pastime, watching TV, can also be addictive. That's official according to Dr Payne A. Ford and his new book *The Reality of TV*. 'The term TV addiction is a very real phenomenon,' said Dr Ford. 'I call it TAD, short for Television Addiction Disorder.'

Psychologists define 'substance dependence' as a disorder characterized by criteria that include: spending a great deal of time using the substance; using it more often than one intends; thinking about reducing use or making repeated unsuccessful efforts to reduce use; giving up important social, family or occupational activities to use it; and reporting withdrawal symptoms when one stops using it. 'All these criteria apply to people who watch a lot of TV,' Dr Ford said. 'That does not mean that watching TV is the problem. TV can teach and amuse, it can provide much-needed distraction and escape. The problem arises when people strongly sense that they ought not to watch as much as they do and yet find themselves strangely unable to reduce their viewing.'

The amount of time people spend watching television is disturbing. On average, individuals in the industrialized world devote 3 hours a day to the pursuit — fully half of their leisure time and more than on any single activity save work and sleep. At this rate, someone who lives to 75 would spend 9 whole years in front of the tube. Why is this when in a Gallup poll (1999), 2 out of 5 adult respondents and 7 out of 10 teenagers said they spent too much time watching TV?

To study people's reactions to TV, Dr Ford conducted Experience Sampling Method experiments in which he monitored the brainwaves of people watching television at home. The participants watching TV reported feeling relaxed and EEG results show less mental stimulation, alpha brainwave production, during viewing than during reading. What surprised Dr Ford is that the sense of relaxation ends when the set is turned off, but that feelings of passivity continue. 'Survey participants commonly reflect that TV is a vampire that absorbed or sucked out their energy. In contrast, they rarely indicate such difficulty after reading. After playing sports or engaging in hobbies, people report improvements in mood. After the screen goes blank, people's moods are about the same or worse than before.'

According to *The Reality of TV*, habit-forming drugs work in similar ways. A tranquillizer that leaves the body rapidly is much more likely to cause dependence that one that leaves the body slowly, precisely because the user is more aware that the drug's effects are wearing off. Similarly, TV viewers' vague learned sense that they will feel less relaxed if they stop viewing may be a significant factor in not turning the set off. 'Viewing begets more viewing' said Dr Ford. 'Surveys in the US consistently show that roughly 10 percent of adults call themselves TV addicts.'

So what is it about TV that has such a hold on us? Dr Ford points to our biological 'orienting response'. First described by Ivan Pavlov in 1927, 'the orienting response is our instinctive visual or auditory reaction to any sudden or novel stimulus. It is part of our evolutionary heritage, a built-in sensitivity to movement and potential predatory threats. Typical orienting reactions include dilation of the blood vessels to the brain, slowing of the heart and constriction of blood vessels to major muscle groups. Alpha waves are blocked for a few seconds before returning to baseline level. The brain focuses its attention on gathering more information while the rest of the body quiets. The orienting re-sponse may explain remarks such as: 'If a television is on. I just can't keep my eyes off it.'

In 1986 Stanford University and University of Missouri researchers studied whether the simple formal features of television – cuts, edits, zooms, pans, sudden noises – activate the orienting response, thereby keeping attention on the screen. By watching how brainwaves were affected, the researchers concluded that these stylistic tricks can indeed trigger involuntary responses. 'It is the form, not the content, of television that is unique. The format of ads or MTV or kids' cartoons activates the orienting response continuously.'

The University of Manitoba extensively studied those who called themselves TV addicts on surveys. On a measure called the Short Imaginal Processes Inventory (SIPI) researchers found that the self-described addicts are more easily bored and distracted, less creative, less patient, less tolerant, and more lonely and anxious than the non-addicts. The addicts said they used TV to distract themselves from unpleasant thoughts and to kill time. Other studies over the years have shown that these people are less likely to participate in community activities and sports and more likely to be obese than moderate or light viewers.

Dr Ford said, 'The most convincing parallel between TV and addictive drug dependence is that people

212

experience withdrawal symptoms when they cut back on viewing.' Nearly 40 years ago the University of Chicago collected fascinating individual accounts of families whose set had broken – this back in the days when households generally had only one set: 'The family walked around like a chicken without a head.' 'It was terrible. We did nothing. Children bugged me. Tried to interest them in games, but impossible. TV is part of them.'

Dr Ford said, 'We need more studies of the effects of withdrawal from TV. I tried to run one but I couldn't get any of my TAD sufferers to stay in cold turkey for more than a week.' If that doesn't convince you that TV is a TAD addictive I don't know what will. But will it stop you watching? No, like me, you can't help yourselves, you're hooked. Addicts every one.

Episode 1

. . . CONTINUED FROM THE LAST EPISODE OF THE LAST SERIES

In media res getting hotter and hotter-headed, I try
to wrestle my way out of the chokehold, but Theo Cosby
the bouncer is a big guy and won't let go of me. He
stands his ground in the corridor outside the Green
Room, the bicep vice-grip tightening, strangulation.
'Don't make me hurt you, nigga.'

I relent. No air = no chance.

Cruel fact of life: *The A-Team* is more likely than
not to be overpowered or outsmarted and captured on
any given mission. The major challenge lies in the
ingenious method of the breakout.

'What were you doing in there?' Theo asks.

I manage to wheeze, 'She's my sister.'

'So you're a concerned relative?'

A cough. 'Yep.'

'I got you,' Theo says. 'But I'm going to let
you go now. You pull anything and . . . Don't try
it.'

I've enough air left in my lungs to hiss, 'OK.'

Theo releases me. He needn't have worried – I'm too
busy coughing and spluttering, trying to get my
breath back for a 'backstaged' *Ricky Lake* fight
against a massive opponent that even B.A. would never
have been able to throw against a wall, over a table,
no way.

Theo opens the Green Room door and yells, 'Yo!'

Wesley Snipes II struts out of the Green Room.
'What's up?'

'Get YoYo.'

'You want me to call security too?' asks Wesley
Snipes II.

'No. This is about the show.'

Wesley Snipes II hustles off in the direction of
MASTER CONTROL. He returns with a jittery YoYo.

'OK. Who's this f**king joker?' YoYo demands, his
big gold-ringed hands flashing multiple gang signals
in my face.

'He's the brother of one of those crazy Sisters,'
Theo answers.

'That right, nigga?' asks YoYo.

Maybe it's because I'm still short on oxygen, or
scared, but I'm kind of hypnotised by his
hyperbolical hands. 'Yep.'

'Let me guess,' YoYo says. 'You don't want her
going through with this mass assisted suicide thing?'

'Mass assisted suicide?'

'Of course, you wouldn't know . . .' YoYo slaps his
forehead. 'Mind-f**k!'

'S**t, nigga,' Theo says, slapping his forehead
too.

Wesley Snipes II slaps his forehead too.

'Know *what*?' I say, resisting the *Temptation* to
slap my forehead. It's not in the memes, those social
memes.

'You want to find out?' YoYo says, clapping a hand
on my shoulder. 'You want to confront your sister?'

Given that I don't seem to know anything about
anything: 'Yep, I guess.'

'So what's your name?'

'Kirk Rush.'

'Hold your right hand up, Kirk.' A black-power fist.
I hold up my right fist.

'You're on the show, my man.' YoYo punches me on the knuckles.

It's sore, but I'm going to be on TV, live TV, or at least a show that's recorded live in front of a studio audience: even real live TV has a ten-second delay on the feed.

'MC,' YoYo says to Theo Cosby. 'Lock him in the Sin Bin and bring him out on cue, yeah, yeah.'

'The Sin Bin?' I say.

'Believe me, it's for your own good, nigga,' YoYo answers, and lopes off up the corridor bodyguarded by Wesley Snipes II.

'This way, homeboy.' Theo bouncer ushers me away from the Green Room. Away from Denise, down the corridor. He leads me to a door that has a misnomer on it – CONTROL 2. 'In there,' he says.

I walk into the Sin Bin. I scan the minimalist room the way the Team do, for potential weapons or tools I can use to get out. There's simply a blue sofa for me to sit on. And a glass-topped coffee table. And a CCTV camera mounted on the wall over the door to spy on me taking off my janitor's overalls, a humiliating peep show to hike up the ratings.

No way out. This is no Stephen J Cannell production.

'I'll be back real soon. Somebody from make-up might stop by in between.' Theo closes and locks the door from the outside.

Episode 2

No make-up artist comes.

And I'm sweating, getting paranoid about how I'll look on TV let alone CCTV, sweating more. My face will be all shiny under the studio lights. Self-reflexivity: what am I going to say to Denise, Sister of Mercy? Where's the script? And I'm looking at the com-link, really dying to order KITTSCH to locate me and drive through the walls of the studio into the Sin Bin and rescue me. The top secret invulnerable molecular-bonded shell should be able to withstand half the building collapsing in on it.

And what's this mass assisted suicide thing? They could at least give me a TV to watch the show, to find out where I'll slot in . . .

And when is Harvey Guck going to get on the cell and tell me the good news? That my career has taken off. The future, it's a killer to BLANK that out.

And where the hell's Theo Cosby? *Real soon* my ass. I kick out at the coffee table. I get up and slide out of my janitor's disguise. Let them watch!

And what's YoYo going to do out there on the stage – shoot me? Shoot Denise? Shoot Doctor Death?

And where *is* Doctor Death, why wasn't he in the Green Room with the other guests?

Thirty minutes of killing waiting: an example of what passes for suspense on TV, like you don't know what's going to happen.

Episode 3

CLICK: The Sin Bin is being unlocked. Theo the bouncer sticks his head around the door. 'Heads up!' he says.

So I get up, pull my T-shirt and shorts costume into some kind of shape. And then I walk out of the Sin Bin into the piercing light of a steady-cam.

Theo plucks my baseball cap off my head and clips a radio mic onto the U-neck of my A-Team T-shirt.

The cameraman backs off as Theo leads me down the narrow corridor, tracking through a door to a YoYo re-rap of 'Insane in the Membrane', and onto left-stage. Blinding lights: for a moment I can't see a thing through my squint. Then I make out the Sisters of Mercy and Denise sitting centre-stage. There's an empty red bucket chair beside Denise which I assume is for me.

'Big up for our surprise guest, Denise's brother, Kirk Rush,' announces YoYo from out in the middle aisle of the crammed audience amphitheatre. 'He came here to try to save her from herself.'

The hundred-strong audience cries out: Yooooooooooooooooooo!

Theo shakes his fist at them in encouragement as he leads me to my place.

I sit down. I can see Denise stiffen, trying to ignore my presence. I wonder what's been going on in the show.

'So, Kirk,' YoYo says, 'what do you want to say to your little sister Denise here, who has just stated on

221

national TV that she wants to die, tonight?'

'Uh?' I look across at Denise. She's so bloated and so jaundiced, and she's refusing to look back at me. Then I look at the camera, the one with the red light on it, directly. Fatal mistake. She wants to die *tonight*? I search for the words. My mind is BLANK. I know I'm dying on stage myself and right in a set-piece scene.

'Is she doing the right thing?' YoYo prompts.

Morticia Addams chips in: 'Absolutely. And it is her right to do—'

'Who asked you, ho?' yells YoYo, pointing the gat-mic at her, the red dot of the laser on her forehead. 'When I want you to make noise I'll point. Now, Kirk, my main man, is she doing the right thing?'

The red dot flicks onto my chest. 'Nope,' I answer.

'You tell her, brother!' someone in the audience shouts. It really doesn't feel right airing this in public but this is the way viewers become better people by learning from bad examples.

YoYo skips down the steps to the stage. 'You don't think she should be f**king checking herself out?'

I'm looking at Denise, the black rings round her eyes, but nothing, not a word, from her or the Sisters. 'Nope, I don't,' I say.

YoYo lopes over to me and kneels down, on one knee. 'And why's that, bro'? You religious?'

'Nope.'

YoYo sighs.

The audience sighs. The bulk of them – and many are obese *Couch-Potatoes* and still believe in God so they feel sorry for me, a lost soul. It's an unwelcome pity for an Angeleno.

'Social morality then. You're worried about how euthanasia might be abused by the WASP elite.' He's waving his gat-mic round my mouth.

'Nope.'

'Then you crashed this show because you love your little sister and you care about what happens to her, isn't that it, nigga?'

Denise shoots me a furtive glance – is it a warning not to answer that or a plea to answer it? I don't know. 'I suppose so, yep.'

YoYo stands up. 'How do the rest of your family feel about this decision?'

'They don't know anything about it,' I say.

'That's because they don't listen!' Denise shouts.

YoYo turns round to the audience, nodding at the cameras, holding his arms out in a cross. 'Hit it.'

The audience chants Yoooooooooooo-Yoooooooooooooo!

The star of the show lopes back off the stage becoming one with the audience. 'So Denise, you've been lying to us, bitch?'

Boooooooooooo!

From his position in the middle of the audience, YoYo: 'You told us that your family supported your decision.

Denise finally speaks up: 'My only family are my Sisters.'

YoYo tut-tuts. 'That's not true. There's your bro' sitting there.'

'I don't have a brother,' Denise says. 'I never did.'

There's a sharp intake of breath into a hundred mouths; the whole audience felt that one. *To Tell the Truth* hurts so bad. Denise the wasted ex-model suicide-to-be has lost any of the sympathy, let alone the empathy, she gained in the earlier segment of the show. Characters need sympathetic audiences so I feel sorry for her and for myself because we're such antipathetical A-holes.

'I mean,' an embarrassed Denise explains, 'we never got on.'

'We're going to commercials,' YoYo says. 'Don't channel-hop, keep it Hip-hop. After the break, I'll be rapping on Doctor Death himself. Yeah.'

The red light on the camera in front of me goes off.

'Denise,' I say, 'can we just talk?'

She doesn't get a chance to answer: Theo, Wesley Snipes II and the set crew sprint on stage and shift the bucket seats, with us in them, to opposite sides of the semicircle.

Out in the audience, make-up people are all over YoYo, trying to dull down the sweat-sheen on him.

I can see placards being handed out to people. One reads: PRO-LIFE, NOT PRO-DEATH.

On the big screen behind us, centre-stage: snow, then the blurred tanned face of Ricardo Montalban, or rather Ahab Khan, then snow, then the piercing lined solemnity of the Doctor.

The producer's voice over the speaker: 'And ten, nine, eight, seven, six . . .'

Silent finger countdown of the floor manager: five, four, three, two, one . . .

Cue neon audience APPLAUSE sign.

Yooooooooooooooooo!

YoYo raises his fist. 'You're still watching *The YoYo Show*. We're about to have a head-to-head with one of *America's Most Wanted*, Doctor Death.'

Booooooooooooooooo!

'So, Doctor Death, you f**king hear me?'

Glittering Aztec eyes on the big screen. 'Yes. Good evening. And YoYo, I'd like to point out immediately that I object to being referred to as Doctor Death.'

YoYo lopes down onto centre-stage, below the big screen. 'Yeah, yeah. Down to business, nigga. You've

224

been involved in fifty homicides all round the world, that right?'

The doctor is impassive. 'No. No homicides. These were medicides or, if you prefer, assisted suicides.'

The Sisters of Mercy are impassive observers of the big TV screen, but the studio audience is anything but passive; they believe they have a say in this: Booooooooooooooooo! And they have placards to wave like: RESPECT THE SANCTITY OF HUMAN LIFE.

'So what's the difference, nigga?' YoYo asks the Doctor – as if he knows the answer, as if it's all black and white.

'A medicide is when a doctor helps a person end their suffering. It is an act of mercy.'

'It's still illegal though, except in the Netherlands, yeah?'

'Right now US federal law in theory does not allow a person to knowingly aid in the ending of another person's life. In practice doctors do this all the time. You only have to look to Oregon, and the Futile-Care Protocols hospitals have already adopted nationwide to relieve their financial burdens—'

'So you're saying the white men in white coats already have a culture of death going down?'

'No. That's why we are campaigning heavily for legal recognition—'

'But you're campaigning for a double-oh-seven licence to kill, aren't you?'

'I wouldn't put it that sensationalist way, and I'd like to say that I'm not the one talking into the barrel of a gun.' The pure *Fantasy Island* leer of Mr Roarke.

'Uh-huh. Uh-huh. I got you. Do you believe that all life is precious, Doctor Death?'

'Absolutely. That is why federal law should be

changed to allow people the right to die with
dignity.'

'Dignity. That's interesting, yeah. Where's the
dignity in dying in the back of van, or as a job lot in
a deserted building, like serial killed?'

The Doctor frowns deeply. 'I have to operate
covertly in order to help the people who need my help.
If the medical establishment was truly, openly
allowed to help people die, we could be doing it in
hospitals, and homes, in comfort, all over the
country.'

'What about God - you're playing God, aren't you?'

Booooooooooooooooo!

The Doctor's eyes narrow. The Wrath of Khan: 'I'm a
scientist. Primitive ideas of God don't come into it.
What we should be trying to create here is a new moral
paradigm to replace the out-of-date Judaeo-Christian
values of the past.'

Booooooooooooooooo!

Placard: NO KILLING TO CUT COST CENTRES.

YoYo believes he's on a roll. 'So what about the
Hippocratic oath? Doing no harm to your patients.
Preserving life, huh, you know what I'm saying?'

The Doctor shrugs. 'What is the point in keeping
someone alive when they are terminally ill, in great
pain, and you are only prolonging their suffering?'

'There's no such thing as painkillers?'

'I didn't say that—'

'But isn't it a fact that you're not only
wasting—'

'I don't waste anyone!' The Doctor holds up his
index finger like the slick Dynastical Zach Powers
from *The Colbys*. 'This isn't like states executing
criminals on dubious grounds of deterrent.'

That throws YoYo. 'Isn't it a fact—'

The Doctor talks over him: 'Don't you find that

226

somewhat paradoxical, YoYo – that if you are a criminal the state has a right to kill you, but if you're a law-abiding citizen you have no right to end your own life. The logical conclusion of this is that your life does not belong to you. It belongs to the state, as your dead body does after your death, at least up to the point of post-mortem.'

'OK, OK. That's an interesting point, sucka,' YoYo concedes, 'especially when most people executed are black. But that isn't the issue here. Isn't it true that you are putting down people who aren't terminally ill? Like dogs? Because of poor quality of life.'

The Doctor is back on the defensive. 'I will help anyone who needs my assistance.'

'Like Sister Denise here?' YoYo refocuses the debate onto the personal tragedy angle.

'Yes, like Denise – who has shown a lot of courage, and has been through the terrible ordeal of chronic illness which most healthy people couldn't bear to imagine.'

'It's your diagnosis that Denise should die along with these other martyrs tonight, on your death machines, on Net TV, in this David Copperfield-type mass assisted suicide attempt of yours, yeah?'

'Not my diagnosis. That's the informed path she has chosen for herself.'

YoYo pivots and points his gat-mic at Denise. 'Like, why do you want to die on Internet TV, Denise?'

Denise is taken by surprise but answers quickly, 'I want to make a statement—'

'Which is.'

'For death to be liberating we have to liberate the dying.'

YoYo turns back to the big plasma screen. 'Doctor Death, have you checked to see if Denise here is depressed, or maybe you know, treated her with anti-depressants?'

'In my opinion Denise was of sound mind when we talked last and fit to sign her DNR order.'

'Doctor Death, why is it that most of the people you have helped to die happen to be female – you know what I'm saying?'

The Doctor sighs, turns up his hooked hawkish nose. 'I'm not going to dignify that with a response.'

'Well, we have Denise's brother here. Kirk Rush. And he has something he wants to say to you, nigga.' YoYo points his red-dot laser-sight at me.

Yoooooooooooooooooo!

As the studio camera focuses in on me, red light, it all ceases to be a debate between life and death. From the passively observed profound, it comes down to me, and the only things I can think of to say are Hannibalesque hammy lines: 'You need to be taught a lesson, pal. You're not above the law. We ought to run you out of town.'

That's popular with the audience: Yoooooooooooooooooo!

But . . .

But the *Dark Shadows* Sister rushes across the stage, and throws herself at me, black robe flowing, claws and teeth bared.

I barely have time to throw my hands up in self-defence before the bucket chair flips and I'm totally on my back. Vampiral claws rake across my cheeks. She's screaming, 'Ahab Khan is a saint, a saviour!'

It takes bouncers Theo and Wesley Snipes II, and YoYo, to drag her off me and hold her back.

YoYo tells her, 'Just calm down, bitch. It's a dog's world.'

She slaps YoYo in the face, a stunning blow.

So, Theo and Wesley Snipes II wrestle her down onto the floor.

So Morticia Addams and the one from *Buffy The Vampire Slayer* attack. And because I'm on my hands and knees with a back that has buckled, I can't see if Denise is involved in the fearsome demonic kung fu melee.

It's certainly no staged fight for ratings. YoYo, nursing his cheek, shouts to the floor manager, 'Call security, chump!'

It's only resolved by Doctor Death commanding, 'Sisters, calm yourselves; this isn't helping our cause.'

The Sisters of Mercy stop their martial arts.

This allows a shaken Theo and a scratched Wesley Snipes II to herd them offstage right.

Bleeding from my cheeks, I shuffle off by the other exit.

Only YoYo remains centre-stage, trying to placate the audience, who are hurling abuse and a half-ripped placard DEATH COMES QUICK ENOUGH WITHOUT ANY HELP at Doctor Death on the big screen.

Episode 4

I miss Denise in the studio corridors. I run to catch up, but those damned Sisters of Mercy are pushing her into a black stretch limo in the NBC car lot. I have to get into KITTSCH and give chase. There's always the car chase, it's obligatory action, even if you're carrying a spinal injury.

'You're injured, Kirk,' KITTSCH states the obvious as always. 'Do you want me to drive you to hospital?'

'Nope, good buddy. I want you to follow that limo. Super Pursuit Mode!' SPM was a series four addition to KITTSCH's armoury, when the budget stretched to more advanced onboard crime-fighting gadgets like the C button, where C is for Convertible.

KITTSCH takes off, speed reverse, J-turn. 'As you wish, Kirk. There will be heavy traffic. This is rush hour.'

The limo is at the Alameda exit, turning right. 'Just don't lose them, KITTSCH. Denise is in that car.'

'Your sister is in that car?' a smoke-SCREECHING of tyres.

The acceleration presses me into my seat – which hurts my back. 'Yep, pal. And she's in great danger.'

KITTSCH can't break the law willingly so it does a handbrake turn round the one-way system in the studio lot and streaks out into the slow-moving crawl on Alameda. 'Do you know where they're going?'

I pick out the limo up ahead – it's hard to miss –
gliding past Walt Disney Studios. 'Nope.'

'We will have to keep them in line of sight
then.'

'Yep.' I test the cuts in my face with my fingers.

KITTSCH weaves through the heavy traffic up to
behind the limo, then slows down to keep pace. 'Do you
want me to utilise the laser on the rear tyres?'

'Nope.' Like that's going to work. 'No ramming
either. This is strictly surveillance.'

The limo crosses two lanes into the slow lane.

KITTSCH tailgates. 'It is highly probable they
will be making for the Golden State Freeway, Kirk.'

'OK.'

The limo takes the ramp onto the Golden State
Freeway.

I'm head-down, trying to find some painkillers for
my back, preferably some easy-to-swallow Advil, in
the glovebox, when KITTSCH reports: 'It seems we are
not the only ones in hot pursuit. *Street Hawk* is also
engaged.'

I sit up and look in the rear-view mirror. Sure
enough, a black attack motorbike, a modified Honda XR
250, is tailing us. And the biker is dressed in black
leathers with silver trim. And he's holding something
in his left hand.

'He's got a gun, Kirk!'

Before I can react, he's five, four, three, two, one
hyper-thrusted up past us to draw level with the limo,
and swerved in close: brilliant blue flashes against
the tinted glass.

This isn't Jesse Mach, yet another injured-cop-
gone-crime-fighter. It's a lone paparazzo, taking a
chance staking out the studio streets, looking for a
big bucks tabloid shot of what some star's doing in
the publicity of their back seat. If that shot is

syndicated all over the world, fortune and glory, kid, fortune and glory.

The limo swerves towards the all-terrain bike, defensive driving.

The paparazzo doesn't expect that. Holding on to the camera, driving one-handed, he oversteers away, and then overcompensates to try to right the bike, drifting into us . . .

'Going to Ski Mode,' KITTSCH announces.

Flipping up on two wheels isn't going to stop a crash, so I yank the steering wheel right, and WHAM! career into the safety wall.

So much for Collision Avoidance – KITTSCH scores along the concrete wall for fifty feet. So much for the passive laser restraint system – my head whiplashes with a CRACK against the driver's side window. So much for the impenetrable molecular-bonded shell – in a daze I can see my side of the hood has crumpled under testing. And so much for Super *Trivial Pursuit* Mode – by Hollywood standards the chase is pitiful and the aftermath a joke. To make things worse, there's no getaway: KITTSCH won't respond, won't start, floods, and the limo and the bike are getting lost in the Golden State smog and traffic up ahead, and I've lost the soul, the elusive anima of the whole piece, my muse, yep, Denise.

Episode 5

A rare, caring rubbernecker in the rush-hour traffic must have got on their cell because *ChiPs* are quick, quicker than any ambulance-chaser, to respond to the smash. Two cruiser officers on new BMW bikes, not Kawasaki 1000s, pull up behind KITTSCH. The remake of 7-Mary-3 pulls his S&W 68 and covers the remake of 7-Mary-4 as he dismounts, and in his knee-length motor officer boots marches up to my car.

'Get out of the car, sir,' 7-Mary-4 orders, RAPPING on KITTSCH's trunk with a black-gloved fist.

This isn't exactly in keeping with the spirit of the original 1977 show or the '99 remake – officers rarely drew their weapons, and if anybody died it was because of an accident or due to a disease – so I hesitate.

7-Mary-4 draws his S&W and aims it in at me. 'Get out of the car, sir.'

What happened to the friendly disarming smile and the paunch of Ponch? Where had Jon Baker's boyish charm and innate sense of fairness disappeared to? I get out of KITTSCH, hands up.

'Place your palms on the roof, sir, and spread your legs.'

'I'm hurt here, officer. I haven't done anything wrong.' I can see a shrunken version of myself, face bloody, protesting my innocence in his aviator sunglasses. 'Some guy—'

'Assume the specified search position, sir.' An S&W

233

4006 Tactical Semi-Automatic gesture.

I assume the presumed-guilty position and am summarily frisked.

'He's clean,' 7-Mary-4 calls to his partner.

7-Mary-3 holsters his gun and comes over. 'How'd this wreck happen, sir? Have you been drinking?'

'Nope.'

7-Mary-4: 'Are you using drugs?'

'No.'

'7-Mary-3: 'Did you fall asleep at the wheel?'

'No.' I can't work out who's playing the good cop and who's playing bad cop. Those are the rules. And if there's no good cop . . .

7-Mary-4: 'Did you take your eye off the road?'

'A biker cut me off.' I decide to BLANK the rest of the story. The cops won't do anything to prevent Doctor Death's crime from happening. That's up to crime-fighters who operate above the law.

7-Mary-3, incredulous: 'A biker?'

'Yep.'

7-Mary-4: 'Did you get his number?'

'No.'

'7-Mary-3: Do you want to file an accident report?'

'What good would that do?'

7-Mary-4 shrugs: 'Do you require medical assistance, sir?' He's looking at my face.

'I don't think so.'

7-Mary-3: 'Have you sustained any injury, sir? Because if you have banged your head we can't allow you to drive off the freeway.'

I want to get out of there, so it's story-within-a-story as well as character-within-a-character time: 'No. These scratches weren't from the smash. My girlfriend, Angela, is *Crazy Like A Fox*, you know?'

7-Mary-4: 'Is your car still mobile, or do you need Dispatch to arrange a tow?'

'It's flooded. I could try starting it one more time.'

7-Mary-3 checks the front and wing of KITTSCH: 'You do that, sir.'

'I get back into KITTSCH. I tell it straight, in a whisper, 'You better start or I'll never speak to you again.'

Even though it's damaged, KITTSCH starts. A small miracle, animism or whatever. I drive off, powered by bathos.

Episode 6

The Truth is Out Where. I'll find her next episode.
Chugging along in the write-off that is KITTSCH, I
have to believe that in the same way-out way that
Agent Fox 'Spooky' Mulder's has to believe it. Out
beyond conventional wisdom into unexplained
phenomena, all I have is my desire to find and save my
missing little sister. This is how I get through *The
X-Files*, putting the I back in the FBI, acting the
lone investigator who can't do anything without a
little help from my friends and of course my trusty
cellphone which is BLEEPETY-BLEEPING the familiar
reprise of 'The Man Who Sold the World'. Caller ID
check: Special Agent Harvey Guck. 'What's up Harv?'

'Hi, kid. How's things?' Harvey's vocal cords
rattle with liquid nicotine.

'OK,' I lie.

'Where are you?' He sounds like the Cancer Man.

'In the car,' I answer.

'Well slow down, *amigo*. I talked to Biff fifteen
minutes ago.'

'Yep?'

A nasal smoke sigh: 'These Mad Bull people, they're
like connected to Temporal, an even bigger mega-
consortium than Universal, which frankly means they
have him by the balls.'

'I knew it!'

'They have their own writer in mind. To get the
project off the ground Biff had to agree, so—'

'I'm out of the picture?' The powers that be were always planning to get rid of me.

'That's the long and short of it, I guess, yeah. I'm sorry.'

'But Biff said it was going ahead as planned.'

'If it's any consolation, they're going to totally screw the whole thing up. I pity the poor bastard who gets that gig; he'll just be a patsy in a big conspiracy.'

'I was counting on that job, Harv.'

Harvey coughs, swallows the tar back down. 'Listen, there's better jobs out there, kid.'

'Better than *The A-Team*, where?'

'As long as you're still hanging in there, we're in with a shot, yeah?'

'If you say so.'

'Hey. It could be worse – you could be dead, kid. I'm flying to this happening tonight in death Valley where four women are publicly committing suicide.'

'Four women, committing suicide?' The truth is now in here, in my mind.

'Yeah. Anyway, listen, I'll be doing the rounds, spreading the good word about you, and we'll talk soon.'

'Did you just say four women were committing suicide?' All we have are our questions . . .

'Yeah, kid.'

'That has to be the Sisters of Mercy.'

'The *what*, kid?'

'This Death Valley thing, the suicides, I want in. Can I come?'

'Sorry, kid, it's strictly an invitation-only event.'

'Where's it being held then, tell me.'

'That's classified information, top secret.'

237

'Where is it, Harv? I won't accept secrets; I need access.'

'Why do you want to know so bad?'

'My sister could be one of the four women committing suicide, Harv!'

'What?'

'You remember. I told you she was missing and I was trying to find her?'

'Yeah . . .'

'Well, I did. And we were on TV with Doctor Death, Ahab Khan.'

'Say *who*?'

'Ahab Khan!'

'Where do I know that name from?'

'He's all over the TV, one of *America's Most Wanted* fugitives.'

'Jesus. Well look, in that case, the happening's at this place called Death Castle. I don't know exactly where it is, but I heard Kirk Douglas used to own it.'

'OK. I'll have to find it, somehow.'

'How? Even if you do, you'll never make it. The show starts at nine. It's six fifteen now.'

'There has to be a way, Harv!'

'Wait a minute. Look, the chopper I hired to get there takes off from Burbank-Glendale-Pasadena Airport at seven. Can you make it there?'

I BLANK the fact that a chopper means flying. 'If I can make it out of this jam that's only fifteen minutes away!'

'I'll meet you on the helipad at a quarter to.'

Proof positive: we are not alone.

238

INTERMISSION 7

Captain's Log, Supplemental (Star Date 90008-256.
whatever): What if Ensign Denise in *Another World*
waits - and I, James Tiberius Kirk II, latter-day
host of *911: Rescue* know waiting can kill, especially
when you're on a transplant list - but what if she
waits another five years till there are advances in
steroids and a reduction in the side-effects? What if
she waits seven years till xenotransplants (organs
from genetically modified pigs) are on trial? What if
she waits ten years till they have rejuvenation up and
running (restarting organs with an injection of
embryonic stem cells from aborted foetuses)? What if
she waits fifteen to twenty more years till they can
clone you and grow replacement organs in moulds,
ready for insertion? What if she waits fifty to a
hundred years in cryo-stasis like Walt Disney and
aliens come down to the *3rd Rock From The Sun* and
instead of destroying us, give us the cures for
ageing, all diseases and death? What if, what if, *what
if* the screenwriter's *Passion*, the tool for solving
the puzzles of the medium, considering all the
possibilities, utilising the imagination, is in
reality a two-word curse? *What If?* projects up the
past in a new light, yep, and the present, and the
future, but only up to a certain soap-sudded-out
point, then you have *One Life to Live*. One confession
to give, over and over and out.

Episode 8

Cruel fact: even supercars break down. I manage to
nurse KITTSCH out of the jam, off the freeway and get
ten or so blocks up Vineland Avenue, but then, with a
KERCHUNK, the engine dies. It must have been more
damaged than CHiPs 7-Mary-4 estimated. In spite of me
repeating, 'KITTSCH, don't do this to me, good
buddy,' like a mantra, it's gone.

I get out, and with my back aching, push KITTSCH
into the kerb. I lock it and tell it, 'I'll be back for
you.'

I look at my watch – the setting sun glinting off
it – there's only twenty minutes to get to the
airport. I have a distance of about thirty blocks to
cover. I try flagging down a Mercedes convertible with
a midget black kid like the one from *Different Strokes*
driving but, because of the cuts on my hitcher face,
no joy. I think about phoning a taxi – that'll take
too long. I consider running, but there's only one man
on earth that could get there in time. Colonel Steve
Austin. His iconic bionic ironic legs never tire
because they run independently on plutonium power
cells. With that ridiculous metallic CREAKING special
effect, I give it a try.

But . . .

Something's wrong (in addition to feeling like I
have a knife in my back): I can't seem to get past the
15 m.p.h. barrier, even when I imagine that that wild-
as-hell bionic Big Foot is chasing me.

And another thing, after ten blocks my heart rate must have reached 200, in the shade too.

And another, after twenty blocks, on Victory Boulevard, I'm down to a loose-limbed jog, dripping sweat, in total slo-mo (no special effects).

At twenty-five or so, I stop to lean against a palm; I've lost all feeling in my legs – like they've been amputated and replaced by automata that have given me radiation poisoning.

At the gates of Burbank Airport, I collapse. I'm reduced to being Colt Seavers. *The Fall Guy*, dying for a living on TV. I get up, but I have barely enough breath to ask the security guards, 'Where is the heliport?'

Rejects from *Police Academy*, they give me a lot of directions, which I follow, but I only have two bounty-hunting-stunting death-defying minutes to get to the chopper.

Episode 9

The rotor blades on the Aerospatiale Gazelle are already spinning, the waves of ripped air beating down on the tarmac and making a mess of the desperately smoking Harvey Guck.

I slog-jog up to him, and am buffeted about by the downforce.

Harvey grips my arm, and yells in my ear, 'What the Guck happened to you?'

'My car broke down.' The sweat-sodden T-shirt and shorts become ice packs in the moving air.

'We nearly left without you,' he screams into my ear. 'You're taking my VIP place. The pilot knows the Castle.'

'Thanks, Harv,' I shout back.

'No problemo!' Harvey smiles and salutes awkwardly, like good deeds don't come naturally to him either.

I'm shivering as I make for the door of chopper number N77GH. My teeth start to chatter as I swing the door open and climb in. As I flop into the one empty seat by the door, I let out a gasp; it feels like my clothes have frozen stiff as Arctic rags. The pilot, who looks incredibly like Roy Scheider, must be wondering if I have hypothermia, or a fever, or a white ook habit – how would he know I'm trying really hard not to let the sleeping B.A. giant in me awake?

The pilot hands me a helmet.

I take my baseball cap off and put the helmet on.
'Are you OK, Lymangood?' he asks.

Lymangood? 'Yep.'

'Then buckle up. It's take-off time.'

I fasten my seat belt.

'Blue Thunder to control tower,' says the pilot,
'we are taking off.'

'Roger that, Blue Thunder, you are clear for lift-
off.'

Lift-off is sudden and vertigo-vertical. I shut my
eyes, and keep them closed tight.

'You're scared of flying, rookie?'

'Yep.' My teeth are still chattering.

'Don't be. This chopper is a star.'

'Yep?' As I recall the heli-star of *Airwolf* had
crashed and burned on a post-show commercial flight I
don't see the link between celebrity and personal
safety in real life. *The Surreal Life*, yep. Real Life,
nope.

'Yeah. I bought her cheap when that crap TV *Spin
Off* series was canned. Reconverted her for commercial
flights. Still have all the kit though.'

'Yep?' My eyes are closed so tight tears are
squeezed out.

'I hated that Bubba and Ski so bad, didn't you?'

'Yep.' My back begins to cramp up.

'But you liked the movie – with Murphy and
Lymangood flying the ultimate weapon in the state
surveillance and crowd control armoury?'

'Yep.' I need painkillers.

'It was a good high concept. That's why I called
you Lymangood.'

'Yep.' I need my Celebrex, diazepam, anything.

'Did you know that the original higher concept for
the movie was that the Vietnam-vet pilot Murphy is a
paranoid schizophrenic who suffers devastating

243

hallucinations in which he becomes the Norse thunder god Thor, and devastates LA with bolts of lightning shot from the chopper?'

'Nope.' But I'm only too aware that TV is full of unbelievably bad ideas.

'Sometimes when I'm up above this city of sinners, like now, over the Valley, I get that urge too.'

'Yep?'

'Yeah. I wish I had that twenty-millimetre electric Gatling gun that fires four thousand rounds per minute, was protected by one-inch-thick armour plate and bullet-proof glass, could fly on whisper mode, could use that CCTV one-hundred-to-one zoom lens . . .' The pilot whistles.

'Yep?'

'Yeah. The only thing I wouldn't need is that jet-turbine boost to do that three-sixty-degree loop, I used to be a stunt-pilot see, and with a bit of stick this baby can do that all on her own. Wanna see?'

'No.'

'Yeah, maybe that wouldn't be such a good idea.' From then on the stunt-pilot stops opening his big mouth and letting anything fall out.

It isn't till Blue Thunder is SCREECHING at 170 m.p.h. low over the poison oaks and sagebrush and cheat-grass of the chaparral that I dare to open my eyes into two slits. It's like this, with a 10,000-yard stare, I bear silent, massively passive, slit-witness to the vast terrifying tumbleweed emptiness of the Mojave Desert.

In the helmet: 'I'll head north-northwest from here. Best to avoid China Lake Naval Weapons Centre or we'll be dodging SAMs all the way to this Castle of yours, eh, Lymangood?'

I close my eyes again. My hands grip onto the seat white-knuckle tight. 'Yep. Whatever.'

Some time later the stunt pilot says, 'Mr Guck paid for a tree-top flight over the redwoods, and you're missing it.'

I tell him, 'The only redwood I want to see is Robert.'

'Don't you want to see any of these *buenas vistas*?' the pilot asks.

'Nope. Thanks.' My idea of a Buena Vista is less connected to the wilderness, much more TV – it's owned by Disney.

Determined to be my basin-and-range guide, to give me value of *Highlander* Harv's money, to cram in a crumby voice-over sequence whether I like it or not, the pilot announces, 'We're hovering over the jagged ridge of the Panamint Mountains. It's sunset. The tips are blood red . . . Not too many people get to see this.'

I grimace, which feels weird if your eyes are shut. 'That's OK.'

'We're swooping down into the deepest hole in the Western World, Death Valley. To the east you can see the steep escarpments of the Funeral and Black Mountains . . .'

I also miss the flyover of the bleached-out Eureka dunes, the Mesquite flats, and the Racetrack and the Grandstand of Death Valley, 'which apparently the Shosone Indians used to watch their horses racing around'.

I don't open my eyes till he announces, 'We're landing at Death Castle, a keep that was constructed in Germany in the 1800s, appropriated by an eccentric Irish collector in the 1900s, deconstructed and shipped to America, the shore of the dry lake, reconstructed and restored by 1984 . . .' And I can't see the castle because of the dust storm of pathetic unintentional fallacy the touchdown stirs up.

INTERMISSION 10

Captain's Log, Supplemental (Star Date 59835.90.
whatever). An ABC *General Hospital* anatomy of a
kidney: a kidney is kidney bean-shaped, about five
inches long, three inches wide and one inch thick. It
weighs all of six ounces. It contains one million
nephrons, little filters. The kidneys are located in
the abdominal cavity, one on either side of the spinal
column, at about the level of the thoracic vertebrae.
If it is healthy, each day a kidney will sift 200
quarts of blood to:

1. Remove toxic wastes from the body.
2. Drain excess water.
3. Control blood pressure.
4. Regulate red blood cell production.
5. Keep bone structure strong.

   In the *General Hospital* way of looking at things –
thinking from within the box – the kidney serves
another seemingly vital function. The implied viewers
generally understand that it's a metaphor, part of
the mixed-up ABC language of daytime TV. It will CLICK
that this symbol ironically represents integrity,
even if they've critically no idea what socratic
irony is or, like me, James Tiberius Kirk II, what
integrity is supposed to be. Or not to be. That is the
question. Whether it is nobler in the mind to suffer
the slings and arrows of outrageous *catachresis*.

Episode 11

The dust clears sufficiently for me to see the white
ghosts of three other choppers parked by the side of a
narrow strip of asphalt, along with two white stretch
limos, ten or so other cars and a blue sixteen-wheeler
juggernaut with IXION TV stencilled on the trailer.

I take off my helmet, CLICK the seat belt open, and
get out of Blue Thunder.

The pilot tells me, 'I'm to wait here for you.'

'OK,' I reply, not paying him any attention,
absorbed instead in the spectacle of Death Castle
itself, a multi-spired, bone-white *schloss*
transplanted straight out of the introduction to an
old Disney movie to the most inhospitable place on
earth. All that's missing is that cartoon fairy
flyover, a twinkling smile, the magic wand, a cascade
of shooting stars.

As I walk through the iron-wrought castle gates,
into the small grove of Joshua trees within the
limestone walls and up to the tuxedoed security on the
doors, I'm wondering how I'm going to get Denise out
of this fortress. I know how to get in, that's Mickey
Mouse, but getting out will require special forces
ingenuity beyond even that of the Team. Angus 'Mac'
MacGyver, with all his issue-orientation, will be the
key. He knows what a climax should look like. He's
worked for the Phoenix Foundation, an all-American
think tank dedicated to righting wrongs, defeating
bad guys all around the world and rising from the

247

ashes again and again, into infinity and beyond.

'Mr Guck,' says a bodyguard who looks and talks
like Arnold Schwarzenegger's long-lost barbarian
brother Conan. 'Ve've been expecting you . . .'

'Yep. Me too.' A Richard Dean Anderson wise-
crack.

Conan Schwarzenegger looks at me funny as if even
Hollywood humour is alien to him, then escorts me into
the banqueting hall of the castle. 'Ve've been
expecting you in a suit.'

'Ah, well, the dog ate mine.' I shrug, a glint in
my eyes. All my pseudo-scientific wizardry isn't going
to help me with that one, unless I wrestle Conan out
of his tux without him realising it and pummelling me.
That isn't exactly going to happen.

'OK, Mister Guck.' Brawn relents to the force of
brains, the way it should be. 'I take you into ze hall
vere happening takes place.'

I follow Conan into a huge hall with vaulted
ceilings. Three rings of black plastic seats surround
a circular stage in the middle of the floor.

'You have front-row seat. (beat) I'll be back.' He
indicates my place.

I sit down in the front row and watch as ten IXION TV
personnel put the final touches to the stage, ringing
it with overhead lighting so the four gurneys in the
glaring light laid out like the spokes of a great
wheel.

The seats begin to fill up with dark-robed Sisters
of Mercy and some other guests. I'm soon joined in the
front row seats by a Bollinger-guzzling party of VIP
guests: Ryan McBride, Griff Walker, Donna Marco and
Madonna, half the cast of the ill-fated *Baywatch
Nights*. Thankfully, no Mitch Buchanan, hunky-chunky
lifeguard turned night-club cop, because there is
only so far you can stretch credulity.

Two technicians in white coats wheel two canisters
into the circle of light, lifting them over the snake-
slither of TV cables. They set the canisters up
beside two gurneys, masks at the ready, levers at the
ready. On the side of each canister: CO GAS aka carbon
monoxide, THANOTRON INC. These are prototypical home-
lab death machines.

Another VIP is sat down by Conan Schwarzenegger,
behind me, to my right. Out of the corner of my eye he
looks suspiciously like FBI Agent Dale 'Coop' Cooper,
munching on a bag of doughnuts, supping on a strong
black coffee, waiting for final justice to be meted out
to the killer of Laura Palmer.

The two technicians wheel in two more simple
THANOTRON INC. death machines. These two are IV racks,
hanging three clear bags of liquid. For 'self-
administered' lethal injections.

I'm not packing my usual Swiss Army knife but the
'Mac' in me is in no doubt I can sabotage these
machines. If a Hershey bar can stop acid leaking out
of an industrial tank, if calcium metal can blow open
steel doors, if a mullet-'n'-bullet formula doesn't
jump the shark?

'Why are you here?' 'Coop' asks me, quietly as a
Tibetan *Monk* with the caffeine jitters.

'To see,' I lie. I'm here to *do* – and where the Team
would need an acetylene torch, a paper clip would do
me.

'You look familiar. Have I see you before?' 'Coop'
asks.

'I don't know.'

'You sure? My name is Kyle McClachlan. I'm a (beat)
realtor.'

'Real estate huh.' This guy isn't into real estate,
coffee and doughnuts, no way.

'Yeah.' I see 'Coop's eyes wander over to Donna

Marco's surgically enhanced Twin Peaks. He smiles.
'What do you do?'

   Launch conversation stopper: 'I'm a Green Beret.'

   'Oh. Really. Seriously?'

   'Yep. And now I've told you, I'll have to kill
you.'

   'Uh, right.' He sits back in his seat, this strange
BLANK smile on his face, and finishes his zoom juice.

   'Yep.'

MacGyverism: based on how the State of California
executes its murderers by lethal injection, those
three IV bags should contain in order of use:

1. sodium pentathol, a barbiturate that puts the
   condemned to sleep.
2. pancuronium bromide, a muscle relaxant which
   paralyses everything but the heart.
3. potassium chloride, an electrolytic interrupter
   which stops the heart dead.

The IXION TV crew finishes setting the stage and
exits left. The two technicians also finish preparing
the death machines and exit left. The hall is only
half-full of the Sisterhood. Here's a window of
MacOpportunity to wreck everything. Rip open the bags
with my bare hands, or my teeth. Smash the valves of
the canisters. All before the steroidal Conan
Schwarzenegger gets hold of me. But . . .

   This is no Henry Winkler production featuring an
action-adventure Fonzie kids love, dispensing
grandfatherly wisdom in MacGyverisms.

   Doctor Death makes his entrance to a round of
applause, his white coat billowing as he strides up to
us guests. He is followed by a jittery steady-
cameraman.

   I try to keep my head down in case he recognises me
from my contribution to The YoYo Show.

'Ladies and gentlemen, witnesses, greetings,' says
Ahab Khan, his genetically engineered smile glowing
in the TV lighting.

The *Baywatch Nights* cast stand up and toast him. I
can't help thinking how much the real Harvey Guck
would have enjoyed falling in with their company,
Young Americans, the wealthy healthy of *The O.C.*,
using a brush with death as a means to get off on life.

MacGyverism: death by lethal injection looks
peaceful, almost humane, but inside the inert body
the organs convulse as they are starved of oxygen. The
same suffering is true of death by gassing. Suffering
is not pain, pain is not necessarily suffering. The
process of dying may take up to thirteen minutes – if
a victim is unlucky enough to be in the hands of a
really sadistic executioner.

'The Sisters' helicopter is landing as I speak,'
Ahab Khan says perfunctorily. 'We're ready for them,
running right on schedule. Are you all ready?'

It occurs to me that if I'd continued my Super
Pursuit of the limo, KITTSCH and I'd likely have lost
the Sisters as they took off in a helicopter. It's
funny how things work out.

'Yeah!' chorus the *Baywatch Nights* crowd, thrilled
to be on their own pay-per-view TV show. 'Bring it
on.'

'Yeah,' states 'Coop'.

I can feel Ahab Khan staring at me. He obviously
wants an answer from each one of his select audience.
Without looking up, I shrug. 'As ready as I'll ever
be.' For a second I think my wise-ass mouth might have
given me away again, but . . .

Doctor Death is not as switched-on as my arch-rival
Murdoc (never to be confused with Murdock with a K)
and he goes on talking – 'The Sisters of Mercy would
like to thank you for your contributions to our cause.

The money will be used for campaigning nationwide. Much appreciated.'

The *Baywatch Nights* cast start to kiss and fondle each other, switching partners, swinging with ease.

Doctor Death leaves the warm-up/chill-out at that and walks off.

Right then, I overhear, barely a whisper, 'Coop' talking to himself: 'Stand by, stand by . . .'

I look around and see 'Coop' talking to his lapel: he's wired!

'Coop' puts his index finger to his lips. 'Shhh, soldier or . . .' The finger slits his throat.

I nod. The Lynchian irony doesn't escape me: Kyle McClachlan actually is some kind of elite law enforcement agent running some kind of undercover operation. Either that or he's part of the in-crowd security, a weedy colleague of Conan Schwarzenegger. It's possible. Not everything's possible in the TV world of international-intrigue-gone-neighbourhood-watch, but that certainly is!

The hall is full of the Sisterhood; every seat is taken. There must be a hundred of them. The IXION TV stage crew signal they're ready with their cameras for the Net broadcast.

I lean back in my seat and say, 'Who are you?'

'FBI, and I'll ask the questions from here on in. Who are you, really?'

'Kirk Rush.'

Agent McClachlan's face is so pale it seems to be made of wax. 'You're not Harvey Guck?'

'Nope, but Harv's my agent.'

A curt nod. 'Rush? You're not related to Denise Rush, are you?'

'I'm her brother.'

'You were the loose cannon at *The YoYo Show* recording earlier today, weren't you?'

'Yep.'

MacGyverism: any method of execution has the potential to be relatively quick and painless. The degree of suffering rests in the hands of the executioner.

'Mr Rush, can we count on your assistance?'

'Yep. Tell me what to do.'

Agent McClachlan lays a pale hand on my shoulder. 'I want you to do nothing. Absolutely nothing. Leave this to us; we're trained for every eventuality. OK?'

Since when did action-adventure heroes do nothing? 'Em . . .'

'OK?'

'OK,' I lie. I can't just sit by and watch. I'm a role model for Christ's sake!

'I mean it, We don't want this death cult getting off on a technicality.'

'Yep.' Like the technicality that the Feds are totally penetrated by the alien shape-shifting elite, and that justice is decided on from outer space: *Twin Peaks* spawned *The X-Files* after all.

A final catwalk. Conan Schwarzenegger leads my sister and the three black-robed Sisters of Mercy into the castle hall and onto the stage. The *Baywatch Nights* cast cheers them on with a Mexican wave like this is a football game. The IXION digital cameras roll as they are welcomed on stage by Doctor Death. Denise looks so ill under the bright lights. I can't bear the thought of her being hooked up to that machine.

I get to my feet, out of time with the wave, all Macgung-ho. I figure I'll hit Conan Schwarzenegger with a chair and take it from there.

'Don't,' Agent McClachlan hisses in my ear as he grabs my arm.

'Name one good reason why I shouldn't.' I'm ready

to list my dangerous vigilante precedents: *Have Gun -
Will Travel*, *The Equalizer*, *Dellaventura*, *Vengeance
Unlimited* . . .

'You gave me your word.'

'That's not good enough.' I rip my arm out of his
grip.

'Then try this out for size. We need to wait till
the IV lines are in and the first dose of barbiturate
has been administered. Then we can move in and free
the hostages—'

'The *hostages*?'

'We consider your sister and the others to be
hostages of this death cult, and should he survive we
will be charging Doctor Ahab Khan with four counts of
attempted murder in the second degree. OK?'

'OK.' I won't take the law into my own hands,
unless enforcement fails and that clichéd course of
rising action becomes necessary.

Thing is, Conan Schwarzenegger's bulging eyes
have been watching us. I sit down, and Agent
McClachlan sits down. We both try to look
inconspicuous. But he marches over to us, muscles
pumping up as he goes through a series of aggressive
bodybuilder poses. 'Vot is vrong, gentlemen?'

The *Baywatch Nights* crowd tunes out of the
spectacle of Doctor Death helping the four suicidal
Sisters mount the gurneys and into us at ringside.

'Nothing,' Agent McClachlan says.

That's quite obviously a lie so I say, 'He doesn't
believe in aliens. That's what's wrong. I mean, how
can any sane, rational person not believe that an
Alien Nation is already here on earth and that
we are either a product of a) their selected breed-
ing programme or b) their genetic engineering
programme.'

That puts the humourless Conan Schwarzenegger on

254

the back foot, temporarily. 'Zat is vy you vere fighting Mr McClachlan?'

'Yeah.'

'Yep. Ever since *Roswell*, the government—'

'You vill please stop now.' Conan Schwarzenegger punches the meaty cusp of his left hand.

I relent, much to the disappointment of the bloodthirsty *Baywatch Nights* crowd, who want to see a fight, or at least a beating. 'OK.'

With a grunt Conan Schwarzenegger returns to guard the stage – where Doctor Death is hooking Denise up to one of the lethal injection machines, probably using her fistula to push the line into her grafted artery/ vein. Doctor Death moves on to slide a mask over the face of another of the Sisters on stage. *Entertainment Tonight*.

That's it, cue climax, roll cameras, big-budget action! Sure enough, I hear Agent McClachlan say to his lapel, 'Hostage Rescue Team, move in. I repeat, move in, HRT.' To me he adds, 'Better brace yourself.'

I brace myself as the narrow windows of the castle implode, simultaneous sprays of stained glass. Canisters bounce and roll TINKLING across the floor. Clouds of tear gas HISSING out, making me cough and choke.

The Sisterhood abandon their seats and, shrieking and screaming, stampede for the exit. Stun and smoke grenades BOOM at the entrance of the hall, and black robes fall deaf and blind and unconscious in droves.

The tear gas makes my nose and eyes sting like crazy but I can just see the forced entry of heavily armed, black-suited storm troopers into the mayhem.

The continuous explosions almost deafen me, but I can hear Agent McClachlan shouting to me, 'I'm going to cuff and stuff Doctor Death. Get your sister out of here!'

I stumble around trying to find her but I'm crying uncontrollably. I can't see. I can't hear. I can't smell, taste, and feeling ends when something far more solid than hyper-self-awareness hits me hard on the back of the head – BLANK.

Episode 12

'Where am I?' are my first *doh* words as I come out of my ALOS (acute loss of consciousness) and find myself lying prostrate on a bed, giving the square light on the ceiling a BOOP-BOOP-BOOP-BOOP-BOOP 20,000-yard stare.

'Head's up,' someone says.

A nurse wearing blue *Scrubs* and a white face mask – who has green witchy eyes like Nurse Carol Hathaway – appears to hover over my head, telling me, 'You're in the *ER* of St Eligius', although tonight it feels like the set of *M*A*S*H*. You've been gorked for hours.'

'How did I get here?' My voice is slow, thick.

Another white-masked face, a bespectacled male, Dr Mark Green Mark II: 'You were involved in a major incident. The paramedics did the scoop 'n' run straight from the war zone in Death Valley.'

'They did?'

'*Third Watch* did. Do you remember how you received your injury?' Latex skin, gloved hands, those of Nurse Hathaway stroking my face.

'I don't remember.'

'Do you remember how you got the facial abrasions?'

'Yep, that was my sister.'

Maybe they think I'm delusional because there's a beat before Dr Green II asks, 'Do you remember the SWAT assault?'

The light is flickering, or maybe it's my eyelids. 'Not really.'

257

Nurse Hathaway II: 'I'm not surprised. You have concussion, a bad lac on the back of your head, and for a while there we thought you had C-spine injuries.'

'Lac?'

'A small cut that needed stitches,' Dr Green Mark II explains.

My hand, which weighs a ton, examines the back of my head. It's bandaged up.

'BP is OK. What would you say his GCS is now?' the nurse asks the doctor.

'On the meds, maybe pushing ten. He can take a trip upstairs for an overnighter. Tell whoever's on triage to send the next cult casualty in.'

'Is my spine OK?' I ask them.

'Yeah,' Dr Green Mark II answers. 'The X-rays showed nothing broken.'

'Do you know what hit me?'

The doctor is peeling his bloodied gloves off. 'Off hand, I'd say you took the full force of a stun grenade.'

I try to push myself up. My head is lead.

Nurse Hathaway II: 'I wouldn't do that. AMA.'

'AMA? What has the American Medical Association got to do with me getting out of bed?' I have to ask; you can get lost in all the acronyms, the patient care area jargon, the changing medical policies, the mortality and morbidity of the body, the fabulistic intercontinental capitalistic nightmare of syndicated TV.

'AMA is against medical advice,' tuts Nurse Hathaway II, and wheels me out of the *ER*.

Episode 13

Go figure: next day, May Day, May Day, a consultant by
the name of Dr Mark Craig visits me in my private
room, interrupting my viewing of *The Breakfast Club* –
nope, not the movie, but a cheap and cheerful morning
TV show of the same name with hosts who look like
Emilio Estevez and Molly Ringwald.

Dr Craig is a small man, with intelligent eyes and
a mistake of a moustache that can't be hygienic.
'Good day, Mr Rush,' he says. It's uncanny how he
sounds exactly politely like KITTSCH – except that
this seems to be the personification of William
Daniels.

'Hi,' I say, and put down the tattered but still
glossy *Billboard* magazine I've been idly FLICKING
through.

'How are you?' He picks up my chart, a cursory
glance at my condition.

I plump up my pillows so as to sit up straighter in
the bed. 'OK, I suppose.'

'Good.' He sighs, puts the chart back down.
'Listen, Mr Rush. I hope you don't mind, but Agent
McClachlan informed us that you were Denise's
brother.'

'Yep?' I remotely turn down the TV volume.

'Well, we have a little problem with her.'

'Yep?' Like *who* doesn't! My head hurts. My back
hurts. My face is scarred. I don't have the greatest
healthcare insurance so this will cost a fortune. And

all because Denise's death wish is stronger than anything Michael Winner will ever direct!

'She's in critical condition with pulmonary oedema but refusing treatment, waving around a DNR order signed by Doctor Khan and some other (beat) so and so.'

'OK. That figures.'

'We've managed to run a BUN tox screen and U/A, but when we try to dialyse her – and I should explain that we have a policy of treating suicides, all attempted suicides, in spite of paperwork – she has three times ripped out the lines, and this even when she's incredibly weak.'

'Yep.'

'My options are currently: one, I can sedate her continuously and treat her, though this is dangerous given her toxicity; two, I can see if you can convince her to see sense, and go on dialysis stat.'

'OK.' I turn the TV off. At the risk of repeating myself, I'm a trier when I'm anything.

'You're disposed to coming down to her room and attempting to convince her that this course of action is (long beat) unproductive?'

'Yep,' I say, though I know I don't stand a *Chicago Hope* in hell.

Dr Craig leads me out of my room, out of the private ward, down through a maze of sterilised white corridors in *St Elsewhere* – just like I'd imagined the corridors of Moon Base Alpha in *Zombie Moon*.

As we walk, he talks, letting me into his confidence like I'm one of his young inexperienced residents – Dr Phillip Chandler – instead of a shuffling zombie. He tells me, 'Her KUB tests make me concerned about multi-organ failure.'

'Yep?'

Dr Craig tells me, 'If you hadn't been around, my

260

only real option would have been to regard her as insane, physically restrain her, treat her and take my chances with the bio-ethical lawyers.'

'Yep?'

Stroking germs off his moustache, Dr Craig tells me, 'I'd like to get my hands on this Ahab Khan. All these poor misguided people who get hurt. He gives the rest of us such a bad name.'

'Yep.'

'And he got away! How could they let him get away, huh?'

I shrug. 'I don't know.'

Dr Craig leads me to a T-junction and straight up to the closed door to Denise's private room.

Dr Craig, eyebrows and moustache raised, tells me, 'It's up to you, Mr Rush.'

I open the door and go in. Denise is lying on the bed, inert, oxygen mask on, her left arm pierced by an IV tube. BEEP, BEEP, BEEP: she's hooked up to an ECG machine.

I grab hold of the relative's vigil chair and drag it up to the head of the bed.

Her eyes open slowly, a sigh: 'Oh great, *you*.'

'Yeah me.' A fake laugh. 'You don't get away that easy.'

'Just leave me alone will you.' She waves me away, weakly.

'I will after you listen to what I have to say, OK?'

'OK. Say it and go.'

Only I have no idea what I'm going to say; my only template here is those terminally awful TVM tear-jerkers. 'I know we haven't exactly been close, but I don't want to lose you.'

She swallows hard. BEEP-BEEP-BEEP, her heartbeat increases. BEEP-BEEP-BEEP.

'I know I should have been there for you. I mean Christ, I'm your older brother but—'

'But what?' BEEP-BEEP-BEEP.

'I don't know.' And suddenly I'm crying and it's all gone the way of cliché, sentimental rhetoric. 'I don't know what went wrong, why we had *The Weakest Link*.'

'At least that's honest,' she rasps.

I shrug, and try to stop the sobs from making a fool out of me – that is, even more of a fool. 'I want to make things right between us. I can only do that if you go back on dialysis, sign up for a transplant.'

'It's too late; we're out of time.' She coughs, a spluttering sound. A stutter in the cardio-rhythm. BEEP (beat) BEEP (beat) BEEP.

I get to my feet. 'What's wrong?'

A startled look in her eyes, then BLANK, *that* fast! A flashing red light. The sounding of a CLANGING alarm, and that terrifying, extended-play, medical-drama, your-number's-up sign-releaser BOOOOOOOOOP.

I shout out, 'Help somebody! Somebody help!'

As if they've been waiting in the wings, a resuscitation team smash in, wheeling a crash-cart. A young resident, who's so fine-featured he could be the beloved *Doctor Kildare*'s son, shouts at me and everybody, 'MCI.'

I know from *ER* déjà view that an MCI is a myocardial infarction, in viewers' terminology, a heart attack.

Dr Craig rushes in after the team.

I watch on, bustled to the side of things. Amongst the chaotic swarm of white coats and skirts, I see Dr Craig holding CPR paddles aloft. There's a William Daniels shout, pure nose noise: 'Clear!'

The resuscitation team step back from the bed as the shock is administered to Denise's bloated body,

naked to the waist, paddles pressed onto her yellow
breasts.

Convulsions. But there are no responsive BEEPS from
the ECG, just one long BOOOOOOOOOOP under the CLANGING
alarm.

Dr Kildare calls it: 'Flat line!'

And that's when Dr Craig notices me standing there.
'Mr Rush! Somebody get Mr Rush over there to the Safe
Room.'

A male nurse, *Doogie Howser MD – not*, comes over
and takes me by the arm. 'This way, Mr Rush.'

Somehow I don't have the spirit, or whatever, let's
say the *Will and Grace*, to stay in that room. Doogie
Howser escorts me to the Safe Room and tells me, 'For
your loved one's sake, stay here, OK?'

So I don't see Denise die. I'm not there for her at
the end, any more than I ever was. I just sit there
wishing that this whole run, this series of events,
every damn 'blooperful' episode in my life, is a bad
dream, the bad dream of some autistic kid like the
done-to-death explanation of *St Elsewhere*. But . . .

But, that's just plain dumb.

After twenty killing minutes, and a mug of coffee,
Dr Craig comes into the Safe Room. He's looking as
sensitive and sympathetic and shrugging as a man with
a lot of practice in acting sensitive and sympathetic
and shrugging can be. 'I'm sorry, Mr Rush,' he tells
me. 'We tried, but Denise has just (beat) well, given
up.'

What can I say to that.

Dr Craig puts his hand on my shoulder. 'Do you want
to go see her, say goodbye? Sometimes that helps in
the grieving process.'

'Eh, I don't know. OK?' There's this huge feeling
that this is all my fault. That has to be BLANKED at all
costs, but can't be, and I wonder how I will tell Mom

and Dad their daughter is gone; that unlike Jamie Summers in *The Bionic Woman* there's no getting away from death, there's no cathartic resurrection, no way of changing the channel or turning this TV programme off; that this episode will repeat over and over and over again until the final cancellation of all of us.

Dr Craig leads me out of the Safe Room and to the door of Denise's room. 'I'll leave you alone with her.'

Her body is lying there on the bed, all covered up except for her face. There's this plastic tube sticking out of her taped-up mouth. To help her to breathe. But she isn't breathing any more. She's so still, her body that is. Is it *her* body though? It doesn't look like Morticia Addams. It doesn't look like anybody really.

I feel like being sick, and due to that old Rush family trait and the collapse of the imagination in the face of death, I BLANK out.

Epilogue

Captain's Log, Supplemental (Star Date AD 9/7/2003):
True to form, my parents go to pieces, can't face
Ensign Denise's death, so I, James Tiberius Kirk II,
handle the post post-mortem funeral arrangements with
the kind help of Fisher & Sons. I choose a fancy coffin
off the Net for a knock-down price and they have it
shipped to the Key in *24* hours from *Everwood* in Utah.
I ensure that Denise's wake is held in the funeral
home, in accordance with her abrupt last will and
testament, and not in a church – thus overriding Mom's
mysterious casting of Father Dowling as MC. I book
her a last makeover to get her back looking something
like a model. I invite Len and Mary, Mercury and the
crowd from My Beautiful Laundrette, Linda Gray from
Next Look *Models Inc.*, Ellen DeGeneres/Michelle
Moniker to attend, and they come to drink wine and eat
canapés and make their peaces over the open coffin. No
Sisters of Mercy make special guest appearances, and
thankfully the press and TV crews heed the grieving
family's *Grace Under Fire* request to stay away. With
Mercury's help I get local DJ Don Juan to play an
ensemble of her favourites including Billy Idol's
'Rebel Yell' and Cyndi Lauper's 'Girls Just Want To
Have Fun' and Prince/the Symbol's 'Purple Rain'.
Mercury places the obituary in the *Miami Herald* but I
write her eulogy, and pitch Denise as a great daughter
and sister and all-round wonderful human being. Mom
and Dad so appreciate me not mentioning the words

'suicide' and 'bisexual', and I get lots of lesbians hugging me. When the party's over, I help the undertakers carry her coffin down the aisle to the hearse and, after the cortège to the cemetery, to the graveside. When everybody is done weeping and wailing I take my turn scattering soil on the lid down there, *Six Feet Under*. I do not cry, not once in the whole teleological process; I can't find the tears for the *aporia*. I fly back to Hollywood three days after. I turn down *The Little House On The Prairie* adaptation Harv offers me a fortnight later. I tell him over the phone that I may be an A-hole but I've something else in mind: I'm going to write a novel based on a true story, that will serve as a literary monument to Denise. Harv warns me writing books is crazy. Nobody reads anymore. But what the Guck kid, good luck.

Chris Kerr was born in 1971. He is not a graduate
of the University of Miami, nor is he the writer
of the scripts *The Cybernetic Man* and *Zombie
Moon*. He is currently not working on his next
novel.

Acknowledgements

As Seen On TV was written for my sister who unlike
Denise never gives in to reality. I love you Sue and
for all the good it will do I wish you well.

My parents Margaret and Denis are not Deme and
Ulysses Rush, doubles of Angela Lansbury and Dick Van
Dyke. What a friend we have in Dr Death, *not*.

It must be categorically stated that Kirk Rush is
in no way a reflection of the talented Greg Marcks,
Hollywood writer/director of *Lector* and *11.14*, who
was so lethally honest about my early drafts. Nor is
the fabulously eccentric John Hardwick, writer/
director of *To Have and To Hold* and *33 Times Around
The Sun*.

My beloved in real life, Caroline, is not Angela.
Indeed Angela, my guide in la-la-land to whom I am
seriously grateful, is not Angela. Who the Guck is
Angela?

Harvey Guck, the agent in this novel, is not an
allusion to Simon Trewin, who represents my work with
his considerable subtlety, wit and skill even when I
have lost the *sjuzhet*.

My editor Helen Garnons-Williams bears no relation
whatsoever to Biff McMurray. She is truly charming

and a wonderful editor, full of epistemophilia and such like.

I'm sorry Cain, Zeb De Vache is not you even though you auditioned for the bit part. If only you'd filled in my death questionnaire and given me material to work with. Thanks for the tour of the dark side of LA. You lived up to Colin McAlpin's pitch.

Muchos gracias to Kevin O'H, in whose spare room this anti-meta-fan-fiction or *whatever* began, and to Rob my brother-out-of-law, whose bedroom I finished the first cut in.

I am seriously obliged to my friends Helga and Laura who taught me gutter Spanish, some of which leaked into the text. Some day I will learn the rest of the lingo, I hope.

Last but not least – cheers to author Ellen Slezak. You and comedy Brian are the best for showing me the sights and taking me to LAX so I could get the hell out of there!